An Uninvited Ghost

Night of the Living Deed

"Witty, charming and magical."   *—The Mystery Gazette*

"A fast-paced, enjoyable mystery with a wisecracking but no-nonsense, sensible heroine . . . Readers can expect good fun from start to finish, a great cast of characters and new friends to help Alison adjust to her new life. It's good to have friends—even if they're ghosts."

—The Mystery Reader

"A delightful ride . . . The plot is well developed, as are the characters, and the whole is funny, charming and thoroughly enjoyable."   *—Spinetingler Magazine*

"A bright and lively romp through haunted-house repair!"
—Sarah Graves,
author of the Home Repair Is Homicide Mysteries

"[A] wonderful new series . . . [A] laugh-out-loud, fast-paced and charming tale that will keep you turning pages and guessing until the very end."

—Kate Carlisle, *New York Times* bestselling
author of the Bibliophile Mysteries

"Fans of Charlaine Harris and Sarah Graves will relish this original, laugh-laden paranormal mystery . . . [A] sparkling first entry in a promising new series."

—Julia Spencer-Fleming, Anthony and Agatha
award-winning author of *One Was a Soldier*

"*Night of the Living Deed* could be the world's first screwball mystery. You'll die laughing and then come back a very happy ghost."

—Chris Grabenstein, Anthony and Agatha
award-winning author

Chance of a Ghost

E. J. COPPERMAN

BERKLEY PRIME CRIME, NEW YORK

THE BERKLEY PUBLISHING GROUP
Published by the Penguin Group
Penguin Group (USA) Inc.
375 Hudson Street, New York, New York 10014, USA
Penguin Group (Canada), 90 Eglinton Avenue East, Suite 700, Toronto, Ontario M4P 2Y3, Canada
(a division of Pearson Penguin Canada Inc.) • Penguin Books Ltd., 80 Strand, London WC2R 0RL,
England • Penguin Ireland, 25 St. Stephen's Green, Dublin 2, Ireland (a division of Penguin
Books Ltd.) • Penguin Group (Australia), 707 Collins Street, Melbourne, Victoria 3008, Australia
(a division of Pearson Australia Group Pty. Ltd.) • Penguin Books India Pvt. Ltd., 11 Community
Centre, Panchsheel Park, New Delhi—110 017, India • Penguin Group (NZ), 67 Apollo Drive,
Rosedale, Auckland 0632, New Zealand (a division of Pearson New Zealand Ltd.) • Penguin Books
(South Africa), Rosebank Office Park, 181 Jan Smuts Avenue, Parktown North 2193, South Africa •
Penguin China, B7 Jiaming Center, 27 East Third Ring Road North, Chaoyang District,
Beijing 100020, China

Penguin Books Ltd., Registered Offices: 80 Strand, London WC2R 0RL, England

CHANCE OF A GHOST

A Berkley Prime Crime Book / published by arrangement with the author

PUBLISHING HISTORY
Berkley Prime Crime mass-market edition / February 2013

ISBN: 978-0-425-25168-3

BERKLEY® PRIME CRIME
Berkley Prime Crime Books are published by The Berkley Publishing Group,
a division of Penguin Group (USA) Inc.,
375 Hudson Street, New York, New York 10014.
BERKLEY® PRIME CRIME and the PRIME CRIME logo are trademarks of
Penguin Group (USA) Inc.

PRINTED IN THE UNITED STATES OF AMERICA

10 9 8 7 6 5 4 3 2 1

ALWAYS LEARNING   **PEARSON**

For my father, and anyone who deals in paint

ACKNOWLEDGMENTS

Regular readers of these books must be awfully tired of reading the same names praised effusively and thanked profusely time after time. On the other hand, you're choosing to read the acknowledgments, so clearly it's something you find interesting. For me, it is a necessary and pleasurable obligation. Many people work awfully hard to get my words to you in the best possible light. How could I *not* take time out to notice and appreciate their efforts?

Some very special thanks this time, to start: Maryann Wrobel, the *real* box office manager at the Count Basie Theatre in Red Bank, New Jersey, was kind enough to take me on a tour and show me how the office works. I told her I might write about fictional intrigue and murder connected to a character who had her job, and she smiled. Thank you, Maryann. The Count Basie is a beautiful place to see a show, and I hope to be there again very soon.

Those who offered advice on homemade fingerprint kits: Michael Silverling and Marianne Macdonald could not have been more helpful. The same is true of Dave Bennett, Sue Epstein, Carola Dunn, Sara Hoskinson Frommer, Carl Brookins, Theresa de Valence, Thomas B. Sawyer (my favorite name in all of crime fiction), Tony Burton and Margaret Koch. Thank you, and remind me never to commit a crime when you're around.

Of course, thanks to the invaluable D. P. Lyle, the one and only resource to a crime fiction writer for all things medical, to teach me about arrhythmia and what kind of outlets a toaster would have to go through to electrocute someone. You can't ask just anybody about this stuff, and I have rarely met anyone as selfless. Thank you, Doug.

Thanks, in other matters, to Linda Landrigan, Lynn Pisar, Damon Abdallah, Sue Trowbridge, Dru Ann Love (for getting the Carly Simon reference), Paul Penner, Mikie Fambro (for the ride to the airport), Matt Kaufhold and everyone who invested their money with absolutely no chance of a return in the movie *Scavengers*. You all know who you are, and so do I. Words are insufficient, but all I can offer.

There is no way I can allow you to read these acknowledgments without seeing the name Shannon Jamieson Vazquez, the incandescent editor of the Haunted Guesthouse Mysteries (and the late lamented Double Feature Mysteries), who knows every single time I'm trying to finesse something and never ever lets me get away with it. She is at least as important a factor in your enjoyment of these books as I am.

Thank you to Dominick Finelle, the cover artist for the series who always gets the tone right and comes up with ideas I couldn't possibly dream up, and Judith Lagerman, executive art director of The Berkley Publishing Group, who takes the awful squiggles I send and makes them look like a real book. Kudos to both of you.

And without the tireless work of my agent, Josh Getzler, and Maddie Raffel of Hannigan Salky Getzler Agency, would there even *be* a book called *Chance of a Ghost*? I tend to doubt it. Thanks for putting up with my neuroses and constant demands for attention. Thanks also to Christina Hogrebe of the Jane Rotrosen Agency, who helped get the Haunted Guesthouse Mysteries to begin in my head.

There are, no doubt, many I'm inadvertently omitting, and to each of them, my sincere apologies; it was, you know, inadvertent. But to booksellers, librarians, reviewers (even the ones who don't like me) and especially readers, rest assured authors know that without you, we'd all be trying to find *real* jobs.

Above all, thanks to Jessica, Josh and Eve, who make my life my life. Which is almost exactly what I always hoped it would be, but never expected.

The dream is not always the same; there are variables in the setting and the details. But it always begins with me, either in the house where I grew up or in the enormous Victorian I now own as a guesthouse.

And my father is there.

Even in the dream, I know he's been dead for five years and that it doesn't make sense for him to be completing some home improvement project with me. But that doesn't seem to matter to him, so I see no need to make it an issue.

It's like things used to be—Dad will point out something about the job he's doing so I'll remember it. "See, you want to drive the screws in a little bit deeper than flush on wallboard," he'll say. "That way when you fill the hole with compound, you can sand it smooth, and you won't see a screw head shining through the paint."

We work like that for a little while, and I feel the way I always did when Dad was around—safe, protected and, above all, loved. I learn from him (although in the dream

I have the feeling it's something I already knew), and we share a chuckle over something that we've agreed not to tell my mother.

Then he asks me to find him a tool.

It's not always the same tool; this is what I mean about there being variables in the dream. Sometimes he'll ask for a pair of needle-nose pliers, and I don't have time to wonder what possible use they might have in hanging wallboard. Other times, Dad will say that there's a ball-peen hammer in his toolbox downstairs, and he'd really appreciate it if I would go down and find it for him.

Every time, I have this nagging feeling that I shouldn't leave, but I don't protest or try to get out of the task. I'm not even sure what age I'm supposed to be in the dream. I can't tell if I'm meant to be a child or if he's just treating me that way despite my actually being in my late thirties with a daughter about to turn eleven. Whichever it is, I never question it in the dream, just as I don't find it strange that the house might change from one to the other at this point. If I start out in the house on Seafront Avenue and walk downstairs to find myself in my childhood home at Crest Road, the shift in location doesn't alarm me—it always seems to make sense. I note it, but I don't question it. It doesn't matter where I find myself; the dream always seems to make sense while I'm in it.

This is usually where it becomes an anxiety dream. I head for Dad's toolbox, but it never seems to be where he said I could find it. I start to wonder why he's working upstairs without his toolbox, and why he might've wanted me out of the room for just a moment right now. I go from room to room, searching for the toolbox. In one version of the dream, I don't ever find it. I search until I wake up, frustrated and strangely sad. In another version, I find the toolbox, but the tool Dad has requested doesn't seem to be there, despite how in life Dad organized his tools very carefully and logically. But someone appears to have meddled with the tools—they're not where they're sup-posed to be—and I begin to get nervous. Dad wouldn't treat the instruments of his profession so carelessly. I often wake up anxious after that one.

But the third version, the one I'd been having the most often lately, is the worst of all. In that one, I actually find the tool that Dad has asked for, and feeling like a proud little girl who has accomplished something she's been trusted to do for the first time, I rush back up to deliver the prize. And here, again, there is variation in the dream. Sometimes I can't find my way back to the room Dad was repairing. I rush through the house—or houses—frantically searching for the right door to get me back to him so I can give him the thing he needed so badly and be rewarded with a smile and a "Thanks, baby girl." But I can't ever find my way because the doors never seem to be in the right place, and I wake up just as I think I have finally discovered the right passageway. I'm never happy to be awake after that, and it always takes me a few minutes to shake it off.

In the really horrible version, I find my way back to the room, but Dad is gone.

I wake up in a cold sweat after that one, no matter what.

One

Tuesday

"You're keeping something from me," I told my mother.

We were walking from my car, a 1999 Volvo station wagon that had seen better days even before I'd bought it used, to Mom's one-level "active adult" home, a structure younger than my car. I was helping Mom bring in six bags of groceries, which seemed excessive for a single woman in her early seventies. But there was the threat of snow—a lot of it—overnight, and Mom didn't want to be caught without provisions, just in case every snow-clearing mechanism within a twenty-mile radius suddenly broke down for the next eight days and she couldn't get out. We weren't wasting our time, because the wind whipping around (and seemingly through) us was bringing the air temperature down to about eighteen degrees.

Welcome to the Jersey Shore during an unusually cold January.

"Don't be silly, Alison," Mom retorted, the scarf wrapped

around her mouth muffling her words. "What makes you think there's anything I'm not telling you?"

"It's the way your right eye is twitching. That's the same thing you did when you lied to me in seventh grade when my English teacher was fired for smoking dope in the faculty lounge."

Mom unlocked her back door and we were inside and thawing out in seconds. She closed the door with her foot to stop the arctic breeze and we unburdened ourselves on the kitchen table.

"Mr. Hennity left the system because he wanted a bigger challenge and you kids were just too smart to provide it," Mom attempted. And her right eye twitched.

"See?"

Mom started taking groceries out of the nearest bag and putting them away. I did the same, leaving out all items requiring refrigeration for Mom to organize herself. We had a system, and it went back to when I was eight years old.

"Well, I'm not hiding anything now," she insisted. I decided to let it go. There was no sense in pushing Mom when she didn't want to talk. She'd tell me whatever it was when she was good and ready. Besides, I had two guests back at the house, so I had to get back before this nor'easter, forecast to be bigger than the Blizzard of '88, began bearing down on us.

"I'm surprised you didn't go to get your nails done today," I said, handing her a box of All-Bran cereal, which she placed in a cabinet next to another box of All-Bran cereal. "Isn't that a weekly thing?"

"I get that done on Tuesdays," Mom said. "Tuesday morning." She started separating frozen things from refrigerated things while I concentrated on dry goods like walnuts and whole-grain crackers. "I'll probably skip this week, if we get all that snow."

I put a container of unsweetened cocoa into her baking supplies cabinet and then turned and stopped. "Today is Tuesday, Mom."

Mom looked positively stunned. "It is?" she asked. "You're sure? Tuesday?"

I squinted at her in confusion. "All day," I said.

"Oh, my," Mom said. "I thought it was Monday! What time is it?"

I looked at my watch. A lot of people rely on their cell phones for the time now, but I like a wristwatch. I'm an old-fashioned gal. "Two thirty," I told her. I was getting a little concerned, to tell the truth. Not because Mom had gotten the day wrong but because of the way she was overreacting to a little confusion about the day of the week. "Are you okay?"

"I'm fine," came the answer, too quickly to be convincing. I didn't see if her eye twitched; she was turned away. "Would you excuse me for a minute?" She didn't bother to wait for a reply (and rightly so—what was I going to do, *not* excuse her?) and headed toward her bedroom.

I stared after her for a long moment, wondering what the heck *that* was about, then went back to putting all room temperature groceries away.

Until I heard Mom talking to someone from behind her bedroom door.

Now that was odd, though not completely unheard of, considering that Mom can see and speak to ghosts. In the interest of full disclosure, I can see ghosts, too, and so can my ten-year-old daughter Melissa. But I'm far behind both Liss and Mom in ability and can't see nearly as many spirits roaming the streets as they can. I'm still trying to decide whether that's a good or a bad thing.

So Mom's talking to someone when I was pretty sure there wasn't anyone else (breathing) in the house wasn't necessarily the strangest thing that could happen. But when I started to make out the words (okay, so I'm an eavesdropper—like you wouldn't listen in if you heard your mother talking to a dead person?), the conversation itself was considerably more disturbing than I'd anticipated.

"Well, I *can't* right now!" Mom was insisting, her voice raised in what sounded like annoyance and frustration. "Honestly, you're like an impatient teenager!"

I hadn't heard my mother use that tone in a very long time. At least five years, probably longer. Not since . . .

Wait a minute.

I listened a moment longer, and heard Mom say, "I *know* it's Tuesday—I just forgot! Now if you'll just—"

I couldn't hear well enough from the kitchen, so I crept into the hallway and started toward Mom's bedroom door. I knew that technically I was infringing on her privacy— okay, maybe not just technically—but there was a familiar ring to this kind of argument, however one-sided, that bore further investigation.

Besides, I figured, I *am* a fledgling private investigator. If I couldn't practice spying on my own mother, who *could* I spy on?

"I understand that you're disappointed," Mom said, a little more calmly. "Why don't you come back tomorrow? It's supposed to snow, and it's not like you have a lot you need to do. . . ."

Now that I was closer, I could just make out another voice responding, "Loretta"—that's Mom's name—but it was at a much lower volume and a lower tone as well. I couldn't make out any other words, but one thing was absolutely unmistakable: It was a male voice.

I'll admit it—at this point, curiosity had overtaken any good judgment I might have otherwise exhibited under other circumstances. I leaned toward the bedroom door, careful not to creak a floorboard or actually come into contact with the door itself.

"All right, then," Mom said, apparently having defused whatever situation she'd been in. "I'll see you tomorrow. Don't make it too early; I want to sleep in."

I wasn't as prepared as I should have been for the bedroom door to then open abruptly and for Mom to be staring me in the chin (she's shorter than I am).

"What are you doing here?" she asked. "How dare you listen in on a private conversation?"

Everything about this situation was bizarre. Usually, my mother would rather sew her own lips shut than suggest I ever did anything less than wonderful. It would have been more typical of her to compliment me on my stealth skills than berate me for being as rude as I honestly had been.

But the fact is, she wasn't acting like herself, and I couldn't quite put my finger on why just at the moment. That was bothering me, because I could feel that there was something very personal and painful at the core of this episode, but I couldn't place it.

"I wasn't listening in," I lied. "I thought you were calling me." I tried to look around her. "Who were you talking to?"

"I was on the phone," she answered far too quickly. "To my friend Marsha."

"You don't have a phone in the bedroom," I reminded her.

"My cell phone," she said.

It occurred to me that I wouldn't have heard a voice over a cell phone from outside the door, but why quibble? It was important not to call Mom out on her obvious evasions, though, because I knew that would just make her clam up more.

"Okay," I said. "I guess we'd better get those groceries put away, and then I should get going before it starts to snow." The snow wasn't forecast to start for some hours, but I had the uncomfortable feeling—which I'd never had before—that Mom wanted me to go.

"I don't need help with the groceries," Mom said, again too fast and too curt. "You go ahead. I don't want to worry about you on the roads."

So I did. I made sure Mom agreed to call me if she

needed anything in the oncoming snowstorm and got into my trusty (and rusty) Volvo wagon. I was on the cell phone to my best friend, Jeannie, before I made it out of Mom's development. (This is the place to note that I was using an earpiece, because New Jersey has laws prohibiting one from holding a cell phone to one's ear while driving, and *everybody* in the state obeys that one. Okay. Maybe not *everybody*.)

"My mother's acting strange," I told Jeannie.

"She's not acting," Jeannie answered. "I love your mother, but she really *is* strange. She thinks she can talk to ghosts."

I couldn't really defend Mom there. Jeannie, you see, doesn't believe in ghosts. She doesn't believe in them despite having seen things happen that could not be explained in any way other than to assume that there is at least one being present who is not visible. She doesn't believe in ghosts even though I've told her they were there, and she doesn't believe in them despite the fact that her husband, Tony, does, and has sort of communicated with them himself. It's a long story. I'd learned over the past fifteen months (since I started spotting spooks) that there are some people who simply aren't going to believe in things they can't see, even when those things were directly in front of their eyes. Jeannie could be the queen of those people.

"Well," I said, sidestepping the whole ghost issue, "that's not the strange part." I told Jeannie what had happened (pretending for her sake that the voice coming from my mother's bedroom had emanated from a live person) and asked her opinion.

"She's got a boyfriend," Jeannie suggested. "She doesn't know how to tell you, and so she's embarrassed and acting unusual." There was the sound of a baby crying so loudly I had to pull the phone from my—that is, I had to move the earpiece away from my ear. "Sorry," Jeannie continued. "Oliver gets cranky when I switch sides." Jeannie's son, Oliver, now four months old, had clearly been breast-feeding while I was talking to her.

"Thanks for that mental image," I said. "Couldn't you have told me he needed a pacifier?"

"Pacifiers are unsuitable substitutes for the real thing," Jeannie said, no doubt rolling her eyes over my thick-headedness. This was not the first time we'd had such a conversation. "They make the child dependent on something that they don't need and create a need to wean the child"—Jeannie always says "the child" when she's dispensing parenting advice I don't need given that I'm the one with an almost-eleven-year-old daughter—"twice later on. That just makes the child cranky and the parents frustrated." Or was it the other way around?

"My mother," I reminded her.

"I'm telling you. She's found some guy and maybe they meet every Tuesday, so she had forgotten he'd be there because she thought it was Monday. And when he showed up, she got flustered and sent him away."

"Sent him away? What, he climbed out the window? Besides, how did he get into the house to begin with?" If she wanted to play that it was a living guy, I could do that.

"Maybe he has a key," Jeannie answered. "Maybe she's living this secret life." I heard gurgling on her end of the conversation. Oliver, no doubt being difficult. It's in the genes.

"Why would he be waiting in her bedroom?" I asked. And I knew I shouldn't have said that even as the words were coming out of my mouth. Suddenly there were new images I needed to get out of my head. "Ewwwww," I groaned.

"Don't judge," Jeannie laughed.

"She's my *mother*!"

"Where do you think you came from, the J. Crew catalog?"

"Jeannie!" I screamed. "Enough!"

It was another ten minutes to my house in Harbor Haven, the hometown I'd returned to after my divorce from a guy we'll call "The Swine," strictly for the sake of accuracy. No snow was falling yet, but I wasn't crazy about the prospect of it. I had guests back at the house, my daughter was being dropped off after school by her best friend's mom and there were these two ghosts to manage.

Perhaps I should explain.

About a year ago, I'd bought the massive Victorian at 123 Seafront Avenue to turn into a guesthouse with money I'd gotten from divorcing The Swine and from settling a lawsuit (don't ask). While I was renovating the place, an "accident" left me with a very bad bump on the head and the sudden ability to see the two spirits, Paul Harrison and Maxie Malone, who inhabited the house.

They'd both died in the house about a year before I bought it—Maxie was the previous owner, and Paul, the newly minted private investigator who'd been hired to find out who was threatening her if she didn't leave the house; threats that turned out to be serious when they were both poisoned—and though it took some doing, the three of us were able to find their killer. But despite our mutual expectations that Paul and Maxie would "go into the light" or whatever once their murders were solved, nothing much seemed to have changed in that regard. So we've had to figure out a way to coexist.

Luckily, right around that same time, I was approached by a man named Edmund Rance, who represented a group called Senior Plus Tours, offering senior citizens vacations with an "added experience" attached. Rance had heard rumors that my guesthouse was haunted—which technically it is— and asked if we could provide evidence thereof at least twice a day in exchange for a steady supply of paying guests during the tourist season (which on the Jersey Shore is at least part of every season except winter, so I was surprised to have even two guests staying with me this week). I prevailed upon Paul, who in turn prevailed upon Maxie, to perform "spook shows," making objects fly around the house and lately adding such touches as musical instruments "playing themselves" and strange substances (usually rubber cement, sometimes corn syrup with food coloring) "bleed" down the walls.

That's entertainment.

But Paul exacted a price for my exploitation of the two ghosts. He'd loved being a PI in life, and even now wanted to keep his hand in investigations—apparently eternity is, in addition to other things, boring—but he'd needed someone living (i.e., me) to do the "legwork."

There had been some negotiations, but I'd ultimately agreed to get a private-investigator's license, and so far had used it twice already. I still wasn't fully on board with the PI life, however—both those experiences had been, to put it mildly, a little unnerving for me. Getting your life threatened will do that to a person.

But back to the problem of what was going on with Mom.

"Okay, I'll let you live your fantasy," Jeannie answered me. "Your mother *isn't* seeing some guy. So what's *your* explanation for what you heard?"

I couldn't tell her that I was pretty sure Mom had been talking to a ghost. I mean, I *could* have told her that, but she wouldn't have believed me, so it wasn't going to get us anywhere.

She took my momentary silence for capitulation. "Aha!" she shouted. "You agree with me that she has a boyfriend!"

"No. I really don't. I was just thinking that it doesn't make sense for some guy to just walk into her house and wait in her bedroom."

"Why not?" Jeannie demanded.

"Because Mom wouldn't do that. She wouldn't trust someone enough to give him a key yet never even mention his name to me. She wouldn't set up some weekly . . . rendezvous in her bedroom just for . . . that. Mom hasn't even talked about meeting anyone. It's too soon since Dad died."

"It's been five years," Jeannie chimed in helpfully.

I pulled into the driveway at my guesthouse and drove

all the way back behind the house to the carport. There was a little overhang there that would shield the car from most of the snow, if I got lucky and the wind was blowing the right way. A girl could dream. "It's been a slice, Jeannie," I told her, "but I have to go batten down my hatches. Is Tony home yet?"

"No, but he'll be here soon. It's the baby's first snowstorm, and we want to make sure he enjoys it with his whole family." At four months, Oliver would be lucky to stay awake until a full inch was on the ground, and certainly wouldn't know the difference, but you can't tell new parents anything.

I hung up my phone and got out of my car, wondering if Murray Feldner, the guy I'd hired to plow snow from my sidewalk and driveway areas, would remember our contract. I'd have to call and remind him. I raised the windshield wipers straight up in the air so they wouldn't stick to the windshield (although I've always harbored a secret plan to leave the car running with the wipers on all through a blizzard), and was halfway to my back door when the realization hit me.

There *had* been something familiar about the way Mom spoke to the person in her bedroom. It *had* conjured up an emotional memory. There was only one person my mother had ever spoken to with such a scolding tone, because she was secure in the knowledge he'd still love her no matter what she said.

The ghost Mom had been shooing out of her house *because I was there* had been my father.

Two

"Your father?" Paul asked. "What makes you think it was your father?"

Hovering over the pool table in my game room, Paul stroked his goatee, which I'd learned was a sign that he found what I'd said worth considering. It also made him look like a very transparent comparative lit professor from a small New England college instead of the ghost of a rather muscular Canadian PI, which is what he was.

I'd told him about my conversation with Mom after checking in with the only two guests I was hosting this week, Nan and Morgan Henderson. The Hendersons, in their late fifties, were not part of a Senior Plus Tour, so they weren't expecting any ghostly happenings, which meant that Paul and Maxie had a winter week off.

"Anything you guys need?" I asked Nan, who had just come back from a walk on the beach, saying the cold weather was perfect for such things (Nan had grown up in Vermont and liked the cold; I'd grown up in New Jersey and wished

I'd grown up in Bermuda, so my sensibility was a little different).

"Not so far," she answered. "We're looking forward to the snow, but I'm wondering what we'll do about meals if we're snowed in." I don't supply meals at the guesthouse—we're not a bed and breakfast, nor a bed and any other meal. I do get my guests discounts at local restaurants in exchange for some accommodations (kickbacks) from the restaurateurs. Hey, it's a business.

"Usually, things don't stay unplowed for more than a few hours," I assured her. "But if we're really stuck for a long time, I'll provide meals. Don't you worry, we won't let you go hungry." Knowing how well I cook, *I* was slightly terrified at the prospect, but it seemed really unlikely, so I moved on. "How was the walk on the beach?"

"Oh, it was wonderful!" Nan gushed. "So bracing to be out there while the wind starts to kick up!"

"Bracing," Morgan echoed. He didn't sound quite as enthusiastic.

"I'm glad you're having a good time," I said.

"A good time." Morgan seemed incapable of forming his own words; he'd just hit highlights from whatever had just been said to him and put a sour spin on them.

"You two should plan on getting some dinner in town tonight, and I'll make sure to have a few breakfast things around in the morning just in case," I said, directing my message to Nan for fear that Morgan would repeat "breakfast things" with a disappointed tone.

The Hendersons went to their room to change for dinner. Melissa wasn't back from her best friend Wendy's house yet, so I went to the game room. At one time I could look for the resident ghosts in the attic, where they had often liked to retreat from the usual chaos that occurred on the lower floors, but I'd converted the attic space into a bedroom for Melissa the previous summer, and now I was more likely to find Paul in the game room or the kitchen, the two areas least often frequented by guests (which led me to think the "game room" might be better suited to another purpose, but I hadn't yet figured out what that might be).

Sure enough, I'd found him in there—Maxie was still in the attic, since she considered herself and Melissa to be "roommates"—and had filled him in on the whole askew scenario at my mother's house.

"Your father," Paul mused. "How do you know? Did you recognize his voice?"

I grimaced to indicate I was unsure. "Not exactly," I told Paul. "He wasn't speaking loudly enough for me to really hear his voice clearly. It was more of a murmur through a closed door. I don't see and hear other ghosts as well as I do you and Maxie."

Paul nodded slowly, digesting the information. "You *have* seen your father at least once since you found us, though," he reminded me.

It was true—or at least, I *thought* it was true. In a moment of extreme duress, not long after I'd met Paul and Maxie, I thought I'd seen—or, more precisely, sensed—my father coming to my rescue. But I hadn't seen his face at all and heard his voice only briefly. And it was the only time.

"I don't know. If he could, why wouldn't he get in touch with me? Maybe I just wanted to believe it was him," I said. "I was new to ghosts then."

Paul grinned a sly grin. "Not like the pro you are now," he said. He likes to gently tease me about my limited ghost-seeing abilities.

"You were a private investigator," I told him, on the off chance that he'd forgotten. "How would you proceed under these circumstances? Suppose I was hiring you."

"To find out what?" Paul asked. "Just go to your mother and ask if she was talking to your father."

I shook my head. "Not the way she was acting. This was

something she honestly didn't want me to know about. She wasn't happy that I was there, and you know my mother—she's *always* happy that I'm there."

Paul tilted his head to the side, which presented an odd image, since he'd been idly listing a little bit that way to begin with. "Yeah," he said. "That is odd behavior for her."

Maxie stuck her head through the ceiling and looked down at us. "What's going on?" she asked. "Planning more renovations? I have ideas." Maxie had been a budding decorator in life and never fails to have splashy ideas for projects I either can't afford or simply don't want to do.

"Calm down," I told her. "The only thing I'm planning on doing is reorganizing the library and maybe trying to widen the doorframe to make it seem roomier. If you have any ideas for that, feel free."

She looked disappointed but held up a finger. "Well, I've always thought you should—"

I cut her off. "Shouldn't you think about it first?"

"Why?"

I ignored her and turned my attention back to Paul. "What do you think I should do under the circumstances?" I asked him.

"I still say asking is the best way to find something out," he responded. "She's your mother. She'll talk to you."

"What's going on with your mother?" Maxie asked with concern. Maxie likes everyone in my family except me.

"We'll recap later," Paul answered her before I could make a cutting remark, which had been my plan. "Just relax, Alison. I'm sure it's nothing serious."

I let out a long breath. "You're probably right. But I'm not going to let it alone."

He gave an enigmatic smile. "I wouldn't expect you to," he said.

"Mom?" I heard Melissa call from the front room. A ten-year-old will never—*never*—come looking for you. They always yell. Yes, even in a house with paying guests and two freeloading ghosts present at all times.

"Game room," I called back, trying to be a little less jarring with my tones. Melissa appeared a moment later with a puzzled expression on her face.

"Hi," she said to the gathering, then looked at me. "Did you know Grandma is here? Her car just pulled up."

My breath caught a little bit, and not just from a childhood reflex because I hadn't made my bed that morning. "I just left her," I said to no one in particular. "Is something wrong?" I headed for the front room.

But my mother appeared in the doorway before I could get halfway there. She acknowledged the ghosts and hugged Melissa, but the expression on her face was strange, much like it had been at her house when she'd realized today was Tuesday—concerned and a little frightened.

"Are you okay?" I asked her. Maxie leaned in a little. She really does love Mom.

Mom's eyebrows knitted. "Of course I'm okay."

I'm sure my eyebrows were now the spitting image of hers. (We do look sort of alike—she's, you know, my mother.) "I was just at your house. What's wrong?"

"I've been keeping something from you," she said.

Three

Melissa was not pleased about being asked to leave the conversation (and the room), but I had no idea which way this scene was going to play out, and I didn't want to have to explain it to my almost-eleven-year-old just yet. But she is an intelligent, wise girl, mature beyond her years, so it took only about ten minutes of whining and cajoling before she agreed to go up to her room.

I suggested the ghosts scram as well, but Mom said they should stay, as what she had to say concerned them, too. Which only puzzled me about six times more than I was already puzzled, which was plenty puzzled. Even if this was about Dad, what did that have to do with Paul and Maxie?

"Okay, spill," I told Mom once Melissa was safely out of the room. "What have you been hiding from me?"

Mom, who is usually anything but a shrinking violet, sat down. "You have any beer?" she asked.

I do keep wine and beer in a mini-fridge (locked, because

I don't have a liquor license and there is a minor living on the premises) in the game room, but that wasn't the point. A *beer*? *My* mother? These two things had never gone together before in my memory. I walked silently to the fridge, worked the combination on the lock and took out a light beer, which I handed to Mom.

She looked at the label. "Nothing imported?" she asked.

I shook my head incredulously. Mom shrugged, opened the bottle of beer and took a rather long pull on it without wiping off the mouth first.

"Okay," I told the person on the barstool, "who are you, and where are you keeping my mother?"

Paul and Maxie hovered near the ceiling, staring at Mom in fascination.

"Oh, don't be silly, Alison," my mother said. "I'm your mother." Then she burped, but at least she looked horrified at her lapse in manners.

I realized that whatever she had to say must be very difficult, so I softened my voice. "All right," I said. "So what is it you need to tell me, Mom?"

She took another swig of beer, seemingly to bolster her courage. "I've been holding this inside, and it's been very painful," she said. "I'm sorry that I didn't tell you."

"Didn't tell me *what*?" That might have come out a touch more irritated than I'd meant it, but Mom didn't react.

"I've been . . . seeing your father," Mom squeaked out, barely audible.

I had sort of known that; this wasn't news. "What exactly do you *mean*, you're seeing Dad? Hasn't that been sort of on and off since he . . . since he passed away?" I've found, especially since meeting Paul and Maxie, that the word *dead* is considered somewhat upsetting. Personally, I don't see how *passed away* is any better, but my philosophy amounts to "don't upset the dead people." Sorry: "the passed away people."

"Of course," Mom said, her tone indicating that were I

among the tools in the shed, there might be some sharper than me. "But that doesn't mean we can't still see each other." Given the company in the room, I couldn't argue the point.

That didn't mean I wasn't going to try. "Okay, so you're seeing him. That's not an emergency, is it?" But for reasons I couldn't identify, my stomach was getting just a little queasy, and Mom's rather horrified expression wasn't helping matters much.

"Now, Alison," she said, her tone a trifle pained for my unfortunate ineptitude, "I know you're not able to connect with the spirits the way Melissa and I can, but you have to come to terms with that. I'm able to . . . relate to your father in ways that you can't."

That brought up images I would have paid cash money to erase, so I switched gears, perhaps with less smoothness than the average Ferrari. "I'm not really able to see him at all," I said, a little unintended bitterness in my tone. "He never comes to see *me*."

Mom looked down at the mouth of the beer bottle. "I know," she said. "I don't understand that. He loves you so much."

"He's got a funny way of showing it."

I'll admit it; I was hurt. If there was one advantage to my newfound ability to see spooks, I had thought, it would be the opportunity to renew my relationship with Dad. But aside from that one momentary sighting only a few weeks after I "met" Paul and Maxie, I'd never laid eyes on my father's spirit. I'd never had a conversation with him since the waning days in his hospital room.

Nobody had ever called me "baby girl" again.

My father and I shared a special bond when he was alive. He called himself a handyman, although he was closer to a building contractor, and taught me everything I know about home maintenance and construction. I wouldn't have dared buy the Victorian at 123 Seafront and converted it into a guesthouse if Dad hadn't brought me up to understand the inner workings of a building—"so you'll never have to rely on some man to do it for you."

We spent a good number of Saturdays together at his friend Sy Kaplan's paint and hardware store, Madison Paint. (The fact that Madison Paint was not in the town of Madison, but in Asbury Park, was irrelevant; Sy had imported the name from his first location, which also wasn't in Madison, but was on Madison Avenue in Irvington. But that's another story.) Dad loved to hang out in the back room, where Sy kept a pot of coffee going all the time, and talk to the other contractors, mostly painters, who came through. They traded stories and complained about customers, but they treated me like a member of the tribe, never like a little girl. But I think Dad must have said something about curbing their language, because I very rarely heard any "inappropriate" words from any of the men.

Most Saturdays would be spent there unless Dad had a major project going, in which case I'd go along with him to the site in question. Mom didn't object, I guess because I was home with her after school every day during the week, so she saw this as Dad's time to get to know his daughter. Not to mention, time for her to get things done by herself.

"He has his reasons," Mom responded. "He won't tell me what they are, but I know it's hurting him not to talk to you."

I didn't want to tear up and complain because I couldn't speak to my dead father. Everybody loses a loved one sooner or later, and the vast majority never hear from that person again. I had no right to whine. So I sucked in my lips and bit them a little, then turned toward Mom.

"This isn't about me," I said. "It's about you. So you've been seeing Dad. I take it this has been going on for some time."

Mom nodded. "Almost since he passed on," she admitted. She'd never been specific about how often she'd seen him or how she could summon Dad, and now I was kicking myself for letting that go all this time. But the lip biting was helping, so I did it again.

"Why are you telling me about it now?" I asked.

"Because now your father is missing, and I want you to help find him," Mom said.

Four

It took a while for that to sink in. "Missing?" I asked. "How can a dead man be missing?"

The private investigator in Paul had awakened, leaning forward and suddenly all attention. He had clearly decided to take over the "client interview." "Slow down, Loretta," he said to Mom in a soothing tone. He'd once told me that saying "slow down" was better than "calm down," which only got people more agitated. "Tell me what's happened."

His tactic obviously had the effect he'd desired: Mom exhaled audibly, looked in what can be seen of Paul's eyes (ghosts are only sort-of opaque) and put a businesslike expression on her face.

"I've been seeing Jack every Tuesday for a few years," she said. "He'd appear in the house, like clockwork, right around eleven in the morning. Once in a while I could sort of call him, you know, talk to him aloud and he'd hear me if he was close enough and then show up. That's what happened the night he came to help Alison."

I'd been so caught up in this convoluted tale that it hadn't occurred to me until now: "Wait. You were talking to someone when I was in your house today. And it wasn't your friend and it wasn't on your cell phone. If that wasn't Dad, who was it?" I asked my mother.

"I'm *getting* to that," she answered. "I'm more worried about your father right now." What did *that* mean?

I didn't get a chance to push the point. "Why do you think your husband is missing?" Paul butted in and asked Mom.

"He hasn't shown up for the past three weeks," Mom said. "And believe me, he never missed a week. I'd go to bed extra early on Monday nights because I knew he'd be there on Tuesdays, and I'd need my rest."

"Mom," I reminded her, "your daughter is in the room."

"Oh, Alison," she scolded. "Really."

Paul did his best to steer the conversation back to the primary topic. "Your husband, Loretta. You say he stopped showing up on Tuesdays. Isn't there any other explanation? Could he have forgotten or simply been distracted?"

"By what?" I asked. "He's been dead for five years." Then I remembered that I was in the presence of other similarly deceased people. "Sorry."

As had become practice, they ignored me. Mom's eyes narrowed as she thought, and she shook her head negatively at Paul.

"I don't think so," she said. "You don't know Jack like I do. He'd never forget and he'd never not show up without telling me."

"Still, that doesn't really classify him as 'missing,'" I noted, having decided to join 'em rather than try to beat 'em. "Dad wouldn't ever leave without saying where he was going, but if he got caught up in something, he could lose track of time."

"There's more," Mom said, once again casting her eyes toward her brewski and looking uncomfortable. "I made the acquaintance of another gentleman."

"You're two-timing Dad?" It slipped out. Or more like it forced itself out at warp speed.

Mom looked up sharply. "Of course not!" she barked, her eyes flashing. "It never got . . . serious. We're just friends."

"Wait," Maxie said. I took in a deep breath, because anything Maxie was likely to interject here was not apt to be helpful. "This other guy . . ."

"His name is Lawrence," Mom said. "Lawrence Laurentz. He's the one you heard me talking to this afternoon, Alison."

"Lawrence Laurentz?" I asked. "Did his parents stutter?" Now you know the truth: I'm not tactful.

"Lawrence," Maxie said, as if I weren't there. "Is he alive, or is he like us?" She gestured toward herself and Paul.

"Lawrence is like you and Jack," Mom answered. "He passed on about six months ago."

Paul decided to regain his authority as the lead investigator. "So how is it that you think your friendship with Mr. Laurentz led to your husband being missing?" he asked.

Mom looked serious. "Well, Jack hasn't been showing up for a few weeks, like I said. And I was going to come to you, Paul, and see if you could contact him." Paul has the ability to sort of telepathically communicate with other ghosts; sometimes it works and sometimes it doesn't. He and I call it the Ghosternet. "But Lawrence came to me a few days ago and said something was wrong with Jack and that he could help. I told him I was sure Jack would show up today, but today Lawrence was there again, not Jack." She looked at me. "He was there to tell me that he knew why your father hasn't been coming by. He said Dad was being kept away; he made it sound like Dad's being held against his will."

I turned toward Paul. "Is that even possible?" I asked.

He gave me a "how would I know?" look. "I never got the handbook for the deceased," he said. "But you know that we've seen things stranger than what Mr. Laurentz was suggesting."

That was true; there seemed to be no rule book overseeing the afterlife. In our short time inhabiting the same house, Paul, Maxie and I had seen ghosts who could move freely about the planet and others, like Paul, who were bound to a certain area of real estate. Maxie had recently developed the ability to leave my property but couldn't actually transport herself independently with any speed faster than a brisk walk. She'd taken to materializing in my car on occasions I was going somewhere, which had almost caused a few accidents along the way. Maxie is anything but subtle.

"So let's assume that your friend is telling the truth. Do you think he's the one holding Dad hostage?" I asked my mother.

"I don't know. After you left, he came back and we talked more, but I got so upset that I wasn't thinking clearly," she admitted. "Lawrence said he could get Jack out of whatever predicament he's in, but he wants something in return."

That kind of talk always raises my suspicions. "Oh, really," I said. "What is it he wants from you?" My mind wasn't wrapping itself around this one comfortably. What could a ghost want? They can't spend money. They can't take ransom.

"It's not me he wants something from; it's you," Mom said to me.

I could feel my eyes narrow. "What is it he wants?" I asked.

"He wants you to find out who murdered him."

This had a familiar ring. When I'd first met Paul and Maxie, that was the very request they'd made of me, and it hadn't been easy to fulfill. I was in no hurry to try doing something like *that* again.

Paul sighed before I could. "I understand his torment," he said. "But how did he know about Alison's ability to see people like us? Does he know she has a private-investigator's license?"

Mom finished her bottle of beer and looked away, pretending to search for the recycling bin she knew perfectly well I kept next to the fridge. "I might have . . . mentioned something about it," she said, making sure not to establish eye contact with me.

Maxie stifled a giggle. When she died, Maxie was a twenty-eight-year-old who had probably topped out at sixteen on the maturity charts. Things hadn't changed much since then.

I decided to pretend not to notice Maxie and turned toward Mom. "So you've been bragging about my detective skills to your dead friends?" I asked.

"Maybe a little. But you know, you don't give yourself enough credit."

Sometimes it is very difficult not to roll one's eyes heavenward. In this case, I found it impossible. For one thing, I know I'm not a good investigator—Paul does most of the brainwork, and I do the legwork—and for another, Mom wouldn't know a good detective if she met Sherlock Holmes at the clubhouse of her condo complex. Which I wasn't sure she hadn't.

Before the top of my head could blow off, Paul floated between Mom and me. "Do we have any details, Loretta?" he asked. "Do we know exactly when Mr. Laurentz died and how he was murdered?"

Mom seemed much happier dealing with Paul, so I took a seat and considered having a drink myself but didn't want to open a bottle of wine just for me. I'd have to look into wine six-packs.

"I met Lawrence at the clubhouse in our development about two months ago, and he began coming around to the house every once in a while right after that. He said he had died a little over six months ago. Last June," Mom reported dutifully. "He says he was electrocuted, but that the police think he had a heart attack or something."

Paul's eyes perked up. "Electrocuted? How?"

"He says someone threw an electric toaster into his bubble bath."

Maxie guffawed, and this time I was grateful. It covered my own involuntary yelp quite nicely. Mom gave Maxie a disdainful look.

"The man was murdered, Maxine," she reminded her.

"Sorry, Mrs. Kerby." Maxie sounded like a third grader being admonished by her teacher, but her grin was unmistakable.

Mom huffed a bit, but Paul refocused her attention from Maxie's (and my) insolence to his questioning. He seemed genuinely interested. Paul likes nothing better than an unsolved mystery. It's one of the few things about him I find completely annoying.

"How could Mr. Laurentz not know who threw a toaster into his bath?" he asked. "He would have seen the person enter the bathroom, surely." Paul speaks with such lovely syntax, owing to his British/Canadian background. Or maybe he's just really polite.

Mom squinted, an indication that she's concerned she's about to say something that will be open to ridicule. I'm afraid Dad and I were rather merciless in our teasing when I was growing up, though in a loving way. Even Melissa, who is smarter than all of us and who loves her grandmother dearly, occasionally giggles at the things my mother says.

"Lawrence said that the person who threw it was invisible," she declared.

In this crowd, that's not so outrageous a statement, but I heard a stifled giggle from the game room doorway, and there stood Melissa, confirming her grandmother's fears that what she'd said would be received with something other than complete reverence. Liss was holding the iPod touch her father had given her a few months before as a bribe. But under her arm was her school laptop.

"You were supposed to be in your room," I said.

Melissa shot a guilty glance at Maxie, who quickly shut the laptop she had, let's face it, stolen from me. Scowling, I walked to the spook, who did not think to rise up to the ceiling to avoid me.

"What are you doing?" I intoned.

Maxie made a sound with her lips that indicated she was unconcerned with my authority. She opened the computer and turned the screen toward me.

It showed Melissa's Skype name but nothing on the main screen because Liss had closed her laptop. On the tiny screen-within-a-screen below was a picture of the game room and the assembled therein in this case, Melissa, Mom and me, because the ghosts did not register on the laptop's web cam.

"You Skyped this to Melissa?" I said. "When I'd sent her upstairs?"

"Oh, grow up," Maxie said.

"I was worried about Grandma," my daughter tried.

"Go to your room," I said.

"Mom!"

"Not you," I said to my daughter. I turned toward Maxie. "You."

The ghost looked at my face, huffed and flew up into the ceiling.

Five

That had been a lot to absorb, and I wasn't feeling very absorbent at the moment. So I reminded Mom that we were expecting a great deal of snow and encouraged her to head back to her town house. I told her Paul and I would confer on the Laurentz matter and I'd get back to her after the oncoming blizzard was shoveled off my front walk and my driveway. It was already starting to get dark outside.

Unfortunately, Paul had heard me tell her about the "conferring" and thought I actually wanted to do so as soon as Mom had left. I'd really just been trying to stall, forgetting Paul's weakness for unsolved crimes.

I asked Melissa to call Murray Feldner about the plowing (partly to get her to go elsewhere in the house and partly because I figured she'd guilt Murray into it) and Paul followed me into the kitchen, staying directly behind—and a little bit above—me.

"An invisible person throwing an electric toaster into a

bathtub!" he marveled. "It seems impossible, but we've seen stranger things happen, haven't we, Alison?"

I ignored him in pursuit of dinner, figuring I should probably feed myself and my daughter sometime soon. The refrigerator, more fully stocked than usual, contained a loaf of bread, some eggs, milk, an actual bag of lettuce, orange juice, English muffins and one Red Delicious apple. There was some meat in the separate freezer downstairs and bacon in the meat compartment here in the fridge. In other words, I was completely ready to make breakfast. And a salad with lettuce and an apple.

It was, as I said, better than usual. Yeah. I know. Would Sun Star Chinese Noodle deliver once the snow started falling?

"I really didn't think we were going to talk about this now, Paul," I told him. "I've got to plan for my first major snowstorm with guests in the house. I have to deal with possible meals cooked here and activities for them if we can't go outside tomorrow." (Actually, I wasn't that worried because I know how quickly this area digs out from even heavy snow and was fairly sure I wouldn't have to do more than maybe cook breakfast, turning the place into a B and B for all of one morning.) "Can't the crazy ghost who thinks he got fried by a toaster wait?"

I wasn't looking directly at Paul, but I got the impression—don't ask me how; sometimes it's an intuitive thing with the ghosts—that he stopped in what would be, for a living person, his tracks. "You don't want to investigate this case?" he asked. "Your mother is concerned. She thinks your father is being held somewhere against his will."

"And I think she's being a nut," I countered, walking into the kitchen and heading directly for the refrigerator. "My father doesn't show up to one of their clandestine little rendezvous and right away she buys the story of some mentally disturbed spirit—no offense—who tells her a goofy story. Give my dad a few days to come back, and you'll see there's nothing wrong."

"I don't understand your attitude," Paul said. "You don't seem concerned about your father at all."

"I'm not," I answered. "I'm sure he's fine, wherever he is."

I walked to the silverware drawer, where we keep the take-out menus. I pulled out the one for Harbor Pizza, deciding that Chinese food wasn't good blizzard fare. Calzones. Now *that's* what you eat during a blizzard. I'd have to check the freezer for ice cream, too. You're supposed to be cold in a blizzard, right?

"This is about his not visiting you, isn't it?" Paul asked.

I slammed the drawer closed. "*No*," I said with a little too much emphasis. "It's not about my father's not visiting me." Definitely ice cream. With hot fudge. But no cherries. Maraschino cherries are an abomination.

"I think it is. I think you're angry at him for coming to see your mother once a week but never coming to see you. And I think that's why you don't want to discuss this case we've been hired to—"

I pivoted to face Paul directly but had to crane my neck upward to do it. "We haven't been *hired* to do anything!" I shouted. "*We* can't be hired to do anything! You're dead, and I'm an innkeeper, not a private eye! This is a ridiculous pretend game we're playing, and it's almost gotten me killed more than once. I'm not doing it again; is that understood?"

Paul's eyes had widened at my first howl. "Alison," he began.

I cut him off. "Is. That. Understood?" I repeated.

He pointed his finger at a spot behind me and then vanished. I spun to see where he'd been pointing, which, as it turned out, was the kitchen door.

There stood Nan and Morgan Henderson. And they were not looking like they had complete confidence in the woman whose house they'd be sharing for the next several days, possibly with a great deal of snow prohibiting travel in the area.

In fact, they looked downright alarmed. Nan had her hands gripping Morgan's left arm, and her knuckles were a little whiter than I would have preferred. Morgan, for his part, had involuntarily bared his upper teeth in a snarl meant, I think, to keep the crazy lady at bay until reinforcements could be summoned.

"I'm so sorry," was the only thing I could think to say. The three of us stood there for a long moment. No doubt they were expecting a more detailed explanation for my behavior. I would have been happy to provide one. But let's face it—I had nothing. I thanked my good luck I hadn't been holding a carving knife when they'd walked in.

"Is something . . . wrong?" Nan asked. "You sounded upset."

"I was just . . . I had . . ." Was I going to tell them that one of the household ghosts had been annoying me with his insistence that we investigate the death of a man in a bathtub so I could find my deceased father, who was apparently being held against his will in some sort of bizarre posthumous blackmail scheme? Somehow that seemed like a bad strategy. "I've had some family difficulties," I finally managed. "I guess I was just venting. I'm sorry. I thought you'd left for dinner, or I wouldn't have made so much noise."

Nan had pasted a frozen smile on her face, similar to the sort typically seen on the terrified girl when confronting the serial killer in slasher movies. "Oh, don't worry," she said. "It's fine." It was a wonder she didn't start backing toward the door, but she held her ground.

"Fine," Morgan parroted.

"No, seriously," I argued. "I don't want you to think I do that all the time. Please, I want you to feel comfortable here."

"We're comfortable," Nan's mouth said, though her eyes

screamed, "We're calling the police as soon as we make it outside." Morgan, at least, didn't echo her words.

"Would you like a recommendation for dinner?" I tried.

"Sure!" she answered, much too quickly and too loudly. I gave them the names of two nice restaurants within walking distance and one that was a ten-minute drive from the house. I was willing to bet they'd ignore all my suggestions and head for the nearest place they could find to plot their escape. But the oncoming snow would probably keep them in my clutches at least another day or two.

Exhaling, I tried to lighten the tension before they could leave. "I'm really very sorry about before," I said with a soothing tone. "It wasn't my best moment, and I promise you, it won't happen again."

Nan seemed to relax a little this time. "I understand," she said. "I've—*we've*—had some trying times ourselves lately. It's why we were so looking forward to this vacation." She couldn't help but give Morgan a sideways glance.

They turned to leave. Morgan mumbled something, and once they were out the door, I almost collapsed into a kitchen chair. I had to remember that my current guests didn't know the place was, for lack of a better word, "haunted." I'd gotten so used to the Senior Plus Tours guests, who *wanted* there to be ghosts, that I'd dropped my defenses. Couldn't let that happen again.

I almost jumped up to Paul and Maxie altitudes when the kitchen door swung open again. But instead of an irate guest or a ghost demanding I find out who murdered someone else, the presence in the doorway was that of my daughter.

"What?" Melissa asked. I must have looked like I was expecting Hannibal Lecter to stop on by.

"Nothing," I said. "Pizza or Chinese?" I stood up to get back to the menu drawer.

"Pizza," she declared definitively. "Can we have ice cream for dessert? That's what you should have in a blizzard."

That's my girl.

Six

Wednesday

In the history of modern meteorology (which really begins in the eighteenth century), weather forecasts have been correct a larger percentage of the time than most people would believe. But it's easy to blame the weather reporter on TV when you're told it will be a lovely day and instead find yourself having to brave a raging monsoon, sans umbrella, from the parking lot to your office.

So it wasn't difficult for me to forgive the blizzard hysteria of last night when I woke up this morning to find what could charitably be called a "dusting" on my front porch. Despite having loaded up on ice melt and bought a new, ergonomically designed shovel, I removed what had accumulated on the porch, sidewalk and driveway with an old broom in roughly four minutes.

As I was putting the broom away, I saw Murray Feldner drive up with the plow attached to the front of his pickup truck and start to position himself at the mouth of my driveway. I walked over and tapped on his driver's side window. He lowered it.

"What's up, Murray?" I asked. It's always best to pretend you're friends with the people who charge you for stuff. It makes it more difficult for them to gouge you. Not impossible but more difficult.

"Here to plow the driveway," he answered. Murray, a guy from my high school football team who might have taken a few too many shots to the helmet, gave me a look that indicated I must be somehow mentally deficient for having asked the question.

"Plow it of what?" I asked. "We got a flurry. There's nothing there."

"Big snow north of here," Murray said, as if that justified his action. "Belleville, Montclair, Bergen County. Foot and a half, I hear. South of here, too. Cape May got a lot." He started to raise the window, clearly having declared the conversation ended.

I had to hurry to be heard. "But nothing *here*," I noted. "There's nothing to plow on my driveway or anywhere else. See?" I pointed to the nothing.

Murray's mouth moved to one side. This might have indicated thought. It was hard to know. "Your daughter called last night. Said to make sure I was here first thing today. Said you had guests."

It was becoming obvious that "obvious" was lost on Murray. "That was when we thought we were getting a lot of snow," I told him. "We didn't get any. You'll scrape your plow. You might damage it."

His eyes narrowed. "Hadn't thought of that," he said. "You don't want it plowed?"

"Not today. Be ready if it *really* snows at some point."

"Okay." Murray nodded and tugged on the Phillies cap he wore all the time except during baseball season, when he wore a cap with the logo of the New York Knicks. "No plowing today. Send you a bill."

It wasn't until he was halfway up the street that I realized he'd just said he was charging me for *not* plowing. I clenched my teeth. We'd have to talk before the next snowstorm.

I checked to make sure Nan and Morgan Henderson didn't need anything, but they hadn't come down from their room yet. (They had, however, returned to the guesthouse after dinner the night before, which was a relief.) This made things somewhat difficult, since I had a few errands to run in town—I didn't want to leave before showing my face to my guests. They already thought I was a raving lunatic; it would be worse if they thought I was an unaccommodating raving lunatic.

Melissa ambled down, looked out the front door and scowled.

"No snow," she said. She must have been really tired and disappointed, because usually she's a chatterbox first thing in the morning. Something she inherited from her father.

"No, sorry, baby," I said in a soothing tone. "Looks like you have school today."

She gave me a dirty look and headed for the stairs. A shower would be next on the agenda.

Before I could make it to the kitchen to start coffee brewing, Paul dropped down through the ceiling, as if he was using an invisible fire pole.

"Maxie has been doing some research," he said quickly. Once Paul gets the idea of an investigation into his head, it's hard to get out, and now that Maxie, our resident Internet expert, was on the case, he probably thought he had some tantalizing piece of information that would make it irresistible to me.

You'd think he'd know me better by now.

"Yeah?" I said. Indifference, not eloquence, was the point here.

He plowed on, choosing not to notice my fantastic display of boredom. "It seems that Lawrence Laurentz did indeed die just over six months ago, and the attending doctor at the emergency room wrote it up as a cardiac arrhythmia."

"So there you are," I said in my best efficient-but-cool businesswoman voice. "Mystery solved. The ghost is delusional."

Paul nodded, which I hadn't expected. I retaliated by continuing into the kitchen, walking directly through him, which is a strange but not unpleasant sensation. Paul's touch is like a warm breeze, Maxie's more like a cooling paper fan.

"Maybe so," he said. I pushed the kitchen door open and let it swing through him as he followed me. "But arrhythmia is not an uncommon misdiagnosis in cases of electrocution. Laurentz's story merits at least a cursory look."

"So go ahead and look," I said. It sounded cold even to me.

Paul's face couldn't have looked more wounded if I'd actually been able to slap it. "You know I can't," he mumbled.

I drew a breath and looked up at him. "I'm sorry, Paul," I said. "You know I didn't mean . . ."

"My problem isn't the point," he said, not making eye contact. Having forgotten why I'd come into the kitchen, I sat down at the chair. I felt like there were heavy weights on the top of my head. "*Your* problem is the point."

"My problem?"

Paul hovered down to try and approximate a level eye-to-eye approach. But he can't really hold still, so I was getting a trifle seasick watching him. "Think about it, Alison. This man is in the same position Maxie and I were when you met us. And he came to you through your mother. Either of those things alone would normally be enough to spur you to action."

I tried to interrupt, but he went on. "And by working on this case, you might get your father out of what sounds like a potentially unpleasant situation. I can't imagine that you don't want to do that."

Suddenly, my eyes felt a little damp. I looked away from Paul. And when I heard my own voice reply to him, it sounded squeaky and quiet. "Then why didn't he ask me himself?" I managed. "Why haven't I ever heard from my dad when he obviously could have spoken to me whenever he wanted? Why doesn't he want to talk to his own grand-daughter? Paul, *why*?" I stopped talking because I was afraid of the next sound that would come out of my mouth.

Paul spoke softly and gently. "Maybe this is your way to find out," he said.

Finding my father: That hadn't occurred to me. My head snapped up. Paul seemed startled by the sudden movement; his eyes widened a tiny bit and his mouth straightened out.

Before either of us could speak, the kitchen door swung open and Melissa slouched in, dragging her backpack behind her and heading for the refrigerator with the manner of a prisoner being led back out into the quarry to break rocks. "What'd I miss?" she mumbled as she opened the fridge in search of something quick and easy for breakfast.

Paul surveyed my face and it must have told him some-thing; he smiled. "Your mom is going to help me investi-gate what happened to Mr. Laurentz," he said.

Melissa's head turned toward me quickly, and for the first time today, she looked enthusiastic.

"I want to help," she said.

Seven

"It's a *conspiracy,* I tell you!" Lawrence Laurentz turned out to be an imposingly tall, probably artificially dark-haired ghost, hovering over the sofa in my mother's living room, looking as theatrical as a box of seven-dollar Milk Duds. The man, I'd guess in his seventies, had a flair for overacting that William Shatner himself would envy.

"A conspiracy?" I parroted back. All I'd asked was what Lawrence had done for a living when he was, you know, living.

This meeting had been hastily arranged through Paul with help from Mom. Mom couldn't summon the dashing ghost herself, but she knew something of his habits. We'd agreed to meet at Mom's house because much like Paul, who couldn't leave my guesthouse property, Lawrence could travel only within the boundaries of Whispering Lakes, the active adult community where Mom lived. (Apparently he'd been a neighbor of hers on the other side of the complex when he was alive, but they'd never met.)

Maxie, who had gotten to come along in her usual way (by materializing in my car after I'd traveled too far to take her back) was with me, too, but Melissa had been convinced—after a good deal of protestation on her part and some old-fashioned threat-making on mine—that she still had to go to school today, though I'd conceded she would be allowed to aid in the investigation when it was possible. Of course, in my mind that still meant "never."

"A conspiracy," Lawrence repeated back, looking down his nose at me. "I am the victim of a vast network of vandals, thieves and"—he paused briefly here—"murderers."

Maxie watched Lawrence openmouthed. It's not easy to impress Maxie, but this guy was a first-class drama queen if ever I'd seen one.

Mom, who had out of polite habit put out a plate of cookies for her guests despite my being the only one who could eat, got Lawrence's eye and spoke in what was for her a soothing tone (to me it sounded like the voice of a police hostage negotiator). "Now, Lawrence," she said. "All Alison asked was about your business."

It had been strangely gratifying to see how pleased Mom was when I'd agreed to investigate Lawrence's "murder." She had such trust in me, however ill-advised, that I'd felt like a heel for hesitating in the first place. So by the time I'd dropped Melissa off at school and seen to the needs of the Hendersons—which were minimal today—Paul had arranged this audience with the ghost.

Once I'd agreed to this meeting, I'd been slightly concerned that I might not be able to see Lawrence. I can't see as many spirits as Mom and Melissa do; my ability is still in the development stage. Which normally I don't find at all worrisome, unless I have to question a dead person. But luckily, I suppose, Lawrence was among the ghosts I could have spotted a football field away—his strength of personality was that strong. If you know what I mean.

Lawrence stopped and considered what my mother had

said. "Of course, Loretta, my apologies," he said, lavishing on the charm. Really, the man should have been wearing a cape. "I am—was—an impresario."

There was a silence. "A what?" Maxie asked.

The elder ghost turned his head slowly, milking the effect. "An *impresario*. I provided entertainment of the highest order to the residents of this"—and here he sniffed to give us a taste of how unappreciated he'd been in this den of heathens—"area."

Mom clucked her tongue. "Lawrence," she chided. "You worked in the ticket office at the Count Basie Theatre in Red Bank."

Lawrence seemed to deflate in the face of Mom's bluntness but then pumped himself up again. "It's true," he admitted. "But I had a ninety-eight percent accuracy score on my evaluations and no customer complaints in fifteen years."

"Impressive," I said. Then, since somebody had to bring this conversation back to the topic at hand, I continued, "So let's talk about what happened to you."

Lawrence regarded me. He didn't look at me; he *regarded* me. And no doubt found me wanting. "I was murdered," he said.

"Yes. That's not a lot to go on. Can you give me a few details? You say you were electrocuted?"

"I was electrocuted, whether I say so or not," he corrected me. "It is a fact."

"The medical examiner's report"—which I had not actually seen, but what the hell—"says you died of cardiac arrhythmia."

He curled his upper lip. "Of course it does. That's what electrocution looks like to a medical examiner. I'm telling you, someone threw an electric toaster into the tub while I was bathing."

I tried very hard not to snicker and believe I would have succeeded if Maxie hadn't puffed out her own lips in amusement. I contained myself quickly, but Lawrence gave me a look indicating that he'd seen my initial reaction. I plowed on. "Are you sure it was a toaster? Did you see who threw it?"

Lawrence looked the other way. "No," he sniffed. "Whoever did it was invisible."

I'd known that was the answer he'd give, so I didn't react. "Invisible," I said. "Like you are to most people now?"

"How many ways are there to be invisible?" Lawrence asked.

Mom picked up a cookie and took a bite, which wasn't characteristic of her; she's a closet eater. "Keep a civil tongue, Lawrence," she said. "Alison is trying to help."

Maxie covered her mouth. She loves it when Mom scolds people who aren't her.

I decided to ignore Lawrence's previous comment. "Did you see anything at all before . . . it happened?" If I'd started to think of Lawrence taking a bath and having a toaster tossed in again, I'd have to picture him in a bathtub, and that wasn't going to do anybody any good.

"Nothing," he said, still not making eye contact. In fact, he floated up a little and the top of his head disappeared. Mom's house doesn't have high ceilings.

"What about the plug?" I asked. That was a question Paul had primed me with before I left for the interview. He's always careful to tell me exactly what to ask, for two reasons: One, he's a control freak, and two, I don't know what I'm doing.

"The plug?" Lawrence repeated.

"Yes, the plug on the toaster," I answered, stuttering just a tiny bit on the word *toaster*. "If you were electrocuted by a toaster "—I couldn't look at Maxie—"it had to have been plugged in. An unplugged toaster wouldn't have done you any harm. Did you see that?"

Lawrence appeared flustered for the first time; he

chewed a little on his lips and didn't speak for a moment, which for him was a long time. He mumbled something I couldn't hear.

"What?"

"I . . . did not see that happen," he answered, regaining some of his swagger. "But I was not expecting a toaster to be thrown into my bath. It's possible I just wasn't looking in that direction. I was reading."

Maxie's eyebrows literally hit the ceiling and kept going as she rose up bodily in surprise. "Reading?" she asked. "In the bathtub?"

Mom gave her a look. "It's not unusual, Maxine," she scolded mildly. "I read in the bath all the time." Another in a series of mental images I really didn't need to carry around with me.

"What were you reading?" I asked. It seemed completely irrelevant, but it was the sort of thing that Paul would ask. He always asks stuff that I think makes no difference and draws information from it. It's really annoying. Best to beat him at his own game.

"*Variety*," Lawrence answered. Of course. "So," he concluded. "That should be enough to begin you on your investigation, no?"

"Not yet," I answered. Maxie had been expecting this (we'd discussed it on the way to Mom's house), so she smirked slyly. "We haven't discussed my fee. I won't be doing any investigation unless we reach an agreement on the other issue."

Lawrence, sensing the trap being sprung around him, dropped his voice an octave. "*What* other issue?" he asked.

"My father," I told him. "I do nothing for you until I see my father."

Maxie hovered down to position herself between me and Lawrence. She said nothing, but the look on her face (which I could sort of see through the back of her head) unmistakably said, "Don't do anything stupid."

Lawrence, however, did not appear to be contemplating any kind of violence; he looked absolutely stunned. His eyes bulged a bit and his mouth formed an O that made it appear someone had hit him hard in the stomach. After a moment in which his eyes seemed to be looking for a way out of their sockets, he focused on me and said, "I'm afraid that won't be possible." Well, that certainly ended the argument.

I twisted my mouth up in an expression of scorn. "Then I'm sorry, but it won't be . . . *possible* for me to help you out. My father is my fee. And I don't work unless I know that the client has the funds available to pay."

Paul had been clear about playing hardball on this point. So I was making a concerted effort not to look at my mother, who as a rule plays Nerf ball. She surely looked desperate, and seeing that would have something other than a positive effect on my confidence.

"It's not possible for me to simply *produce* him," Lawrence said, regaining some of his composure. "This is a process, and it takes time. Have a little patience."

"I don't understand the process, Mr. Laurentz," I said. "But I am very concerned that I get some proof you *can* produce my father when you want to. So far, all I have is your word, and I don't really know you, do I?"

The ghost raised an eyebrow so archly Olivier himself would have been intimidated. But I was mad, so it only caused slight goose bumps on the back of my left arm. I took that as a victory.

"Your father is confined to a space I can't adequately describe," he said with a great air of authority. "He is not suffering, but he cannot move about the way he could before."

"Why are you holding him?" I asked.

"I am not. He is, as far as I can discern, operating under his own will."

There was a long silence while we digested that tidbit. I assiduously avoided looking at Mom, but from behind me, I could hear her gasp.

"He's doing this to *himself*?" she whispered.

Lawrence nodded. "I can communicate with him, but I am not able to go to him or to bring him back." He turned toward me. "So you see, Ms. Kerby, I cannot comply with your demand. I can't bring your father to you. But I can get messages to him and bring back his replies."

I shook my head. "That's not enough, Mr. Laurentz," I said. "Why should I believe you?"

Paul had advised me to watch Lawrence very carefully—he had told me, as he always does, to "look at the subject's face when you confront him with something he wasn't expecting. That's when you get the good information." What I saw, perhaps for the first time since we'd started talking, was Lawrence without any pretense, without the act.

And he looked very sad.

"I'm sorry, Ms. Kerby," he said. "I can't think of one reason why you should."

Well, that was a real nonstarter! If I actually started to feel sorry for the guy who was keeping me from Dad and making Mom miserable, how could I possibly refuse to help him? Since what I really wanted was to turn him down, I used my favorite tactic when trying to refuse someone something—I pretended Lawrence was my ex-husband Steven, The Swine. Just picturing The Swine's face with Lawrence's words coming out of it was enough; I was sufficiently pissed off to deny Dorothy a visit with Toto.

I was about to swing back toward him, angry, but as I turned, I saw Maxie looking worried and staring over my left shoulder. And that led to a major mistake on my part.

I looked at my mother.

For the first time since I'd known her (which was admittedly my whole life), she looked her age, plus a few years. Her eyes were wide, her mouth had little lines around it and she was pale and drawn. She looked, in a word, terrified.

I continued my turn toward Lawrence.

"We'll take your case," I told him.

Eight

"There's no record of a Lawrence Laurentz dying suspiciously," said Detective Lieutenant Anita McElone, sitting behind her desk in the bull pen at the Harbor Haven Police Department. There was commotion all around her, but McElone, who knew me from a few previous cases, was calm and still. She could be really annoying that way.

"He died alone," I said. "That means there has to be some report on it. It was about six months ago, at Whispering Lakes in Manalapan."

McElone raised an eyebrow. "And you're not talking to the Manalapan police because . . . ?"

"Because I don't know anyone there, but you know me and love me, and you'll help me," I told her.

"Well, I *know* you, anyway." McElone and I have an interesting relationship: It's not exactly a friendship, since we've never seen each other except about a crime. And it's not really a professional interaction, since she's a cop and I'm just an innkeeper with a private-investigator's license.

Not to mention McElone is fairly convinced that I'm a screwup who gets in the way a lot, which—if I'm being honest—is not all that far off the mark.

Let's call it mutual respect. Without the "mutual" part.

"Could you please look up the medical examiner's report?" I asked. "There has to be one."

McElone would have rolled her eyes if she were any less dignified. Instead, she simply gave me a look indicating her day would be considerably easier if I'd just go away. "I told you. I already looked it up. There's no report of a Lawrence Laurentz dying in Manalapan. Is it possible you spelled the name wrong or something?"

That hadn't occurred to me. "Let me check," I told her, and got out my phone. Lawrence had promised to stay at Mom's until I could check in, so I texted my mother (we're so twenty-first century) and asked her to pass on the question.

"Why are you looking into this?" McElone asked me while we waited for the reply from Mom. "Who's your client?"

This is always a tricky question when dealing with a client who is, technically, deceased. Police officers—especially McElone, who avoids coming to my house because she says it "creeps her out"—tend to look askance at someone who says she communicates with the dead. And the smart-asses always want to know why you can't just ask the "vic" who killed them and cut out the middleman.

Luckily, I'd been around the block with McElone a few times before and had prepared for the question. "You know I'm not supposed to say," I told her. "But between us, I was hired by . . ."

I had timed it nicely, because that was when my phone chirped with the news of a text message coming from Mom. I pulled out the phone and opened it. The message read, "L sz 2 sk bt Melvin Brookman." Mom has embraced the abbreviated language of texting; I am old-school and write full sentences. Mom's next text read, "L sz his rl nm." The lack of punctuation in texting is enough to drive me mad. The lack of vowels was worse. But it translated into "Lawrence says it's his real name." After a while, you get the hang of it. Sort of.

"How about a Melvin Brookman?" I asked McElone, while texting back to Mom, "Why?" I'm a multitasker.

McElone dutifully clicked away at her keyboard, waited a moment and nodded. "There's a Melvin Brookman who died of arrhythmia in Manalapan last summer," she said. "The ME's report doesn't really seem all that interesting. Heart problem. Found in the tub. No evidence of foul play. I can print out the pertinent parts if you want it."

"I want it," I said. "Thanks. Is the ME sure it was natural causes?"

She shrugged. "There's nothing here to indicate there's anything to be suspicious about." She pulled a few pages out of her printer and handed them to me. "Now, are you done with your side job for today? Can I start doing some actual police work?"

"In this town? Did a rash of jaywalking break out all of a sudden? It's winter. There's nobody here."

The phone buzzed, and Mom had texted back, "ts hs stg nm." I had no idea what that meant and decided against texting while I stood to leave.

"There's enough crime going on for us," McElone said. "Besides, we have to dig out after that humongous blizzard we had last night." She never even broke a smile.

"Thanks for the ME report," I said.

"Don't mention it," McElone told me. "To anyone. Hey. You never answered me. Who's your client on this?"

"Close relative of the deceased. That's all I can say."

Her eyes narrowed. "I think you're wasting your time with this one. The guy died of natural causes."

He says otherwise, I thought. Instead, I said, "I hope so," thanked McElone again and walked outside.

Despite the lack of snow, it was still freezing cold, but

the kind of debilitating, mind-numbing cold we tend to get with our hard ocean winds this time of year. Standing outside the police department building, I texted Mom, "What's an stg nm?" And I'd like it pointed out for the record that I went the extra mile and used a real question mark.

Less than a minute later came her reply. "Stage name," it read.

I returned home to check in with Nan and Morgan Henderson, who were not acting quite as much like they were in the care of a deranged person but appeared (Nan, anyway) disappointed not to be snowed in. They said they had decided to take the opportunity and visit Asbury Park (like many tourists, they wanted to go to the Stone Pony, under the mistaken assumption that it was the first place Bruce Springsteen ever played professionally, and I did not disabuse them of the assumption). That meant they'd be out until after dinner, which left me time to consider what the hell I was going to do about Melvin Brookman, aka Lawrence Laurentz, aka the nut who could reportedly lead me to my father.

"A stage name?" Paul asked. "Was this Laurentz fellow an actor?"

"I don't think so," I answered. "I'm taking a break from trying to decipher Mom's texts, and I don't have the strength to call right now. But from what he and Mom tell me, he was a ticket taker in Red Bank. Do you think it would work to widen this doorway?"

That last question was aimed at Maxie, who was hovering near the library ceiling in a horizontal position like Cleopatra on her barge. For all my reluctance to puff up her ego, Maxie *had* been an emerging interior designer when she died, and she's got a talent for it. She likes to consult on any changes I make in the house, and I've given up being annoyed when her ideas are better than mine; it's inefficient.

She put her hand to her chin in a (literally) transparent overdone dramatic gesture of thought. "It would open up the room," she said, "but you don't have a lot of space on either side. How about making the window larger instead? That would add light."

Paul, trying hard to be the resident gumshoe, frowned at the turn the conversation was taking. "Then why would he have a stage name?" he asked, ignoring the topic Maxie and I had begun.

"I haven't a clue. You have my notes—I couldn't record him; you know that. He seems to have a view of himself that's, let's say, a little overinflated. He was probably an aspiring actor who lives with the fantasy."

"*Exists* with the fantasy," Paul corrected. He stroked his goatee, which he thinks is a sign that he's deep in thought but which actually makes him look a little pretentious in a cute way, like a little boy who pretends to be a grown-up.

He looked up at Maxie. "What was your impression?" he asked.

Maxie looked surprised to be asked. "The guy's hilarious," she said. We waited, but that was it.

Paul turned his attention back to me, shaking his head slightly. "From your description, he sounds flamboyant but not delusional, as far as I can tell. There's probably another explanation."

I mulled a few thoughts over and turned toward Maxie. "The problem with putting in a larger window is that it would require outside work on the siding, which I don't want to do in the winter, and this is supposed to be my winter project while I don't have many guests. Besides, a bigger window cuts down on wall space, and in a library full of books, wall space is especially important."

Maxie considered and nodded. "It would definitely require work outside and might be expensive," she agreed. "Maybe better overhead lighting in the room itself? Recessed or track?"

Paul sighed loudly. It was a day, it seemed, for theatrical gestures from dead people. "Are you even paying attention?" he asked me. "We're trying to investigate a murder here."

"No," I answered. "We're investigating a *death*. There's no evidence yet that this guy was actually murdered." I turned back toward Maxie. "Yeah, but the room still feels a little tight and claustrophobic. I can't move the walls, but I can widen the entrance. I'm going to ask Tony about it."

Maxie scowled. "Do you have to?" she asked. Maxie doesn't really get along with Tony Mandorisi, Jeannie's husband and my contractor guru. It's because Maxie first thought Tony was cute and flirted with him in a manner that seriously creeped Tony out. With good reason, I might add.

"I want to make sure I do it right, and the only other reliable contractor I know is my father," I answered. Going again from ghost to ghost, I looked over at Paul. "I don't suppose you've been able to raise my dad on the Ghosternet, have you?" I asked.

"Oh, am I still part of the conversation?" Paul pouted. Honestly, men. Don't pay attention to them for six seconds and they think you've forgotten they exist. "No, I've tried to contact your father frequently since we met with your mother last night, and I've gotten no response. But that doesn't really mean much. As you know, I've tried to get in touch with him before, and I've never really been able to establish a connection. My ability to communicate with other people like Maxie and me is still evolving, I suppose."

"Well, keep trying. I need to know if this Laurentz guy is telling the truth about Dad."

"Give me a day or two to think about it," Maxie said, gesturing at the library door. "Maybe I can come up with something else." I nodded, and Maxie vanished through the ceiling.

Paul cocked an eyebrow and considered me. "Can we

go back to discussing the case now that your interior design seminar is over?" he asked.

"Don't get snippy," I told him. "It's your fault I'm in this investigation business to begin with."

"Some would see that as a good thing," he answered. "But nonetheless. Given the interview you did with Lawrence and the information we have that he changed his name from Melvin Brookman, I think we have to consider another possibility."

"It's a stage name. The guy's a kook," I said. "Why do we need another possibility?"

Paul floated down to eye level to emphasize his point. "Melvin Brookman wasn't an actor; he had no need for a stage name. Why does a person change his name?" he asked. I hate it when he asks a question in an effort to educate me. What I really hate about it is that he's always right.

"Why does a person ask questions when he already knows the answer?" I countered.

"Alison." Paul forced eye contact. "Why does a person change his name? Think."

"Because he doesn't like the old one," I suggested. We'd known someone named Alice who'd changed her name to Arlice simply to be more exotic.

"Perhaps," Paul said, clearly thinking that was not the reason in Melvin Brookman's case. "What else?"

"For professional reasons?" That was an outright guess.

"Lawrence was, as you put it, a ticket taker in Red Bank, New Jersey. No one he worked with would even ask his name. What else?"

One of my tricks when trying to solve a problem was to think of something else, so I considered how long I had before I needed to go pick Melissa up from school. (If you're interested, I had three hours and fifteen minutes.)

"Because he doesn't want someone to know who he is," I said. I have no idea where that came from.

Paul smiled, the successful teacher with a somewhat dim pupil who was finally grasping the concept. "And why would a man not want people to know his real name?" he rephrased.

I didn't like the answer I was about to give. "Because he might have a criminal record," I said.

"Excellent," Paul beamed.

"Not really," I answered. "That criminal is a ghost who spends a lot of time in my mother's house."

Nine

The prudent thing to do would have been to call McElone to ask if either Lawrence Laurentz or Melvin Brookman had criminal records. But that would have required my talking to McElone again and asking her for another favor, and quite frankly, that was more than I was willing to do just at the moment.

Instead, I cleaned a few rooms in the house and then picked Melissa up from school, and her first words on getting into the admittedly frigid Volvo (the heater is nominal at best) were, "So where are we in the Laurentz case?"

This was not the conversation I'd been prepared to have with my ten-year-old, but have it we did, as Melissa is a force of nature and not to be ignored or defied when she gets up a head of steam. I filled her in on what I'd found out, which was not much.

We drove to Jeannie and Tony's house in Lavallette so I could ask Tony about the library door, and because we hadn't seen baby Oliver in at least a week. The doorway was a small project I thought might not require Tony's in-person inspection, just a short conversation, and Liss likes visiting the baby, too.

Once we arrived, and after the shedding of coats and the inevitable showing off of more baby pictures (while the actual baby was right there on his mother's lap, making the procedure seem somehow redundant), Liss sat on the floor with Oliver while Jeannie watched her shake rattles in front of him and Tony and I moved to the dining room so I could explain my construction issue and get his advice.

I described the doorway—which Tony had seen many times before—and what I wanted to accomplish in the library, but Tony's eyes were looking into the living room, watching Melissa on the floor with his son.

"Are you listening?" I asked him.

He turned to me and his face had an expression of desperation I'd never seen on it before. "You've got to get her out of here," he whispered.

Okay, there are protective parents and then there are people insulting to my daughter. "Why can't Melissa play with the baby?" I asked quietly, so my completely blame-free daughter wouldn't overhear.

"Melissa? What are you talking about?" Tony's brow furrowed.

"You just told me to get Melissa out of here," I reminded him. The lack of sleep must have been eroding his brain.

"No, no," Tony insisted. "Not Melissa. *Jeannie*. You've got to get Jeannie out of here!"

One of us was speaking a foreign language, and I was beginning to suspect it was me. "Jeannie lives here. You want me to get rid of your wife?" I asked. Forget that Jeannie was my friend long before I met Tony and that I'd actually introduced them. This was a really inappropriate time to suggest they shouldn't live together anymore.

"You don't understand," he pleaded. "It's been four months and she won't do *anything* except watch the baby."

"I thought Jeannie was going back to her job after three months," I said. The one time I'd asked Jeannie about it, she'd ignored me and asked if I thought Oliver's toenails needed clipping.

"I thought so, too," Tony answered. "But she says she can't bear the thought. They call her and she keeps putting it off. She gets up four times a night with him. She won't let me get him back to sleep at night. She won't let me feed him in the morning. She won't let me play unsupervised with my own son. Alison, she needs to get out and remember she has a life!"

"She won't let you do anything?" I asked. "She won't let you change diapers?"

He huffed. "No, that she occasionally manages to delegate. But I get out of the house every day, I get to go around and see people and fix things and be something other than Ollie's dad every once in a while. Jeannie *won't leave*."

"Easy, Tony." I was once again following Paul's advice about avoiding the words *calm down*. "I realize Jeannie's been a little obsessive since Oliver was born, but—"

"A *little*?" Tony's Adam's apple was the size of a grapefruit; I watched it rise and fall. "Alison, please. You're her best friend. Look at her."

I glanced over as Jeannie subtly picked up the rattle Melissa had been waving in front of Oliver's face. She wiped it off with a cloth diaper (after considerable agonizing, Jeannie had decided on cloth diapers for in the house, and disposables only when traveling) despite its not having touched anything except Liss's fingers. Then she set it back down on the immaculate play mat while Liss rocked the baby in her arms. But that wasn't good enough for Jeannie. She picked the rattle back up, took a baby wipe from a dispenser, ran it over the rattle, then reached into a drawer, pulled out a bottle of hand disinfectant, wiped the rattle again and set it down.

While doing all this, Jeannie said, "Make sure you support his head," to Melissa, who was supporting Oliver's head with both hands, despite the baby's best efforts to shake his head free. Oliver was four months old, after all, not four days. Despite his mother's protests, he could raise his head whenever he wanted.

"Okay," I told Tony. "I get your point. But what can I do?"

"*Get her out of here*," he repeated. "What are you doing this afternoon?"

"Visiting you. Then I'm taking Liss back home and I have a quick errand to run on an investigation I'm doing."

"Perfect!" Tony shouted—well, breathed with enthusiasm. "Take Jeannie with you on the investigation! She loves when you ask her to help with that stuff!"

"It's late already," I protested. "I might not even do it today. I have guests . . ."

"Alison," he said in a voice weighted down by weariness and desperation. "If you don't take Jeannie out of here, she's going to spend the night taking Ollie's temperature."

That didn't sound good. "What's wrong?" I asked.

"Nothing! That's the point!"

"Okay." There was no sense fighting it. "Let me see what I can do. But you're going to help me with my library doorway."

Tony's face looked so relieved I felt like I'd helped starving orphans get adopted by billionaires. "I'll do the library door for *nothing*!" he said. "Thank you, Alison!"

"What're you talking about?" Jeannie called from the living room, where she was rechecking the baby-proofing on one of the socket plugs that the baby couldn't reach. "What are you two plotting?"

"I'm just giving Alison a little carpentry advice," Tony said, and even though that was technically true, his tone was so forced that even I didn't believe him.

I took Tony by the arm, giving him a look that indicated I should do the talking and marched him into the living room. Melissa was nuzzling Oliver's belly, which produced the desired effect of making him laugh. Jeannie was watching and visibly stopping herself from reaching for a box of aloe-enhanced tissues on the table next to her seat on the couch.

"I was telling Tony about the case I've agreed to investigate," I told Jeannie. "It looks like it's going to be a bear." Melissa looked up, her expression puzzled. I sent a "go with it" look her way, and she smiled and went back to making Oliver laugh.

"You're taking a case? Voluntarily?" Jeannie knew I wasn't that keen on the whole investigation thing, but since she refuses to believe in Paul and Maxie, I've given up trying to explain to her the truth about my motivations for getting the private-investigator's license.

"It's the off-season, and I could use a little extra cash," I told her instead. "I didn't think this one would be a big deal, but it's proving to be more puzzling than I thought." I turned away from her at that point because I wasn't sure I could sell that line of crap without breaking into a ridiculous grin.

"Oh, really?" Jeannie said. I'd have expected to need more of a lure than that, but she took the bait eagerly. "What's the case about?"

It seemed safe to turn back and face her. Melissa grinned at me from out of Jeannie's line of sight, and started to play with Oliver's feet, which were currently snug in a blue woolly-looking sleeper. He giggled.

All I had to do now was reel Jeannie in.

"It seemed like it was going to be a simple case, just confirming that a man in my mother's residential community had died of natural causes, but now it seems like maybe he didn't," I told her. "His sister called Mom to ask for my help, and now I can't figure out what to do next."

"Is this what all the intrigue with your mother and her mysterious visitor was about yesterday?" Jeannie asked. Um . . . sure! I nodded. "What have you done so far?" Jeannie asked.

"I checked the medical examiner's report. There's nothing

unusual there, but even if there were elements that would point to a crime, they probably weren't found since it's obvious they weren't looking for anything unusual." Indeed, the report McElone had given me was incredibly routine and superficial.

"So what makes you think there was anything to find?" Jeannie wanted to know. It was a good question, especially given the fact that telling her I'd heard it from the corpse himself seemed just a little bit pointless.

"This was a man whose heart problems were under control," I said, which was true, according to Laurentz/Brookman. "He'd had some prior heart issues, but nothing major. He wasn't under stress at the time and he'd had a completely clean medical checkup three days before he died."

Jeannie shrugged. "It happens," she said.

"Yeah, but his sister thinks it didn't just happen. She told Mom she thinks somebody electrocuted him."

"Please don't speak of such things in front of . . ." Jeannie cocked her head toward Melissa, sitting on the floor.

"Liss knows about the case," I told her.

"I meant Oliver," Jeannie corrected me. Of course.

"Sorry," I told her, despite the fact that it would be a miracle if Oliver even knew his own name yet. "But I'm so stumped, I'm not thinking straight." Was that too over the top?

"It's all right, but I really don't want him exposed to violence this early in his life," Jeannie said, apparently in earnest. Nah, the top was so high Shaquille O'Neal couldn't get over it with a trampoline.

"What do you think I should do? In the case?" I said, before she could lecture me further on the proper way to speak in front of a four-month-old baby.

Jeannie pursed her lips and nodded. This was her "thinking" face. I'd seen it applied to everything from whether she should have the chocolate chip muffin to whether she should marry Tony. (She'd ultimately decided yes to both.)

"The obvious thing would be to find out whether this man had any enemies," she said. "See if there was anyone with a reason to want to, you know, not be nice to him." Her gaze was at her son, who had fallen asleep on the baby mat.

"That's brilliant!" I said, not loudly enough to wake Oliver, as that would undoubtedly break the mood. "Exactly what I should have been thinking." Normally, I'd have thought "brilliant" was a bit much, but Jeannie was on a roll.

"Glad I could help," Jeannie said, beaming.

I walked over to her and took her hand. "What would I do without you?" I asked. Then I turned away and saw Tony's alarmed expression as I did. I gave my head a small shake to indicate he shouldn't worry. And I waited three seconds.

Jeannie said, "Hmmm . . ."

I had her.

"Do you really need help on this case?" she asked in a very quiet voice, no doubt intending not to disturb her baby's slumber. "Is it really a tough one?"

I kept my back to her and struggled to control my grin. "Toughest I've ever taken on," I said.

Jeannie looked at me, then at Oliver, who was drooling on the baby mat. She swooped in with a tissue and wiped it up, waking her son, who started to cry. So Jeannie picked him up and held him close to her shoulder, patting his back. My hopes of a wider entrance to my library, with no work done by me personally, sank.

Jeannie grinned. "I think I can help you out," she said. Before I could answer, she turned toward the entrance to the dining room, where her husband was standing. "Tony!" she said. "You can help Alison with her case, can't you?"

Tony looked like he was trying to break the Guinness Book of World Records mark for longest dropped jaw. If the floor hadn't been there to hold it up, no doubt his chin would have been in the basement. *"Me?"* he asked.

"Sure. You don't have that much work right now." Oliver stopped crying as Jeannie bobbed him up and down.

"But I do have some," he answered. "And I think it's just the thing for *you* . . ."

"Me?" Jeannie echoed. "I can't just leave Oliver with a babysitter all day. This is a very important moment in the child's development. He's only just started eating a little solid food, and he might actually be"—she whispered—"*a little behind* on his motor development. I need to be here."

Tony's eyes darted from me, to Jeannie, to Melissa, to the clock; nobody was offering him an out. Almost all in one word, he blurted, "Well, take the baby with you!"

There was an uneasy silence, followed by a strange gurgling sound that turned out not to be emanating from Oliver but from my own throat. Because Jeannie was smiling.

"That's a *great* idea!" she said.

Ten

I managed to convince the new parents—after failing to make my case that investigating a possible murder could be dangerous for an infant—that I'd be doing no detecting at all until the next day, which I hoped would give me time to think of a way to extricate myself from days of sleuthing with an obsessive mother and a nice little guy who might burst into loud, easy-to-locate tears at any given moment.

I don't know a great deal about murder investigations, but I'm pretty sure that would be bad.

Melissa and I drove home from Jeannie and Tony's, Liss texting her BFF, Wendy, about something that went on in school that day—or the utter tragedy that there had actually *been* school that day, after the buildup that had convinced them they'd be sledding and throwing snowballs instead—and me musing on how I'd gotten hip-deep in playing detective for a guy who, let's face it, was already dead.

Nan and Morgan Henderson had not yet returned from their dinner, so the evening was spent in consultation with

Paul and Maxie, then reporting in to Mom, who passed on our complete and utter lack of new information to Lawrence Laurentz (whom I still suspected might be a dangerous lunatic or criminal, neither of which I wanted keeping company with my mother for the duration).

I'd have to ask McElone to check him out the next day. Not calling her today had been a cowardly mistake. And one I would, under similar circumstances, no doubt make again.

When my guests arrived back at the house around nine, I believe I might have added to their suspicion that *I* was a dangerous lunatic by suggesting, in an ill-fated attempt to keep myself in their good graces, that we have karaoke night.

"Karaoke night," Morgan parroted, with his usual deadpan.

"It sounds . . . lovely," Nan attempted. "But we have early plans tomorrow, so I think we'll turn in."

"Early plans?" I asked.

"Yes," Nan said, hustling her husband out of the room without further elaboration. I hoped the early plans didn't involve finding other lodging possibilities. I began to fear the lousy reviews these two would be posting on TripAdvisor.

That night, when lying sleepless in bed, I thought mostly about my father.

I simply didn't believe the part of Lawrence's story in which Dad had supposedly exiled himself from the rest of the world—ghost and otherwise—for no discernible reason. It was odd that he hadn't come to see Mom for weeks, especially without letting her know that would happen. It wasn't like my father, dead or alive, to cause us worry.

That had been, perhaps, the most difficult part of his battle with the cancer that killed him. He detested seeing Mom and me so concerned about him, so sad that he wasn't getting better, so terrified that the prognosis was dire. Particularly because it proved to be correct.

"I don't want you to worry about me, baby girl," he'd said to me the last time we spoke. I saw Dad a few times after, but he was asleep every time—he'd been in terrible pain, on morphine, and had barely registered recognition when I walked in the door of his hospital room. "I want to know that you'll take care of your mother."

"Mom will be fine," I'd told him during that last conversation, regretting the message that she would get by just dandy without him. "She's a lot tougher than you give her credit for. All we're thinking about now is you getting well."

Dad shook his head. "That's not going to happen, Alison," he said. When he called me by name, I knew he was serious. Mostly, it was "baby girl."

"Sure it will. You'll get stronger." He gave me a look that indicated something less than complete confidence. I was lying, and we both knew it. He was in such pain that he could only talk for a minute or so at a time, and on enough morphine to make fifty addicts happy. It didn't seem to be helping. He drew in a lot of quick, unexpected breaths when the pain struck especially hard.

I hate hospitals, by the way. Even when I gave birth to Melissa—the only happy time one spends in such a place— I hated the hospital and left the minute it was possible. There's only so much hope you can summon on linoleum floors and under dropped ceilings. Whenever I was in a hospital room with Dad, we'd discuss what we'd have done to liven up the décor. Tops on the list were hardwood floors and incandescent lighting. Florescent sucks.

Again, he shook his head. "You don't have to sugarcoat it for me," he said. "I know the deal, and I've had a good life. I got no kicks coming." That was a quote from his father, my grandfather, that we both loved. "But you take care of Mom, okay?"

"Dad . . ."

He fixed his gaze on me. "I promise I'll try as hard as I can, but you have to promise to take care of Mom. Okay?"

I fixed my gaze on him. "You promise. You'll never give up."

"Promise. Now, *you* promise."

I was putting such effort into not crying that I could only nod and say, "Okay."

Dad had then closed his eyes and was snoring within a minute.

Tonight, wondering about his absence five years after his death, I finally let the tears go. But they weren't because Dad had died. They were tears of self-pity because I now knew he could have come back to call me "baby girl" again, and with only one exception, he hadn't.

"Larry Laurentz?" Penny Fields put on a show of trying to remember her co-worker when I spoke to her on Thursday morning. It was clear from her amateur performance she could have answered the question without hesitation, but felt it was best if she seemed less concerned. "Oh yes. Poor man. Went very suddenly, if I remember correctly."

Penny, who was the box office manager for the Count Basie Theatre, stood about five foot one but had an authoritative presence when she wasn't being unconvincing in her manner. She'd agreed to talk to Jeannie and me after we'd barged our way through the front door and gone through three different employees before finding someone who'd worked with Lawrence at the box office. The Basie had a low rate of turnover; the box office staff was very stable, she said.

"Yes," I agreed. "It was extremely sudden. And I'm wondering what kind of man he was." I'd told Penny that I was a private detective but had foregone the whole maybe-it-was-murder scenario as potentially off-putting, substituting instead the idea that Lawrence had left "a little money" in his will, and I was tracking down the next of kin.

"I didn't know him very well," Penny answered. She

tapped some keys on the computer keyboard in front of her; I thought she was looking up Lawrence's employee record, which might have been helpful, but as it turned out, she was looking at a page regarding the upcoming Stevie Nicks concert at the Basie. That wasn't helpful, except perhaps to Ms. Nicks.

"Well, what can you tell us about him?" Jeannie asked. She was standing near the door to the box office, which was a very cozy (that is, small) sort of room. The box office consisted of three windows in the lobby, through which people would receive tickets; computer terminals (one in front of each window, and a few in cubicles in the cramped area to the rear); telephones situated on each desk in the cubbyhole section; some boxes on shelves in which preordered tickets were waiting in envelopes marked with the patrons' names and a coffeepot, out of sight of the paying customers, in a far corner by the door. This was not a recreational area.

Jeannie had apparently noticed that Penny kept dotting her nose with a tissue, had decided that she was no doubt carrying typhoid and was keeping Oliver, who looked woozy, as far away as possible. Clearly, Jeannie was not going to be a ton of help on this case.

"He was an older gentleman, probably around seventy, but he was very vital and knew a lot about theater," Penny said, concentrating on cataloging the areas of unsold seats for the once and future Fleetwood Mac vocalist. "I think it bothered him that we didn't do more plays and musicals here, that it's more often concerts, you know?" She clicked onto a page advertising the Flying Karamazov Brothers.

"Was he friendly with anyone who worked here?" I pushed on. "Anyone who might have been special to him?" I had to keep the fiction of a possible inheritance alive, even while trying to find out if Lawrence had made any mortal enemies during his time at the Basie.

That distracted Penny from her web browsing. "Friendly?" she echoed, and then stifled a rueful chuckle badly. "I don't

think Larry would condescend to be friendly with anyone
who would work in such a dismal corner of show business.
He clearly considered himself meant to be hobnobbing with
the talent, not the staff." She shook her head, seemingly to
herself, and looked back at the computer screen. "And the
fact is, we never have contact with the artists."

"I thought you didn't know him well," I said quietly.
Jeannie switched Oliver from her left shoulder to her right
expertly, without so much of a whimper from the baby. Jeannie, however, now that her son was getting a little larger and
she hadn't worked out since before he was born, grunted a
little.

Penny's head twitched a little, uneasy at having been
caught in an unguarded moment. "I didn't," she said in a
clipped tone. "That was just the aura he gave off. I'm sorry,
but I don't think I could tell you anything else." She stood
up in an effort to signal to us that the interview was over.
But I wanted a little more time, particularly since Penny
seemed to want me out.

"Oops," Jeannie said. Then she did that thing where the
parent holds up the child and sniffs at his diaper, which
would bother me much more if I didn't recall doing it myself
when Melissa was that age. "I'm afraid someone needs to
be changed. Do you mind?" She pointed at the counter next
to the coffeemaker while clearly measuring the distance
visually, to ensure that Oliver wouldn't be anywhere near
anything dangerous. Then without waiting for a response,
she reached for her diaper bag, conveniently hanging off
the handle of Oliver's stroller, a contraption that probably
had its own area code. Jeannie had her changing mat spread
out on the counter (after wiping the counter down with a
disinfectant wipe) before Penny could protest or suggest
she move to the ladies' room.

I smiled at Penny with a look that said, "New mother;
whatcha gonna do?" "It sounds like Mr. Laurentz wasn't an
especially popular figure while he was working here," I

said. "Was it just his attitude, or were there some people who didn't like him more than others?"

Penny looked like she'd bitten into a chocolate dough-nut and found it tasted like fish. "I don't like to speak ill of the dead," she said.

"It's okay. He can't hear you." I knew that for a fact, since Lawrence was nowhere nearby. There *was* another ghost in the room, however, one who must have been from the 1930s based on his overcoat and hat. He looked to be in his fifties and was floating along horizontally, looking as close to asleep as the dearly departed can get.

"Well, all I can say is that when the news that Larry died got back to the department, there were some people who really weren't all that sad." Penny blinked a couple of times and drew a breath through clenched teeth.

"Like who?" Jeannie asked as she put a new diaper on Oliver.

"Oh, I don't want to name names," Penny said.

Jeannie gathered Oliver from the countertop, rolled up the changing pad and then grabbed the used diaper, which she had closed up tightly. She leaned toward Penny, although not too close because the woman still had a sniffle.

"Should I just drop this in the wastebasket?" she asked.

Penny gave us three names before we left, and in thanks, Jeannie put the diaper into a biodegradable plastic bag and disposed of it in the restroom.

Maybe it wouldn't be so bad having her along on the investigation, after all.

Eleven

"Why haven't you interviewed the three theater employees yet?" Paul asked me later that day.

Nan and Morgan Henderson, having clearly decided to hang in with me at the guesthouse, were back from their day of . . . I admit it, I didn't ask. Now I was making tea in the kitchen for them. I'd put on the oven, too, because the kitchen is drafty, and I figured I'd justify it by baking something. So at the moment, I was cutting up squares of premade chocolate chip cookie dough. Paul, hovering over the center island (incidentally with his head inside the exhaust fan), saw this as a sign that I was not completely engaged in our investigation.

"I have guests to take care of," I said very quietly—no sense in attracting the attention of said guests and once again convincing them that I was off any number of rockers. "Jeannie had to go home, and I had to come here. This is my business first, and we have an agreement about that, Paul. This place is how I keep a roof over my daughter's head. Any snooping has to happen when my responsibilities here are covered."

I turned on the CD player in the kitchen to cover any further conversation and slipped in a Beatles CD. *Rubber Soul.* You can't beat the classics.

Paul stuck out his bottom lip, but he knew he had no argument. "We agreed to that, I know," he said. "But I'm concerned that you don't care enough about this investigation." I felt it was probably best not to mention how I'd sobbed myself to sleep the night before thinking about Dad, but that would certainly have indicated that I did indeed have an emotional stake in what was going on.

"Here's the thing," I said, figuring I could tap into Paul's detective mind instead. "Whether we find that Laurentz/ Brookman guy died of a heart problem or if he was a victim of a vicious Pop-Tarts killer, my priority is finding my father. What else should I be doing?"

Paul loved nothing better than to be consulted on a difficult puzzle. If Sherlock Holmes were a dead Canadian with fairly impressive musculature and an incongruous goatee, he'd be Paul. He put his hand to his chin in the characteristic pose of contemplation. Men love to be observed being natural.

"I have attempted again to contact your father and didn't succeed," he told me. "We need to know more about what his ghostly routine was like before this strange interruption. Have you asked your mother?"

I idly picked up a piece of cookie dough and ate it. This was because I didn't want to look Paul in the eye, and also because cookie dough is delicious.

"I've never really talked to her about Dad since he died," I said as John Lennon sang about crawling off to sleep in a bathtub. "She didn't deal well with the way he was when he died, so weak and defeated. It wasn't the way either of us wanted to remember him."

"And since you've been able to see people like me?" Paul asked.

"We've never spoken about it," I told him. I set a kitchen timer for ten minutes, in accordance with the instructions on the dough wrapper (which still had some delicious dough stuck to it, too), then picked up the cookie sheet and put it in the oven. "I used to think it was just because it was too painful for Mom."

"And now?"

I steeled myself and faced him. "Now I think it was because she was embarrassed that Dad was continuing to have a relationship with her, but he didn't ever get in touch with me or Melissa."

Paul nodded slightly. "You knew your father well," he said. "Why do you think he would choose to stay away from you and his granddaughter?"

I shook my head. "It doesn't make any sense. Maybe there's something about being . . . Paul, do you feel any different than you did when you were alive?"

He narrowed his eyes in thought. "I'm a little less aware of physicality, of course," he said. "I don't worry about weather or temperature. I don't get hungry. I'm not afraid of being hurt when I have the chance to think about it. I don't really have a sense of presence. I don't need to sit or lie down most of the time. I'm not really . . . here."

"You've told me most of that before. I mean emotionally. Do you not care about things now that were really important to you before this happened to you?" I think I held my breath a little waiting for his answer.

"You're asking me if I think your father stopped caring about you and Melissa when he died," Paul said. He made a point of staring into my eyes. *"No."*

"Then it's a mystery. What can I do?"

There were still eight minutes left before the cookies would be done, but the aroma of baking cookies had already permeated the room, and I was mentally dividing them up among my guests and my daughter. It's also possible that I had one or two staked out for myself. Or three.

Paul scowled again. "You need to get past your disinclination to speak to your mother and find out how your father was spending his time previous to this incident. You need to determine if there's a place he would go—away from most living people, I would guess—if he were really determined to disappear effectively for reasons we can't yet understand."

That all made sense, but there was something he wasn't saying. "And once I find all that out, what do I do?" I asked.

This time Paul looked away to avoid my reaction. "You take Maxie there," he said.

"Maxine?" Mom asked. "Why Maxine?"

We had assembled, once again in my kitchen, for a war council that could be held out of the earshot of Lawrence Laurentz. I'd stashed the cookies—the ones I hadn't eaten or given to Melissa when she got home—away for after dinner, which Mom would prepare. Mom reported that the theatrical ghost wasn't always in her house, but she couldn't be sure when he was there and listening because he'd gotten good at moving through the walls to be out of Mom's sight when he didn't want to be detected.

Maxie, tickled with the idea that things would be left to her, was grinning as she hovered in the area of the stove. Paul, pretending to sit on the center island so he could be the focus of the conversation (a tactic so far turning out to be less than stellar), was doing his investigator-face thing. Melissa, home from school and not to be denied a place at the table this time, actually sat at the table.

"Because Paul can't leave this property, and we can't trust Lawrence as far as we can throw him, which isn't far since we can't actually touch him," I explained. "It appears Dad doesn't want to see me, so he might leave if I'm visible. So Maxie's our best bet."

That wasn't easy to say. The fact was, I wasn't crazy

about the prospect of placing all my hopes for finding Dad on Maxie, either. She wasn't the most responsible being who ever existed, and her concept of problem solving generally had an element of improvisation to it, with the end result usually being that Maxie had no plan B. She often didn't even have a plan A.

"Well, I don't understand how we're going to find him to begin with," Mom said, avoiding the Maxie issue.

I sat down next to Melissa and put my fingers to my temples. This was an indication of thought. "First, we have to figure out what state of mind Dad might be in, why he'd want to isolate himself," I said. "I know Dad pretty well, at least when he was alive, and I can't figure it out. Do you have any ideas?"

Mom isn't still when she thinks. She cooks when she thinks. Luckily, she'd brought the makings for oven-fried chicken and mashed potatoes, so she started to bread chicken legs and was silent for a few moments. Then she stopped, her fingers full of Panko bread crumbs, and turned to look at me. "Your father is not a man given to worrying about himself," she said. "He wouldn't hide out of fear. He wouldn't abandon us if he didn't have to."

"He pretty much abandoned me and Liss." It really just slipped out. I was as surprised to hear myself say that as Melissa, whose eyes widened.

"I asked him," Mom answered, her face turned away from us but her voice a trifle unsteady. "He always said that it wasn't that he didn't want to see you; it was that he couldn't."

"That doesn't make any sense," I told her.

"I know," Mom answered. "Believe me, there have been some . . . tense words between us, but he won't, or can't explain. There's something he's not telling me, too. He just won't discuss it, but it's hurting him. A lot."

"It doesn't make sense to *you*, Alison," Paul interjected. "You don't know what your father's situation might have been. That's what we're here to find out. Loretta, how does your husband normally spend his time? Before this happened, what was his routine?"

"When he was alive, he worked during the day," Mom said. "At night, we'd usually watch television or play cards. It's funny, you don't think those are the things you'd miss."

"But you could still do those things with Grampa," Melissa said. "You said he came by every Tuesday. You could still watch TV or play cards."

Mom took the cookie sheet on which she'd placed the chicken legs and some breast pieces and slid it into the oven. She was careful to concentrate on her cooking and not anyone else present, which wasn't easy considering the arrangement of beings in the room.

"We did that sometimes," she told her granddaughter. "Once in a while."

"Why just Tuesdays?" Paul went ahead. "What did Mr. Kerby do the rest of the time after his death?"

"I don't know," Mom answered. Her voice sounded clipped and uncomfortable. "He didn't tell me."

She turned toward the kitchen counter, but I stood and walked to her. I stopped her in her tracks and took hold of her forearms gently.

"We're trying to help him, Mom," I reminded her in a quiet voice. "You can't hold back now."

"I'm not holding back," Mom said. She extracted her arms from my grasp. "I just don't *know* why Dad didn't tell me much or why he only showed up once a week. He changed when he crossed over. I don't really understand it. He seems like the same man in many ways, but he's sadder and somehow more secretive than he used to be. It worries me, Alison."

I looked up at Paul. I knew his natural inclination now that Mom had opened up would be to push the issue, but she was hurting and I didn't want to press on anymore. I knew how much it had pained her to say even that much about Dad that wasn't glowing and upbeat.

"What are our options, Paul?" I asked. "What kind of . . . spatial dimensions are there to search? Where do we look?" If I could focus the conversation on the nuts and bolts of finding Dad, I might be able to spare Mom some discomfort.

Paul read the urgency in my voice, sighed and shrugged. "Our best bet now is to do two things. First, I can start sending out messages to other spirits and see if your father has been seen anywhere other than this immediate area." He started to stroke his goatee again.

"What's the other thing?" I asked.

"Take Lawrence Laurentz at his word and hope that solving his death will lead us toward your father."

"That means another look at the medical examiner's report and some questions on the investigation. I don't know any cops in the town where Lawrence died, so I have to talk to McElone again," I said with a moan.

But my daughter stood up and put on the most determined face I'd ever seen her wear, which was saying something. This was a girl who had held her ground for six straight days when told that she couldn't attend a midnight showing of a Harry Potter movie, and had worn me down.

"No," she said. "You find Mr. Laurentz's co-workers. *I'll* talk to the lieutenant."

Twelve

Melissa's logic, which was admittedly the logic of a ten-year-old girl, was persuasive, if not airtight. She'd go to police headquarters after school and tell McElone she was writing a report about her mom the private investigator, was following my current case and wanted to help. Making her eyes look wide and innocent would not necessarily be outside the realm of tactics utilized. I, meanwhile (she said) could divide the names and addresses of possible Lawrence haters with Jeannie, and we could cover three fronts at the same time, thus proceeding with maximum efficiency and using every asset of the agency.

There are times I truly do wonder who's raising whom around here.

I was counting on the skills of Maxie Malone and my Stone Age laptop to answer the question of Laurentz/Brookman's possible criminal record before Liss ever got near police headquarters. After all, Maxie had developed into quite the Internet research artist and had the added advantage of not needing to sleep like Melissa and I did.

Mom, apparently feeling left out of the impending on-slaught, gathered her things to go but volunteered to bring dinner again the next night and to try to question Lawrence whenever he showed up about anyone's possible motives for knocking him off. (So far, his only comment about the people he'd worked with at the Basie was that they were "unwashed masses," which didn't help much.) Personally, having spent just over an hour in his presence, I considered it something of a surprise he had lived long enough to qual-ify for residency in an active adult community.

Around this time, Nan and Morgan Henderson returned, so I served some tea and cookies and listened to their sto-ries of a trip to the Hereford Inlet Lighthouse in North Wildwood, which Nan had considered atmospheric and beautiful, and Morgan repeated "atmospheric and beauti-ful" in a way that made it sound dreary and soul-sucking. Both claimed great weariness, and retired early—Nan was now on a lighthouse kick and wanted to go to Absecon and Barnegat the next day, though Morgan had apparently talked her out of driving all the way to Cape May, almost three hours each way—and went to their bedroom on the first floor. But Nan was still eyeing me oddly, as if concerned that I would start talking to the walls angrily again. My best efforts at convincing them I was stable and hospitable were seemingly for naught.

I sent Melissa to her room to sleep, consulted with Paul for a little while before fatigue started working on me as well and then I headed upstairs to rest up for what was doubtless going to be a very long day tomorrow. I asked Maxie for an online weather forecast, and she reported that it was going to be cold but, in her words, "too cold to snow" the next day.

After getting washed and ready for bed, I started think-ing about Melissa and the life I'd had a hand in creating for her. She had been seeing ghosts as long as she could remember, much longer than me, but was it a good idea to let her live with two of them in her house? That wasn't normal. Now she was showing signs of interest in doing investigations for dead people, and as much as I adored spending time with my daughter, that couldn't be a healthy pursuit for a preteen. Had I simply let things go because they were easier for me and neglected what was right for Liss?

I mention my long and indulgent musing simply because it helps explain how I could possibly have passed by my dresser at least three times in my preparations for bed without noticing there were words spelled out in the (I admit it) dust that coated the dark cherry wood finish. Normally, one would expect to immediately pick up on the possibility that there had been an intruder in her bedroom, is all I'm saying.

Anyway, written there in the dust were the words, "I KNOW WHERE YOUR FATHER IS."

There was no way I could sleep after that, but I also didn't want to scream my brains out and alarm my daughter, so as quietly as I could, with my heart beating through my chest, I hustled out the bedroom door and ran downstairs to the kitchen. No Paul.

I said his name out loud in a conversational tone a few times. Often that will get him to show up. Not this time.

In desperation, I even called out, a little louder I think although it was unintentional, to Maxie. She didn't show up, either.

Unfortunately, the one person in the house I really hoped wouldn't have heard me, did. Morgan Henderson, in pajamas and (open) robe, shambled into the kitchen and looked startled when he saw me standing next to the refrigerator. He moved his lips back and forth on his face, as if trying to determine which side was the least attractive. It was a tie.

"Your bedroom," he mumbled, or words to that effect.

Excuse me? "I beg your pardon?" I asked. It was the best I could do under the circumstances.

"I thought you were in your bedroom," he said. "I wouldn't have come out if I'd known you were here."

Oh. I hesitated, possibly because I wasn't aware Morgan could put that many words together in a row. "It's okay," I said. "Do you need something?"

"Something." Morgan was back to his usual speech pattern, repeating the last thing he'd heard with a twist of lemon. "Glass of milk. You got?"

Yes, Tonto. I got. "Sure," I said. "Help yourself." I was confident there was milk in the fridge for once, because I'd stocked up for the "blizzard." Besides, we'd had cookies tonight, and it is, I believe, a law that chocolate chip cookies can't be eaten without milk. I pointed to the fridge and reached up to get Morgan a glass from the cabinet over my head.

He nodded when he took it from my hand, as a way to avoid saying "thank you," I assumed. He got the container of milk from the fridge and poured some for himself.

I inched my way toward the kitchen door and was about to leave when Morgan said, "What about your dad?"

I froze again. What was going on here? "What do you mean?" I asked. If he answered, "mean," I'd have to hit him with a frying pan.

"Saw your mom. What about your dad?" Morgan asked, apparently thinking that was an explanation.

"My father passed away five years ago," I told him. *Like it's your business.* No frying pans handy; I wasn't even close enough to grab a carrot peeler out of the drawer.

"Oh," Morgan said. "What happened?"

I don't like it when the guests ask personal questions. "Just now?" I asked, knowing full well that wasn't what he meant.

"With your father. How'd he die?"

"He was ill," I said.

"I figured," Morgan said. "What was it?"

Sometimes such directness takes you by surprise, and you simply answer without the consideration that the questioner has just asked something personal and painful. "Pancreatic cancer," I said.

Morgan shook his head. "Cancer," he said. "Tough." Then he downed the whole glass of milk in one gulp and walked to the sink to wash out the glass, something I would not have expected.

He put the glass in the dish drainer and headed toward me. I froze in panic for a second, then realized he was simply walking back to the kitchen door, where I was standing. I stepped out of the way and he swung the door open.

Then Morgan stopped and turned toward me, shaking his head. "Doesn't make sense, does it?"

He shuffled through the door and back toward the downstairs guest room, not waiting for an answer. It was just as well. I didn't have one.

Thirteen

Friday

"Larry Laurentz was an egomaniac, a prude, a sexist, a snob, a bigot and a bully," said Tyra Carter. Tyra, the first name on Penny's list of people who had worked with Lawrence at the Basie, was now working from her studio apartment as a customer service representative for a tire company. She'd agreed to talk to me (once I'd flashed the private-investigator's license) between calls, but since she was paid by the call, she would not take a break from her work so she was sitting with her headset on.

"But aside from that, he was nice, right?" I responded, stifling a yawn. Suffice it to say that after the discovery that someone was writing in the dust in my bedroom and the encounter with Morgan in the kitchen, I had not gotten a wink of sleep the night before. Paul had eventually materialized in the game room, and I'd informed him of everything that had gone on. His advice had been to keep pressing on the Laurentz investigation while he searched the house for other ghosts who might have had a hand—or a finger—in the message on my dresser.

Jeannie had begged off investigating this morning owing to a routine pediatrician appointment for Oliver, so I was alone. I hadn't loved Paul's suggestion but had no counterargument, so here I was in Red Bank, talking to Tyra, and apparently being too wry for her to understand. Sometimes my dry humor just goes over people's heads. This was hard to believe in Tyra's case, since she had to be six feet tall, but she looked at me and asked, "What?"

"Nothing," I said. "You worked in the ticket office with Mr. Laurentz?"

"Yeah. And it's not a bad job, but there isn't a lot to it, you know? You take ticket orders, put them in the computer, sometimes give actual paper tickets to people who don't print them out at home—most do now because it's free, no handling charge—and make sure you cross the seats off the seating chart for the right show. You don't have to . . . Wait. Hello, this is the Tire Hotline. How may I help you today?"

About seven minutes of tread discussion ensued, after which Tyra clicked off the call and looked at me again. "What was I saying?" she asked.

"Not a hard job, the ticket office," I told her.

"Yeah. But Larry, my God, that man! You'd think that we were sending out, like, gold in the mail. He had a religious experience every time he sold a seat for Hall and Oates or something. The guy honestly thought he had, like, the most important job in the universe." Tyra pursed her lips and shook her head.

"But that's just an annoyance," I suggested. "You didn't hate him or anything?"

Tyra cocked an eyebrow. "You want some cheese or something?" she asked. "I could . . . Hello, this is the Tire Hotline."

I shook my head about the cheese and listened to some

conversation about the merits and disadvantages of an extended warranty on tires. I stood up and looked around the apartment.

The sofa, which I assumed opened up into a bed, was a little worn, but had a hand-embroidered slipcover that no doubt hid a multitude of sins. The lamp had a fringed shade on it, the rug was a tied rope style in an oval pattern, and the small galley kitchen, to my left, was neat, no dishes stacked in the sink. There was no dishwasher, but a small stove, a refrigerator that could easily have held the tiny amount of food I had in mine at home and a microwave oven. I guessed that neither ticket selling nor talking about tires exactly qualified as wildly lucrative vocations.

When Tyra ended the rubberized conversation, I sat back down in the kitchen chair she'd pulled over for me when I came in. She smiled and apologized for the interruption, but I waved a hand to declare it irrelevant. I had another question I wanted to ask.

"Why did you leave the Basie to do this tire work?"

Tyra scowled, a face that actually made her look a little scary. "Well, that's where your friend Mr. Laurentz comes in," she said in low tones. "He got me fired."

I tried not to show my reaction to Tyra, but in my head I was picturing my hair standing on end and my legs sticking straight out, like when someone is surprised in an old Daffy Duck cartoon. "Lawrence Laurentz got you fired?" I repeated.

Tyra nodded. "All I was doing was taking a few tire calls—just a few—while I was working at the box office. I mean, not that many people call in to the box office anymore; they all buy their tickets online, you know. But when there was a call, I always answered it. Still, I needed a little extra money to pay some old bills, so I took a few calls for the tire company. No biggie. Everybody else who worked there covered for me."

A picture was starting to form. "But not Mr. Laurentz," I said.

Tyra curled her lip. "No. Not Larry. Man dimed me out to the manager, said I was neglecting my duties at the theater so I could talk about tires and collect two paychecks. Next thing you know, I'm only collecting one, and it's not the bigger one anymore. Thanks a lot, Larry."

What would Paul say? Try to get her to go a little further. "Must have made you mad," I suggested.

"Mad! I could have killed him!" Tyra yelled. Then she stopped, put her hand to her mouth and grinned naughtily. "Good thing he died of a heart attack, or I'd have just said something wrong, huh?" She looked at me.

"Well, it's possible . . ." I began.

Tyra put up a hand to signal I should stop. "Hello, this is the Tire Hotline," she said.

"I sort of liked Larry Laurentz," Frances Walters said. "But I'm not sorry he's dead."

"That seems contradictory," I told her.

Frances's Whispering Lakes town home was the same model as Mom's, not dissimilar to tens of thousands of other active adult community town homes in central New Jersey, a great many of them near the shore. We not only like to have our own older people live near the beach, we import a lot from New York City and Philadelphia just to be neighborly. In the past twenty-five years, it's become almost as popular to retire to the Jersey Shore as to move to Florida. You can look it up.

In this case, however, the similarity was not surprising: Frances lived in the same complex as Mom, and where Lawrence Laurentz (aka Melvin Brookman) had lived. Her place was decorated with too many knickknacks, the sign of someone who had downsized from a much larger home.

This, again, is not unusual. People who move here often try to cram all the accumulations of thirty or more years into a new home whose walls and closets can accommodate perhaps ten years of memories. It's difficult, and it shows.

"I know," Frances agreed. "I intended it to sound contradictory. It was for effect."

Frances explained how she and her husband had moved here after their children had started families of their own, but then her husband, Phil, had passed away shortly thereafter. Frances, who had danced in the chorus in a couple of Off-Broadway shows, done some summer stock and once had a line in a TV commercial for soup, had left "show business" to marry Phil, and after his death had started doing community theater ("There aren't a lot of parts for chorines in their sixties"). She took a job at the Basie as—and again, I'm using her terminology—"an usherette."

She regarded me closely. "Alison Kerby," she said. "Are you Loretta Kerby's daughter? I've met her at some condo association meetings." I admitted that my mother was, indeed, my mother, and she nodded. "You favor her. She's a lovely woman."

I didn't know where to go with that, so I nodded modestly and plowed ahead. "If you liked Mr. Laurentz, why are you glad he's dead?" I asked.

"He seemed so unhappy," she replied. "He was one of those men who always acted dissatisfied, like life was simply not going along with his plan. And then dying upstairs in his bathroom, all by himself." Not that dying in your bathroom with someone else seemed much more appealing.

"But you liked him," I said.

Frances stood up from the sofa in front of her coffee table—overstuffed with photographs of her children and grandchildren, but I noticed, none of her late husband—and struck a pose looking out the front window, but just barely touching the drape on the right side. No wonder she liked Lawrence so much; he'd been as big a ham as she was.

"Yes, I did. It was I who got Larry involved in the New Old Thespians."

"The New Old . . . what?"

Frances smiled, because I clearly was not very well informed and now she could clue me in. "It's a group that puts on local productions of very high quality, but everyone participating must be at least fifty-five years old," she explained. "The group was started here in the condo community three or four years ago, and I got involved right at the beginning. We perform plays and musicals, mostly in other active adult communities, but sometimes in schools and once in a while in small community theaters. We have a performance tomorrow night, in fact. I'll be at rehearsal all evening. But Larry was clearly very interested in theater, so I told him about the group and brought him to his first meeting."

I managed to hold on to the same vapid grin I'd been giving Frances since I first showed up at her door, but internally, I was fuming at Lawrence Laurentz. In all the private-eye movies and books, the one thing the detective always insists on is that the client provide all the necessary information, and here I was discovering that Lawrence had left out a whole group of people who might have wanted to kill him.

"So he came and was a big hit, I suppose," I said to Frances. It wasn't a question, exactly, but it did elicit a response.

Frances covered her mouth, perhaps to hide a chuckle. "Oh, I'm afraid not," she said in a coquettish trickle of a voice. "Larry had . . . opinions about pretty much every aspect of every production and was rather loudly disappointed whenever he wasn't cast in the lead role."

"How often was that?" I asked.

"Every time," Frances told me.

"Was he a bad actor?" Lawrence seemed like such a larger-than-life personality, so it was hard to believe he wouldn't be a natural on the stage.

Frances appeared to consider the question, and put a finger to her lips. "I wouldn't say that, exactly," she began. "Larry was very good at parts that required large gestures and oversized line delivery. But subtlety was not his forte, I'm afraid, and when we were presenting a musical, well, the fact is that Larry couldn't sing to save his life."

"So he was vocal about his opinion that he should have gotten some leading roles. I imagine that didn't ingratiate him with the rest of the group very effectively," I suggested.

Frances shook her head sadly. "No, I'm afraid not. He just rubbed some people the wrong way. But it was mostly because he did care so much about putting on a really good show. Though not everyone in the group saw it that way."

"How much did they not see it that way?" I asked.

She let out a long sigh and looked at her extremely well-vacuumed rug, the section of it that wasn't covered with furniture or some rather odd porcelain figures of animals. "It was suggested, after a while, that it might be best if Larry leave the group," she said.

Uh-oh. "Who did the suggesting?" I asked.

"Jerry Rasmussen, the president of New Old Thespians," Frances said. "He didn't like Larry, and he was the one who was especially adamant about that. I think everyone else would have tolerated Larry because of me."

"Because of you?"

Frances smiled sadly and looked away, this time out the window again. "I guess Larry had a little crush on me, and they knew it," she explained. "But that got Jerry especially upset."

"Because . . ."

Frances's smile got a little bit broader. I was right. "I think Jerry might have a little crush on me, too," she said.

I was starting to sense a pattern in her thinking. "How did Mr. Laurentz take it when he was asked to leave?" I asked.

She seemed to be searching for her answer in that square

foot of pristine wall-to-wall. "Oh, not very well. At the meeting when it was suggested, he accused Jerry of favoritism, told the group they were jealous of his talents and declared quite clearly that they . . . *we* could all go rot in hell."

"Would you excuse me for just a moment?" I asked Frances. She appeared a little confused at my sudden request but nodded. I walked just out of her view into the hallway to the bathroom, where I pulled my cell phone out of my tote bag and texted Mom, "Is Lawrence there?"

Mom was as quick as she was dependable, and in seconds came the response "yhi." The only problem here was that I had no idea what that meant, so I came back with, "What?" And almost immediately my phone vibrated. "Yes he is." If one could put eye-rolling into a text, it would have been in that one. Seriously, couldn't I get into the twenty-first century?

I sent Mom a quick message back: "Keep him there. I'm coming." I walked back into the living room and smiled at Frances, even as I pictured a whole new group of suspects to interview. This investigation was beginning to look like an endeavor that could take months to clear up. It's rough when pretty much anyone in a twenty-six-mile radius could have committed the crime. If indeed a crime had been committed.

"The tension with Mr. Laurentz—was it difficult for you? Because you had brought him into the group?" I asked.

Frances wiped her eye. Either she really was a very good actress, or the conversation was disturbing her severely. "A few people stopped talking to me. Larry was one of them."

"That must have been very hard on you. Are you still a member of the group?"

Frances looked up, startled, as if I'd asked whether she was still a human being. "Of course," she said. "I wouldn't let some minor personality conflicts get in the way of the show. I'm a professional." One who wasn't getting paid for her work, but then I could certainly empathize with such an arrangement. "In fact," Frances added, "I was thinking of asking your mother if she would be interested, but I had no idea if she had a theatrical background." That last bit seemed intended to reinforce the idea that Mom was my mom. Once again, I chose not to respond.

I'd have to narrow the suspect field a little, however, if I was going to get Paul the information he'd need to figure this puzzle out. Certainly I wasn't going to get to the bottom of it, especially with the entire state of New Jersey capable of having killed Lawrence. We're a very densely populated state.

"Were there some people who were especially angry with Mr. Laurentz?" I asked. "Maybe the people who stopped talking to you?"

"Well, Tyra hadn't been talking to Larry already," she said casually. "And . . ."

"Tyra Carter?" How did *she* fit in?

"Yes. Do you know her? Tyra works the stage crew for us. She's very strong, you know, and she knew Larry and me from the Basie Theatre." Tyra was now linked to Lawrence both at work and through the theater company, and was leaping to the top of the suspect list, if only because I didn't have a reason to put anyone else there yet.

"What about you?" I asked.

"A few of the members stopped talking to me, but most of them understood I'd simply wanted Larry to enjoy himself," Frances said, now able to look me in the eye once more. "But Jerry never really forgave either of us."

Finally! Someone who never forgave! "Jerry?" I asked, trying not to seem too anxious.

"Yes," Frances answered. "A few weeks later, Tyra told me that Jerry had considered asking me to leave the Thespians, too."

This theatrical group was a nest of yentas, as far as I could tell. "Why didn't he?" I asked. "I mean, according to Tyra, why not?"

Frances looked at me with something approaching pity at my dense brain. "The *crush*," she said.

Fourteen

It didn't take long to get from Frances Walters's town home to Mom's, but it was enough time for me to build up a pretty serious head of steam (impressive, given that my prehistoric Volvo wagon had a heater that was more rumor than fact). By the time I was standing in Mom's living room with Lawrence Laurentz hovering in a sitting position over the easy chair, I probably had steam escaping from my ears, and not just because I was wearing two sweaters, a coat, a scarf, gloves and a knitted wool hat.

"Why didn't you tell me about the New Old Thespians?" I demanded as soon as I had unwrapped the scarf from around my mouth.

Lawrence didn't respond right away, so my mother jumped in ahead of him. "The New Old *what*?" she asked.

"Thespians," Lawrence said. "It means 'actors.'"

"Oh." Mom appeared a little disappointed.

"You haven't answered my question," I reminded the ghost.

Lawrence had managed to regain his aura of superiority when correcting Mom, so he looked completely urbane when he said, "I did not mention the Thespians because they did not seem to be relevant. We were discussing my murder, not my avocation."

"You were asked to leave a group of local theater people under what could be described as acrimonious circumstances," I countered. "You didn't think that was relevant? One of those people could have been mad enough to kill, if you really were murdered."

The dapper ghost, looking overdressed in a vest and tuxedo pants, rose a couple of feet toward the ceiling. "Of *course* someone killed me!" he shouted. "I'm dead, aren't I?"

"You don't really think Larry had a heart . . . whatever, do you, Alison?" Mom seemed somehow concerned that I was insulting her guest rather than being—as I would be— ticked off that he was the one speaking to her daughter in such harsh tones.

"All I'm *saying*," I exhaled, "is that so far we haven't found any concrete evidence that someone killed you, Mr. Laurentz. All I have is your story. If you're not going to be forthcoming with me, there is no way I can continue with this investigation." Nothing would have made me happier than to hear Lawrence release me from that responsibility.

No such luck. "Don't forget about your father," he warned me. "I'm still your best link to him."

I did my best to look misty-eyed. "That's very cruel of you," I told Lawrence. "You know that's an emotional point for my mother and me, and you use it to get me to do what you want. I'm starting to think you're not very nice, *Larry*, and I don't think I want to work for you unless I have actual proof you can produce my father the way you say you can."

"Alison!" Mom was appalled. I'm not sure if it was because I was being rude or because I'd had the audacity to call a man of Lawrence's age and stature (in her eyes) by his nickname.

I ignored her exclamation of horror at my bad manners and watched Lawrence closely. His eyes narrowed and he watched me without blinking, obviously trying to determine if I was bluffing. Since I really wasn't, he probably saw something other than what he wanted. He snorted.

"Very well," he said finally. "You need proof? You shall have it." And he vanished; one second here, gone the next.

When a ghost does something like that, it has the immediate effect of making the living people in the room feel foolish. You're standing there staring at nothing for a bit before you realize there's nothing to stare at. So Mom and I started and then looked at each other.

After a minute or so, we realized that we couldn't just stand there, so Mom gestured to me to follow her. "No telling when he'll be back, or even if," she said. "Let's go get some coffee." Mom can solve pretty much any problem as long as she's within walking distance of a kitchen. So I followed her, and lacking any useful purpose, sat in one of the wicker-back chairs at her kitchen table.

I told her about Frances and Tyra. Tyra had suggested subtly (once off the phone) that I never bother her again, which I understood but did not appreciate, but Frances had actually been so interested in my investigation—she called it "life research for a future role"—that she'd given me her cell phone number and asked me to call if she could help. I didn't see how she could, but one thing Paul has impressed upon me is to never turn down someone who wants to tell you things about the case you're working on.

"You know," Mom said out of the blue, "I read that Dr. Wells passed away a few weeks ago." Mom reads the obituaries in about seven newspapers online, including the *MetroWest Jewish News*, the *Catholic Spirit of Metuchen*, and for all I knew, a Baha'i newspaper based in Jersey City.

"Dr. Wells? Which one was Dr. Wells?" All the doctors who'd worked on my dad—the oncologists, surgeons and radiation specialists whom Dad had called "the White

Coat Brigade"—had eventually blended together in my memory.

"The oncologist," Mom said. "The one who was there at the end."

I remembered now—he had been in the room with Dad during his last moments and had signed my father's death certificate. "What did he die of?" I asked, just to fill the conversation.

"Not cancer," Mom answered. "Heart attack, I think." We were silent for a while; Mom got coffee out of a cabinet and started putting some into the basket in her coffeemaker.

"I've been thinking about Dad a lot lately," she said, as if we'd been discussing the subject for hours.

"So have I," I said. "Sometimes I feel like he just died. Sometimes I feel like he never did. Sometimes I'm sad and other times I'm just angry at him."

I thought that would throw Mom—she never seemed to be angry at Dad or me, or especially Melissa—but she nodded. "I know. I get mad at him for dying, too. I know I shouldn't. I've still be able to see him, but . . ." Mom took a breath. "He's not alive. It's not the same thing."

I shook my head. "I'm not mad at him for dying, I'm mad because I feel like he could have gotten in touch with me, now, like he did with you, and he's choosing not to. It feels like he's freezing Melissa and me out, and I can't come up with any explanation for why he'd do that."

Mom sniffed a little, and I saw her stop her coffee preparation to dab at her nose with a tissue, very quickly, as if I wasn't supposed to see. "There isn't one," she answered. "I know your father wouldn't ever abandon you like that if he had the choice, so he must not have a choice."

I didn't get a chance to answer because there was a noise from the living room that sounded like flapping wings, as if a bird had gotten into the house and was trying to fly its way out. "Where has everyone gone?" Lawrence Laurentz shouted. "I have arrived with your proof!"

Mom, having set the coffeemaker up to brew, headed toward the living room and I followed her. There, sure enough, floated Lawrence Laurentz, having changed (I assumed for traveling) into—I'm not kidding—a cape. He looked like he'd been cast in the lead of *Zorro*, as performed by the National Yiddish Theater.

"You wanted to see evidence that I've been in touch with your father?" he insisted before either Mom or I could utter a word. "Fine! Here is your evidence!"

Lawrence reached into an inside pocket, and retrieved a small white business card. He slapped it down on Mom's coffee table. "You see?" he chortled. "There!"

A business card? "That's your proof?" I asked. "What does it say, 'Lawrence Laurentz: Friend of Alison's Dad'?"

"Look at it," Mom said in a hollow voice.

I stopped and looked. Sure enough, it displayed a small logo of a paintbrush and a handsaw, and the imprint read, "Jack Kerby: Handyman." Underneath, the slogan, "No Job Too Small—Reasonable Prices!"

I'd seen it a thousand times as a kid. Dad used to hand them out wherever he went, and he and I played a game with them when I was little. He'd mark one with a little blue dot and then stash it in a stack that held at least a hundred. We'd see how many tries it took for me to find the one with the dot.

This one had a little blue dot on the top right-hand corner.

"Now what do you think?" Lawrence demanded.

My voice was a little weaker than I'd expected it to be. "There's still a little time before Melissa gets home from school," I said. "I think you're going to tell me all I need to know about Jerry Rasmussen."

Lawrence curled his lip. "That worm," he said.

Jeannie met me at Mom's, and despite Lawrence's fuming away about Jerry Rasmussen and the unfairness of it all, Mom and I ignored him and ate lunch with Jeannie. We made small talk and had a very nice Cobb salad. Then Jeannie bundled up Oliver (who had helpfully slept through the whole thing, though he'd stirred slightly when Lawrence became especially emphatic) and we got into Jeannie's new minivan (with extra childproof locks) for the thirty-second drive to Jerry Rasmussen's place. I wanted Jeannie there for this interview—and had wanted her there for the others, but she had given me a lecture on how important frequent visits to the pediatrician are, even if you had a wellness visit just last week.

After listening to Lawrence's description of Jerry Rasmussen, which included the words *simpering, blithering and IQ in the negative numbers*, it was something of a surprise to find the man actually quite accommodating and concerned upon hearing that I was an investigator looking into the circumstances of Lawrence's death.

Mr. Rasmussen, who asked us to call him "Jerry," had done everything to belie the image Lawrence had painted of him short of sweeping me off my feet and asking me to marry him, which was just as well. I'd only been asked once before and had foolishly consented. Besides, Jerry was almost forty years older than I was and in yet another cookie-cutter active adult town home.

It had gotten to a point where every one of these homes I saw was running together in my mind. Even with all the problems and challenges that my Victorian guesthouse at 123 Seafront provided—and they were abundant—I was more glad than ever that I'd bought the old barn to live in for hopefully the rest of my life, assuming I could generate enough income to keep the place running.

Jerry's town home was no exception: There were the high ceilings (with a ceiling fan in each room), the skylights, the extremely beige walls, the entrance hallway with the tile floor, the wall-to-wall carpet in the living room (a different shade of beige), the pass-through to the kitchen . . . Stop me if you've heard this before.

"Is there some insurance question or something like that?" Jerry asked. Oddly, he was the first of today's interview subjects to question me on my motives for investigating the death—apparently of natural causes—of an older man more than six months earlier.

"Something like that," I said.

"Not allowed to say, huh?" he asked, smiling. "Okay, I won't ask anymore questions. How can I help?" He gestured me toward a chair facing his sofa, and he took the nearer cushion on the couch.

I'd clued Jeannie in on my previous conversations with Tyra and Frances, but she still opened by asking Jerry, "Did you know Lawrence Laurentz?"

We'd already established that Jerry did in fact know Lawrence, so the question was pointless, but Jeannie grinned and bounced Oliver on her knee, seemingly thrilled with her participation in the process. Jerry admitted he knew Lawrence—again—and I jumped in before Jeannie could ask him if his name was Jerry Rasmussen.

"I'm told you knew Mr. Laurentz from his involvement with the New Old Thespians; is that right?" Paul had instructed me to let the "witness" expound on the question, so to make the first one relatively simple and broad. Paul had also reminded me on numerous occasions that anyone who commits a violent crime is by definition capable of violence, no matter how pleasant and accommodating he might seem. Which is really reassuring every time I ring a doorbell with that voice recorder in my tote bag.

Jerry nodded. "Yes, Lawrence was a member of the troupe for a while." He folded his hands in his lap and looked at me, smiling with a bland expression, awaiting the next question. He might have been a very well trained golden retriever.

"And he left because the troupe asked him to leave?" I said, watching Jerry's eyes.

Not a flicker. "Yes, I'm afraid so, and he did not take it

all that well. He thought we were kicking him out because we were jealous of his talent." I thought he might stumble a bit on the word *talent*, but again, there was not the tiniest sign of amusement or contempt.

"Was that not the case?" I asked.

Jerry shook his head and looked, of all things, sad. "I'm afraid Lawrence's talents were not, shall we say, as generously supplied as he might have believed them to be."

"He was a ham," Jeannie suggested. Then she looked at Oliver and said into his face, "Ham. Ham, ham. Are *you* a ham? Are you?" Oliver seemed fairly sure he was not a ham but did not answer. I was waiting for Jerry's response.

This time, Jerry did allow a smile but one with regret in it. Wow. If this guy was lying, he was very, very good at it. "That would be one way to put it. But normally, we wouldn't have asked a member who . . . emotes a little too much to leave. We're here to bring the arts to senior citizens, but going over the top is to be expected sometimes."

"So why in Mr. Laurentz's case?" I asked. "If you don't mind a little hamming it up, what made him more of a problem?"

Jerry raised his left eyebrow. "I wouldn't say a *problem*," he began. "Lawrence turned everything into a *situation*. He wouldn't take direction. He was critical of the other actors' performances. He had an opinion on everything, and he voiced it loudly and bluntly, during each rehearsal and in presence of the entire cast and crew. It became . . . a distraction. Members were complaining. I'm the president of the troupe, so they came to me with their grievances. I finally had to act on it, and when it became obvious that Lawrence would not change his behavior, we had to ask him to stop coming to meetings and rehearsals."

I couldn't honestly say the scenario Jerry had described was anything but what I'd expected. From what I'd personally observed of him, I could easily believe that Lawrence would have acted that way, the "professional among amateurs" in the theater group, just because he really believed he knew more than everyone else and that he should let them know it. But Jeannie had never met Lawrence (and wasn't likely to), and I wanted her to have an idea of his personality. Telling her I had observed him myself—other than the fiction that he'd been a friend of mom's—was out of the question.

"I imagine he reacted badly," I said to Jerry.

He stifled a mild snort and looked to the ceiling fan for an instant. "You could say that," he said. "Lawrence accused us—me, mostly—of 'conspiring to demean him' in the eyes of the group, to make him look foolish and feel unwanted. He said it was 'a blatant manifestation of jealousy'; those were his exact words. He left that night, saying none of us would ever see him alive again. And the fact is, none of us did, as far as I know. A few went to his funeral. The poor man. So sudden."

"Did you go? To his funeral?" Jeannie asked, wiping some drool from Oliver's mouth.

Jerry didn't make eye contact. "No. I felt that Lawrence would have preferred I stay away." Then he looked at me, and his gaze narrowed. "But what does this have to do with insurance? Why are you asking about the New Old Thespians in relation to Lawrence Laurentz's death?" Uh-oh; he'd caught on.

"I'm not here on an insurance matter," I told him. "I'm here to clear up some of the circumstances about Mr. Laurentz's death."

Jerry's voice took on a slightly scratchy quality. "So you came to talk to me? Why? Lawrence died of a heart attack, didn't he?"

In my head, I heard Melissa's voice: "Awwwk-waaard . . ."

I gave him the prepared answer Paul and I had worked out: "There are some questions about what happened, and my client is asking me to see what I can find out." I figured that was vague enough to be true but not so vague that it would simply frustrate Jerry.

Or so I thought.

"So you think that something else happened?" he asked, his voice rising about a half octave. "You think he did himself in? Or . . ." His face took on a delighted quality that only world-class gossips can achieve. "Do you think that someone might have killed him? How can that happen? How can somebody give you a heart attack?"

"I'm not saying anything happened just yet," I said, trying to maintain a soothing voice rather than hear his escalate to castrati levels. "I'm trying to determine exactly what might have caused Mr. Laurentz's death."

"Nobody sends out a private detective unless they think something sinister has happened," Jerry said. While I was still marveling at his use of the word *sinister*, he went on, "And if you believe that someone did kill Lawrence, your first stop is at *my* door?" Jerry's voice was reaching pitches that only a dog would be able to hear and alas, I had no dog handy.

"You weren't our *first* stop . . ." I began, before realizing how stupid that sounded.

But Jerry wasn't listening, anyway. "How dare you even consider the idea that I would want any harm to come to another human being, even Lawrence Laurentz!" he ranted. "I'll have you know, I've been a vegetarian since 1986, before it was fashionable! I don't even kill insects I find in my bathroom—I remove them to the backyard! What could possibly make you think I would . . . would . . ." And with that, he put his fingers up to his brow, shielding his eyes.

It was a good show, but I watched. Not one tear fell down Jerry Rasmussen's cheeks, no matter how hard he shook with his feigned sobs. "This is interfering with my process," he managed. "I have to . . . prepare for a dress rehearsal tonight. And my emotional state needs to be . . . restored. I'd prefer it if you two would leave."

The man could act; I'll give him that. He'd almost had me convinced.

Jeannie snorted. "We *three*," she said, but she was already packing Oliver into his snowsuit.

Fifteen

On our way back to Mom's, Jeannie and I compared notes on Jerry, whom she'd found cold. "He never so much as chucked Oliver's chin!" She dropped me back at my car, and we split up so that she could go talk to another of Lawrence's remaining co-workers and then pick Melissa up from school. Since Liss wanted to go and pull her "school project" gambit on Lieutenant McElone, and the conceit of her trying to do something behind my back would be lost if I was spotted dropping her off, it made more sense for Jeannie to do it. My daughter had tried to lobby for permission to walk to the police station from school, but I wasn't about to let a ten-year-old ("I'm almost *eleven*, Mom!") walk for more than a mile to the police station in freezing temperatures all by herself. Call me crazy.

That left me time to check in with Paul before Liss got home. I picked up the mail—which sure enough included a bill from Murray Feldner for *not* plowing my walk—and went in search of Paul so I could play him the audio of the conversations with Tyra, Frances and Jerry.

Paul listened carefully, doing some serious goatee stroking, his eyes at half-mast and his brows coming close to meeting in the middle. He nodded a few times, especially during the Jerry playback, and when all the recordings had been played, he looked at me and did something very odd indeed.

He smiled.

"You're really progressing, Alison," he said, every inch the proud parent. "There was barely a question left unasked, and you reacted to everything they said with an eye toward the investigation and not the emotion of the moment. I'm very proud of you."

It's important to point out that I don't take compliments well. I've never really examined this impulse, not even when I was seeing a therapist after The Swine walked out to seek sun and extreme blondeness in California. But suffice it to say that at this moment, I looked away and focused on how the Tiffany lamp over the pool table really needed dusting.

"Thank you," I mumbled. "Now, what does it all mean?"

"An excellent question." Paul "stood up," which gave the impression of an expectant father in the 1950s pacing in the waiting room while his wife gave birth—two feet off the ground. "We haven't established anything definitively, but it is significant that both the woman from the Count Basie and the man from the theater group admitted they didn't much care for Mr. Laurentz and did not try to hide it."

"Does that make you suspect Frances more, because she claimed that she liked Lawrence?" *Give me another gold star, teacher! I shined these patent-leather shoes just for you and had my mother braid my pigtails!*

But Paul shook his head. "No, I think it would be extremely premature to start prioritizing suspects at this point. For one thing, we don't have Jeannie's report on the people she's interviewing, and there were several others in the theater group, at least, who probably held a grudge."

"Yeah, but that's such a lousy motive," I argued. "The guy was a bad actor, so they decided to kill him? Even if Lawrence was especially obnoxious on his way out—and I'd bet cash money he was—they had already kicked him out of the group. His behavior was cause for a flaming bag of dog poop on his doorstep, not a toaster in his bathtub." And yes, it felt just as ridiculous to say that as it must be to hear it.

"I agree," Paul said. "There must be something more to it than that. Generally speaking, people kill for three reasons: money, sex or revenge. None of those seem to apply in this case."

"I got a creepy feeling from Jerry Rasmussen," I said. "Does that count for anything?"

Paul considered. "Instinct is a factor," he said, pacing. "You would still have to prove anything that would tie him to a criminal act, but you were in the room with the man and I wasn't. If your feelings about him were accurate, what do you think his next move will be?"

Jerry's next move? I was lucky I knew what my *last* move was! Still wanting to impress my mentor, I thought hard, and my stomach froze a little. "You think he might get violent with me?" I asked.

Paul quickly shook his head. "No, no. The next thing he'll do, if he's as calculating as you think, is call you to apologize for his behavior. Expect the call within a day."

"I did leave him a business card. You really think he'll call?"

"If you were right about him. You're a pretty good judge of human nature. I'd bet on it." That was encouraging. Sort of.

"Did you get the feeling Lawrence was telling us everything?" I asked. "He's left out important details before, like the whole experience with the theater club."

Paul smiled at me. "You really are progressing. No, I

don't think he's telling us all there is to know, and it makes me wonder why more than what. He's already dead; what does he have to lose?"

Maxie slid down through the ceiling wearing a trench coat, which is highly unusual for her; she usually favors the tightest clothing possible, as if she were still trying to attract shallow men three years after her death.

"I've got something," she said, and opened the coat to produce my decrepit MacBook from inside the coat. That explained it; the ghosts can carry pretty much any object smaller than a Subaru undetected as long as they conceal it in their clothing. So Maxie could fly directly from the attic through my bedroom and into the game room without having to take human routes. We'd also had some past arguments about uninitiated guests seeing a flying laptop computer on the stairs, so Maxie was actually being considerate. But as soon as she reached her hovering spot, the trench coat disappeared, leaving her clad in some sprayed-on blue jeans and a black T-shirt bearing the slogan, "You Won't Like Me When I'm Angry." Truer words were never silk-screened.

Paul watched her float down. "What?" he asked.

"This New Old Thespians group," she said. "You asked me to look it up." Paul had indeed requested Maxie do some online research on the troupe, and it hadn't taken her long to get whatever information she was talking about.

"Wow—there's really something notable there?" I asked. Frankly, I'd thought anything Maxie could pull up on the Internet about a group of senior citizens putting on the occasional musical would be tame at best.

"You're gonna love this," she crowed. "They got busted six months ago."

"What?" Paul and I said at about the same time.

Maxie held out the laptop for us to see. "Believe it. They were doing a performance at some old people's development—"

"Active adult community," I corrected.

Maxie shook her head to declare it irrelevant. "Whatever. Anyway, so they're putting on this show, and halfway through it the cops burst in and start arresting everybody."

"Why?" Paul wanted to know. Maxie was waving the laptop around with such enthusiasm that one, it was impossible to read the article on the screen, and two, I was worried about buying a new laptop if she dropped it.

Maxie smiled her naughtiest, most self-satisfied smile. "Public nudity," she said in a long drawl.

"Public . . . public . . . *what*?" I managed. So I'm not erudite when taken by surprise. No, shock.

"You heard me," the ghost answered. I'd never seen her look quite so happy. "The performance apparently included a bunch of the cast stripping down to nothing, and there are laws against such things if you don't have the proper permits ahead of time."

I grabbed the laptop out of curiosity and a sense of self-preservation. "Let me see that thing," I said. "That can't be right."

Maxie's mouth flattened out. "Oh, it's true all right," she said. "Do you think I make this stuff up?"

"Oh, stop," I countered. "Believe it or not, sometimes it actually isn't about you." I started reading the article, from the *Home News Tribune*, dated almost seven months earlier. Sure enough, there had been eleven arrests for public indecency, lewd behavior and resisting arrest, at an active adult community called Cedar Crest during a Sunday night performance of . . .

"*Hair*?" Paul asked. "A bunch of people over fifty-five put on *Hair*?"

I shrugged. "They were there the first time, I guess," I said. "But the nudity in *Hair* is only a few seconds. How could the cops know when to show up?"

Paul raised an eyebrow.

"Someone must have alerted them," he suggested. "Someone like—"

"A disgraced former member of the troupe who had been unceremoniously kicked out?" I asked.

Paul shook his head. "We're getting way ahead of ourselves here," he said. "We have no proof. We don't even know exactly when Mr. Laurentz was asked to leave the theater company. For all we can say, this incident could have happened before that or after he died."

Maxie chewed her upper lip. "I don't know," she said. "Larry did die in the bathtub six months ago. The timing fits."

I felt my eyebrows meet in the middle. Something was a little bit off here. "Since when are you interested in these investigations?" I asked Maxie. "You usually complain about having to do the research."

"This one's funny," she said.

"Funny? A man dies, is maybe murdered, and you think it's funny?"

Maxie shrugged. "I have a different perspective," she said.

"Yeah. You should be more sympathetic."

Maxie started to answer but was distracted by a noise at the game room door. Melissa swooped into the room at top speed, backpack bobbing behind her, with footsteps that would have awakened the dead, if they hadn't already been part of the conversation.

"Mom!" my daughter shouted out eagerly. "I just talked to the lieutenant!" Liss stopped to catch her breath. As she did, Jeannie appeared behind her in the doorway, grinning proudly at my little girl. Jeannie was pushing the stroller, and Oliver appeared to be inside it, but with all the snowsuits, it was hard to tell.

Paul and Maxie exchanged the same glance they always pass between each other when a "civilian" enters the room, a reminder that they could say whatever they wanted, but they should not be expecting direct communication from Melissa or me. The fact of the matter was that I could have had an ongoing conversation with either of them with Jeannie there—and had done so in the past—and my friend would simply refuse to believe there was anything the least bit unusual going on. And in my house, she'd be right.

"What did Lieutenant McElone say?" I asked Melissa.

Melissa shed the backpack and her down jacket, as well as a scarf, a hat, a pair of gloves and her shoes. "Well, first of all, she said that next time you should come down to her yourself and not send your daughter with a line of hooey about a school project," she began.

"Did you mention it was your idea and not mine?" I asked.

"Yes, but she said it was just because you're afraid of her."

I made a sour face. "I'm so afraid of her that I'm in her office about every two weeks?" I pointed out.

"She said that was because you're a bad detective and need help from the police," Melissa replied. "And she also said that if you had shown up, she probably wouldn't have told you anything, anyway."

Paul put a hand up over his nose and mouth as if stifling a sneeze. Like he could have a cold.

"So far, this has been a real treat for me," I told my daughter. "Do you have anything in the way of information that *doesn't* contain an insult to me from the lieutenant?"

Paul made a sudden turn away from the right-hand corner of the room, almost in a panic, and I looked to see that Jeannie was sitting down to nurse Oliver. Men. I'm not nuts about watching, but seriously; it was just a mother feeding her child, quite literally the most natural thing in the world.

"Don't let Melissa fool you," Jeannie piped up. "She got more than that. I was watching from across the street in the car so Oliver could sleep in his car seat, and even from there I could see Melissa was great. She ran into the lieutenant outside the station, and I couldn't hear, but when she seemed to be having some trouble getting help, Melissa even pretended to tear up at one point, so the lieutenant brought her inside and gave her whatever information she could."

I looked at my daughter. "You teared up?" I asked.

"Not really," Liss said. "I just sort of sniffed a little when she said she didn't have time for this and looked around like I couldn't figure out what to do. So Lieutenant McElone asked me if I needed a tissue, and I said I didn't have one."

"Which no doubt made her think I'm a bad mother," I suggested.

"You're missing the point," Jeannie interrupted. "Melissa needed to talk to the lieutenant, and she got to talk to the lieutenant."

I *had* been missing the point. I knelt down, although not as much as I used to, and looked my daughter in the eye. "Jeannie's right," I said. "I haven't been giving you enough credit. You did great."

"How do you know?" Melissa, who could make Jack Bauer talk if necessary, smirked at me. "You haven't heard what I found out."

"Speak."

She actually reached into her backpack and pulled out a notebook, which had "Language Arts" scrawled on the cover. She opened it to a page and read from notes she'd taken when talking to McElone. "First of all, Lawrence Laurentz has no criminal record. Neither does Melvin Brookman."

"That is a relief," Paul said to me.

I nodded. "Yes," I said.

"Yes, what?" Jeannie asked.

Melissa's eyes were flashing me a warning I no longer needed. I spun on my heel. "Yes, that makes sense, don't you think?"

Jeannie shrugged as best she could while involved in her current activity. "I dunno," she said. She was changing sides, so Paul was staring at the ceiling and probably would have stuck his head up through it if he hadn't wanted to hear what was being said.

Maxie laughed loudly. Of course, Jeannie didn't hear that.

"What else did Lieutenant McElone say?" I asked Melissa, if only to change the subject.

"This is the interesting part," she told me, grinning. "I didn't even have anything to ask her after the question about Mr. Laurentz, and I was going to say thank you and go home, like you told me to do."

Jeannie nodded her approval. "She's a very good girl," she said. Melissa and I exchanged a look in which we noted that she was in fact not a four-year-old and that Jeannie should know that.

"But . . ." I prompted my daughter.

"*But* the lieutenant said she'd followed up on the medical examiner's report on Mr. Laurentz because you had made her curious," Melissa continued. I noticed Paul going immediately into his Sherlock Holmes stance, standing straight up and cocking an eyebrow in anticipation. "And she said there had been something odd about the report but not the one from the doctor."

"There was another report?" I asked. Paul nodded; he'd been expecting that there would have been.

"Because Mr. Laurentz died alone, the police had to come and take him away, and that's why there was an autopsy," Melissa said, seeming to recite the words by rote but closely checking her notebook for accuracy. "So the officer who came to his house wrote a report and filed it."

"And . . . ?" There had to be more to it than that. A burned-out toaster in the bathtub, perhaps? The smell of scorched toast in the air?

"He didn't find anything unusual," Melissa said.

I waited. "That's it?" I asked. "What did the lieutenant say was odd about the report?"

"The fact that it was filed at all," Liss answered. "It was . . ." She struggled to remember the grown-up term. "Standard procedure, she said, but there was a lot more detail, like the officer filing it thought there was something to report. But Lieutenant McElone read the whole thing, she said, and it all pointed to Mr. Laurentz dying of . . . natural causes."

That wasn't much. "That's really good, honey," I told my daughter. "You did a terrific job."

Melissa looked disappointed. She knows when an adult is patronizing her.

"Wait!" she insisted. "You didn't let me finish. There was no toaster in the kitchen."

Okay. That could mean something, but it was weird. "The cops checked for a toaster? Why would they do that?"

"An officer noticed crumbs on the countertop and a space where a toaster would be," she said. "But there was no toaster."

"Excellent work," Paul said.

I agreed and gave Melissa a hug before pivoting toward Jeannie. "What did *you* find out?" I asked her. She looked up from her task—which really required more work from Oliver—and her eyes went up and to the left. Thinking.

"Not a lot. I talked to Patricia McVale," Jeannie answered. "Goes by 'Patty.' She said she knew and worked with Larry at the Basie, but thought he was kind of a pain, didn't talk to him much. Didn't even know he was dead; thought he'd just been fired." Jeannie saw that Oliver had fallen asleep and started to clean up.

"So not much we can use," I thought aloud.

Jeannie shrugged. "Patty said she heard from someone she worked with that Lawrence was a snitch who got people fired, and she had thought he'd just been gotten back."

I considered. "Maybe he had," I said. "It's secondhand information, anyway."

Paul said, "Melissa, I'm going to have your mom ask you whether Lieutenant McElone told her who the report said had called the police about Mr. Laurentz's death. Who discovered the body?"

I relayed the question for Jeannie's sake. "I have it here," Melissa answered, rifling through her notes. "I know the lieutenant said to tell you . . . Here!"

"Who was it?" I asked.

"Somebody named Penny Fields," Melissa answered. "Did Mr. Laurentz have a girlfriend?"

Sixteen

All that gave us a lot to discuss, but as I drew breath to reply, Nan Henderson called from the front room, "Alison?" Her voice was tentative, as if wondering whether she wanted me to respond or not.

I gave Jeannie and Melissa a look that warned against any further murder-related conversation right now, and I called back, "Right here, Nan. I'll be there in a second."

Jeannie stayed to change Oliver's diaper, but Melissa followed me into the front room, where Nan and Morgan were unbundling from the biting temperatures outside. There was enough outerwear being tossed onto my couch to start a consignment shop. Paul dropped through the floor; he rarely interacts with the guests when he doesn't have to.

"Is there something I can do for you?" I asked when I got there. Melissa, in her (unofficial) role as assistant manager, stood behind me, by virtue of her youth keeping the guests from looking at me like I was a dangerous felon on the loose.

Nan gave Melissa a glance, then looked at me almost timidly. "Yes," she said finally. "I know we're scheduled to stay until Tuesday, but . . ."

That kind of sentence rarely ended well. "Do you need to cut your vacation short?" I asked. "I hope there's no emergency at home."

"At home," Morgan said, apparently to remind us he was still alive.

"No, no," Nan assured me. "It's just, well, we think it's possible we've exhausted the tourist possibilities for the area. I'm sure that during the summer, with the beach nearby, there's a lot to do, but . . ."

I was about to give in and tally up their bill, but Melissa stepped forward. "Oh no, there's plenty to do here during the winter!" she gushed. "Have you been to the board-walk yet?"

"Yes, we have," Nan said. "I love walking on the board-walk in a brisk breeze. And on the beach. But thanks for mentioning it, Melissa." She smiled what seemed like a sincere smile at Liss, and I started to feel badly that I had some-how let the Hendersons down while they were my guests.

"I know you've been touring some of the lighthouses in the area," I said. "How many have you seen?"

"All of them," Morgan answered, sounding like he'd been asked how many hideous diseases he'd been exposed to. "All of them."

"I feel bad," I told Nan. "You came here wanting a relax-ing vacation, and I feel that somehow you haven't gotten what you came for. Please tell me if there's something I can do."

Nan took a guilty glance at Melissa, perhaps wondering if she should say something in front of my daughter. Tak-ing the hint, I said to Liss, "Could you check on Jeannie and then maybe put the kettle on for tea? I'm sure Mr. and Mrs. Henderson are cold and would like a warm drink."

Liss gave me a look like the kind Hendersons had

been giving me for the past few days—an expression that asked if I'd gone mad—but said, "Sure," and walked toward the kitchen to put the water on to boil. Practical girl, my daughter.

I looked back at Nan once Liss was out of earshot. "Was there something you wanted to say?" I asked.

"No, no," Nan repeated. But she betrayed herself. "Not really."

"Go ahead," I said. "Even if I can't do anything to make your stay more pleasant, your telling me about a problem might help with future guests. I want you to tell me if I've done something wrong."

Nan, who had deposited her coat and various other outerwear items on the nearest sofa cushion, pointed to the loveseat opposite. "Perhaps we should sit down," she said.

"Please." We all took seats, Morgan at the other end of the loveseat, me on the ottoman at the foot of the easy chair. "Tell me what the problem is."

"Well, to begin with, what I said was true," Nan told me. "We do feel like we've exhausted our possibilities here. Morgan especially has been . . . saying that he's seen enough lighthouses and tiny seaside museums. It really is a warm-weather area, isn't it?"

"Yes, though it's lovely in the winter as well," I answered a touch defensively. "I do understand your feelings, but I get the impression there's something else."

Nan nodded. "There is." She waited a moment while Melissa walked through on her way to the game room to talk to Jeannie. Liss gave me a surreptitious look indicating her confusion, just about at the time Maxie pushed her way through the wall over the piano (which had come with the house and which no one who lives here knows how to play) and hovered near one of the exposed beams, where a television production crew had hung a flat-screen TV the previous spring. It's a long story.

Once Liss was out of the way, Nan nodded at me again.

"We've both gotten the impression that something is making you tense, and that's been creating a feeling of . . . unease with us. Like we're intruding, and we don't want to intrude."

"Oh no!" I protested. "You're not intruding at all! I'm very happy you're here. It's just . . . well, as I told you the other night, I've been having some family difficulties. It's not a terrible issue, but it has been weighing on my mind. I sincerely apologize if that's been interfering with you having a good time; that's the last thing I'd want."

The couple exchanged a glance; surely they had indeed thought my "family issues" were making their stay uncomfortable. "I don't want to pry," Nan said. "But what's the status of your family situation now? Because if this is going to be an ongoing thing . . ."

"I promise you, you'll never even notice anything going on," I said, probably rashly, since Maxie was already snorting laughter. "Please, tell me what kind of vacation you'd like to have for the next four days, and I'll do all I can to make that happen."

Again, a glance between the two. Morgan, of course, looked unenthusiastic—he was probably seeing more lighthouses in his future—but he nodded.

The whistling from the kitchen indicated the kettle was boiling, but before I could move, Melissa ran through like a track star and pushed open the kitchen's swinging door. Seconds later, the whistling stopped. Nan smiled, perhaps for the first time in days without the undercoating of tension.

"Well, one thing you could do is direct us toward some of the more infamous crime scenes in the area," she said.

Suuuuure . . . "I beg your pardon?" I asked.

She chuckled, and Morgan looked sheepish. "You see, Morgan just retired. He was chief of police in Ringwood, up in Passaic County. He's really interested in unsolved crimes."

"Unsolved," Morgan repeated, nodding.

Nan tilted her head toward him and lowered her voice almost to a whisper. "He had to quit his job because he can barely hear. He usually wears hearing aids, but he thinks they make him look old. So he takes them out and repeats things people say to him like that's a conversation." She rolled her eyes. "Cops."

A real cop, whose brain I could pick without suffering McElone's snide condescension? Gold mine! However, immediately asking him to consult on my case might damage this fragile peace we'd just established. Let him settle in on the idea first. "But you're *not wearing hearing aids now*," I shouted in Morgan's direction.

"New models," he said, giving Nan a look that indicated his displeasure with her sharing his difficulty. "Coming here today."

"Could you watch for the package?" Nan asked. "He's so much less grumpy when he can hear."

"I absolutely will," I said, wondering what a less grumpy Morgan would be like.

Nan raised her voice back to a level that Morgan, who was leaning forward in a vain effort to hear her, could pick up. "So if you could furnish us with a list of some crime scenes we might be able to reach from here . . ." she reminded me.

I looked up at Maxie. "I'll research that on my computer immediately and get back to you," I said. "Give me"—Maxie held up both hands—"ten minutes." Maxie vanished into the ceiling.

"Thank you," Nan said. "I think this vacation just got a lot better for us."

"Me, too," I answered.

Maxie delivered the list to me a few minutes later and I passed it on to Nan. She and Morgan seemed quite pleased with it, although I was now worried about how many notable crime scenes we had in the area. After tea (Morgan had coffee), they said they would get out there and start visiting the areas suggested the next day, but first they went out to do some shopping and find some dinner.

Once they were on their way, and before I could reflect on the welcome, if odd, turn our relationship had just taken, the doorbell did indeed ring, and Billy the FedEx guy delivered Morgan's hearing aids, which figured; he'd have to wait until he returned to de-grumpify. I called for Paul, who rose up out of the basement and without prompting began to take stock of the investigation he thought we were conducting, which I was conducting.

"So let's be clear," he began, stroking his goatee at a fevered pitch. "We've discovered that the box office manager where Mr. Laurentz worked was the person to discover his body and call the authorities. We've also established that there were people who worked with him there who were angry with Mr. Laurentz, particularly Ms. Carter, who felt that he had informed on her and caused her to be fired."

I figured if Paul was going to sum up, I might as well make myself useful—I knew all this stuff already—and began cleaning up the kitchen. There wasn't much to clean, since making tea and coffee doesn't require a huge operation, but it was something.

"Then there was the theater company, the Old New Thespians," he continued without missing a beat.

"New Old Thespians," I corrected. There weren't enough dishes to bother with the dishwasher; I'd just wash them by hand in the sink.

"New Old Thespians," Paul repeated, trying to maintain his rhythm. "Clearly, Mr. Laurentz created a good deal of animosity there, to the point that he was asked to leave the group. But was that enough to anger someone to the point of violence?"

"They got busted for being naked and they think he snitched on them," I reminded him.

Paul nodded. "Yes. We need to find out which ones were involved and how seriously they were punished. That could be a motive. The news report Maxie found wasn't very specific; no names were mentioned. Can you talk to Lieutenant McElone again?"

I put the cups in the dish drainer and wiped my hands with a towel. "I don't have to," I told him, thinking I could ask Morgan. "I can utilize the power of the press."

Seventeen

Saturday

"A bunch of senior citizens stripping down to do *Hair?*"
Phyllis Coates, editor and owner of the *Harbor Haven
Chronicle*, threw back her head and laughed. "Oh, I can't
believe I missed that one!"

"Can you find out about it?" I asked.

Phyllis, as I'd expected, looked at me with mock disdain.
"Can *I* find out about it?" she echoed. "Whom do you think
you're talking to?" Phyllis, a longtime veteran of the New
York *Daily News*, had bought the *Chronicle* as her "retire-
ment plan," and prided herself on being a tough, fair street
reporter. The fact that she was probably old enough to be
my mother (and had been my first employer when I was a
paper delivery girl at thirteen) was irrelevant.

"I think I'm talking to someone really talented and smart
who could do me a great favor if she were so inclined," I
answered. "How am I doing so far?"

Phyllis chuckled. We were standing in her office, which
took up only a small section of the overall *Chronicle* work

space, despite the fact that Phyllis was the only full-time employee of the paper. You'd think her work area would take a somewhat higher priority, but the "outside," as she called it, housed all her previously published issues (aka "the Morgue"), plus advertising brochures, two light tables for studying photographs—Phyllis was just now starting to go digital—and all sorts of other dusty equipment I couldn't identify.

"Not bad," she responded. "Flattery will get you everywhere. Tell me, why are you so interested in this geriatric love-in?" She pulled a pencil out from behind her ear and looked on her desk—which was buried under mountains of paper—for a scrap on which to take notes. Phyllis didn't mind doing some digging for me, as long as she got a story out of it.

I explained the situation briefly, without mentioning any dead people I'd talked to recently. "If I can find out who was arrested and if some people took it more personally than others, it might point me in a direction in the case," I told her.

Phyllis narrowed her eyes, thinking. "You're sure this Laurentz guy was murdered?" she said. "You said the ME's report shows an arrhythmia. People do die from those, you know."

"Actually, I'm *not* sure," I said. "If I were sure one way or the other, this would be a lot easier. But until I can verify it was natural causes, I have to assume it was a murder, or I have nothing to investigate. Is this coffee from today?" I pointed at the half-full pot on her hot plate, which was inadvisably close to one of the many stacks of papers in the tiny office.

Phyllis looked, as if the coffeepot's appearance would give her a clue to its most recent activity. "Today or yesterday," she said offhandedly. I decided not to chance it.

I gave her the date of the *Hair* performance and also the location: Cedar Crest, a forty-minute drive from Harbor

Haven but close to the Freehold area where most of the New Old Thespians lived. Phyllis took note of all of it, then poured herself a cup of the suspect coffee—she's always been braver than I—sat down behind her incredibly unkempt desk and surveyed me closely.

"What's the problem, sweetie?" she asked out of nowhere.

That stumped me. "Problem? I told you. I need to find out about what happened to Lawrence Laurentz."

"Who do you think you're talking to?" Phyllis demanded. "We've known each other a long time."

"I don't have other problems, Phyllis. I'd tell you." I didn't have problems I wanted to *think* about, anyway. . . .

"You're acting funny," she said, then added—not leaving time for me to make a remark about how nobody was laughing—"You're hesitant when you should be enthusiastic yet you're rushing into something when you don't have all the facts. You don't know if this guy was murdered. You don't know why someone would want to murder him. I don't mind helping as long as I can get an article out of it, but this doesn't seem like you. Is there something else on your mind?"

"It's about my dad," I said quietly, surprising myself. I'd had no idea that was going to come out of my mouth.

Phyllis's eyes got sad. "He's been gone a few years now," she said.

I nodded. "Five years. And I know I'm supposed to have moved on by now, but I don't think I have. And this thing with Lawrence Laurentz feels connected to him somehow." I couldn't say it was because Lawrence's ghost had insisted Dad was involved. "It's gotten me thinking about him a lot."

Phyllis drank some of the coffee and barely grimaced at the way it must have tasted. She looked me straight in the eye. "You never get over a loss like that," she said. "Don't believe what people tell you; you don't. And every once in a while, he's going to pop into your mind and make you sad that he's not here. You have to expect that once in a while."

Suddenly I was fighting back tears, successfully, but just barely. "I know. The logical part of my brain is aware of that. But that doesn't make it hurt less." I could also have mentioned that I was upset with my father for not coming to visit me and his granddaughter after he was dead, but making Phyllis think I was crazy didn't really seem like it would be a huge help.

"You know, I think I have a few clips about your dad in the . . . archives," she said, tactfully avoiding the word *morgue*. "Come back in a couple of days, and I'll put something together for you to remember him by when you choose to do so."

At that second, my battle with the tears was lost. I sniffled, let a few drops go from my eyes, but managed not to break down in loud sobs, which I suppose was a pyrrhic victory. "You're a good person, Phyllis."

She patted me on the shoulder. "I know," she said. "But don't spread it around. I have a reputation to uphold."

Paul was right: Later that day, while I was driving home, Jerry Rasmussen called to apologize for what he described as "my regrettable behavior when we met yesterday."

"I don't think you need to apologize," I said, having rehearsed for this once Paul had suggested the situation could arise. "You were upset, and I was saying things that would rightly upset many people." The Bluetooth I was wearing made it sound like Jerry was in Siberia, but luckily, the drive from the *Chronicle* office to the guesthouse would be short. That was lucky, too, because the cup of Dunkin' Donuts coffee I had in the cup holder (I just wasn't brave enough for Phyllis's coffee) would probably be an iced coffee by the time I arrived home.

"Still," Jerry said, apparently trying to convince me that he was indeed an awful person, "I attacked the messenger when it was the message I found objectionable. I regret my actions, and I wonder how I might make it up to you."

I wouldn't have seen that one coming if Paul hadn't exhibited better foresight than I and had already coached me on a proper answer. "Well, you could answer a couple of questions I still need to figure out," I said. "For example, how many of the other New Old Thespians lived in Whispering Lakes, like you and Mr. Laurentz?"

"Well, the group's genesis was actually here," Jerry answered. "Besides Larry, I'm not sure if you met Frances Walters. She lives there." I hadn't told Jerry that Frances had given me his name because I didn't want him to resent her sending a private eye after him—I'd told him only that I'd gotten his address from "another member of the group." This might have been his attempt to confirm it had been Frances, but I wasn't biting, so he hesitated and then went on. "At the time, Marion O'Day was here, too, but she's since moved to Taos, New Mexico, to live with her daughter. And Barney Lester passed away just a few weeks ago."

Uh-oh. "I'm so sorry to hear that. What happened?" I asked.

"Heart," Jerry sighed. "He'd been frail for a long time. I don't think he appeared in a production for more than a year." Well before Lawrence died.

"One other thing," I moved on. "Can you think of a reason someone would want to be rid of Mr. Laurentz?"

"I can think of thousands." Droll.

"Do you know if he left a large estate? Money, property, anything like that?"

"You haven't checked on such things?" he asked, unimpressed with me.

"An investigator asks the same questions sometimes to see what answers she'll get," I explained, parroting something Paul had told me. "So, Mr. Laurentz's estate?"

"You'd have to ask his accountant," Jerry sniffed. "The

man was a ticket seller at a regional theater. I doubt he was sitting on the Hope Diamond and waiting for the right moment to cash in."

As apologies went, it left me just a little unsatisfied.

"I don't see how this is getting us closer to Grampa," Melissa argued. I was driving her to a bowling party for one of her friends from school, and gift in hand, she was still complaining about not doing any investigating today. Meanwhile, my new "official" assistant, Jeannie, had begged off for the day, saying she didn't work weekends, which was not making her husband, Tony, happy. "You and Jeannie talked to a bunch of people yesterday, I talked to Lieutenant McElone, but even if we find out what happened to Mr. Laurentz, how does that help us get Grampa to come back?"

"That is a good question," I admitted. "But I don't have an answer for you now."

"I don't see why I have to sit in the backseat," Maxie interjected. This time, I'd actually asked her to come along, as per Paul's suggestion. She'd have work to do.

"I'm going to see if Phyllis gets anywhere with the theater troupe arrest angle," I told Liss, doing my best to ignore the dead woman in the car with us. "There's nowhere to go with the medical examiner's report. I can go back and question some of the people I've already questioned—especially Penny Fields, now that I know she found Lawrence's body— but I don't know if I'm going to do that today. So that's where we stand in the investigation."

"So why am I going bowling for Justin Krenshaw's birthday?" Melissa moaned.

"You like bowling."

"I don't like Justin Krenshaw."

"Then why are you going to his birthday party?" Maxie asked.

"That's what I'd like to know," Liss answered.

"You were invited," I reminded her.

"Hmmph." That was Maxie, not Melissa. Occasionally I wonder which one is more mature. The rest of the time, I'm positive it's Melissa.

I chose not to listen to the rest of the conversation (Maxie has a way of convincing Melissa that everything is my fault) and pondered Liss's original question: How *was* this getting me any closer to finding Dad or figuring out exactly what was going on with him? And when I searched my heart, the fact was, I cared more about that than I did about what happened to Lawrence Laurentz. I know; I'm a bad person and a lousy private investigator. I have never suspected otherwise.

After I dropped Melissa off at the bowling alley (where her mood immediately brightened when she saw Wendy and a couple of her other friends and went giddily inside), Maxie slithered up into the front seat and sighed contentedly.

"So," she said. "Where are we going now?"

Before I could answer her or even move the car out of park, my cell phone rang, with a number I didn't recognize in the caller ID. I hesitated, but put the call on speaker to be hands-free. And got an earful of an angry Tyra Carter.

"What are you doing talking to Penny Fields about me?" she demanded. "How am I supposed to get my job back if I'm being bad-mouthed behind my back?"

"Since when do you want your job back?" I asked.

"I don't make enough money. I need that job back. So how come you're bad-mouthing me to Penny?"

"I'm not." I thought back over the sequence of events. "Wait. I never even *mentioned* your name to Penny Fields—she gave your name to *me*! What are you talking about? How did you get my number?"

Maxie seemed amused, which was not at all unusual when I was made uncomfortable.

"You gave me a business card," Tyra shot back. "The point is, how come you were talking to Penny Fields about me?"

I took a deep breath and thanked myself for not putting the car in gear. "Listen carefully, Tyra. The only time your name came up in my conversation with Penny was when *she* brought it up. I'd never heard of you before then, and I haven't talked to Penny since I met you. So what makes you think that I'm talking about you behind your back?"

"All I know is that before you talked to Penny, she said I had a chance to come back and work at the theater, and now she says they're full up and there are no jobs available. Does she think I don't talk to the people on staff there? She has a job available—she just doesn't want to give it to me! It's got to be because of something you said."

"Look," I said. "Do you want me to call Penny and ask her? Because I'm telling you, I never . . ."

"No, I don't want you calling Penny!" I pictured Tyra, all six feet of her, standing up with that headset on, looking angry. It was not a comforting image. "Lord knows what you'll tell her this time. But mark my words: If I have to spend the rest of my life trying to tell people how to inflate their tires, you had better start looking over your shoulder, because one day, I'll be behind you." She hung up.

I looked at Maxie, who was not attempting to conceal her glee. "Shut up," I said.

"I'm not saying anything."

I decided while I was parked there to take Frances Walters up on her offer and called her. She knew the people involved better than I did, after all. I told her about Tyra's call and asked her what she thought it meant.

Frances was silent for a long moment, and I didn't get the sense it was because she didn't have an opinion, but because she wasn't sure exactly how she wanted to express it. "I think it means that you should be very careful," she said. "Tyra has something of a temper, and she can still be extremely physical." That didn't sound good.

"Still?" I asked. "What do you mean, still?"

This time I got the impression the pause was because

Frances was trying to determine exactly how stupid I might be. "You know about Tyra, don't you?" she asked. Sort of asked. More like insisted.

"I'm guessing I don't. What do I need to know?"

"You're not driving, are you?" Frances could tell I was calling on a cell phone. I assured her I was parked (we still hadn't had a chance to leave the bowling alley parking lot) and able to withstand any shock. "Well, the fact is, until about a year ago, Tyra Carter was Tyrone Carter."

"She's a transsexual?" If it was true, I had to admit her doctors had done admirable work. You'd only know because of her size and to some extent her voice, if you were more observant about those kinds of things than I was, clearly.

"Yes. And before she managed to come to terms with her gender, Tyra told me that she was a rather, well, excitable man who would occasionally act out his emotional frustration physically."

"Tyrone was violent?"

"Yes, according to Tyra. She never did any jail time or anything like that, but there were arrests after the occasional bar fight. Tyra says it stopped when she learned to go to different bars and says she hasn't had any violent feelings since she finally decided to go for gender reassignment."

I moaned. Now I had to actually worry about Tyra's threats that she'd dog my tracks. I thanked Frances for her help and disconnected the call. "Let's go somewhere safe," I said, more to myself than to Maxie.

"Like where?" she asked.

"The only logical place to go," I said. "A paint store in Asbury Park. Time to put you to work."

Madison Paint had not altered much since I'd last been there, and yet it had changed, or I had; it was like going to your childhood home and realizing it's much smaller than you remembered. The colorful sign hanging on the front of the store was a little shabbier now, illuminated a touch less completely. But the primary colors behind the letters *P-A-I-N-T* were still clean and joyful, inviting the customer in to bring a little variety of color into his life.

Inside, the place was a paint store like most others that weren't part of huge home improvement superstores (and I would know, since I used to work at one of those). It smelled slightly of, well, paint, a smell some people don't like but I do. Whenever Dad was painting a room in our house, even before I was old enough to help, I had a sense of anticipation—that things were going to look new and different. The smell was part of that excitement. I've always loved it.

Inside, the shelves were stacked, though not with gallons of different colors anymore. As Josh Kaplan—grandson of Sy Kaplan, the owner—was telling me, the procedure now was to stock various kinds of primer (essentially a colorless paint), find out exactly what hue the customer wanted and then add the color with a precise formula and mix it on what Josh called "the shaker," a machine that did exactly that to a can of paint.

"Got into the family business," Josh, a tall, curly-haired guy with an ingratiating smile, told me with a light laugh, "after an MBA from Drexel. You can imagine how thrilled my parents are."

I was afraid to ask, but it was sort of central to the reason I was there. "But your grandfather. He's . . ."

Josh grinned. "Oh, he's very much alive," he assured me. "He's ninety-one years old now, so doesn't come into the store on Saturday or Sunday. Says he's semiretired." He shook his head. "He's quite a guy."

Maxie, who had followed me inside, was eyeing Josh with something uncomfortably resembling hunger. She muttered, "He's not the only one." I shot her a scolding look, and she stuck her tongue out at me. This is the level of maturity I live with on a daily basis.

Paul had instructed Maxie to fly through the store, looking for signs Dad had been there. This had been one of his favorite places on earth; he might be using it as a refuge. She materialized through a shelf of spackling just as I was introducing myself to Josh and shook her head.

"I'm betting you're not here to talk about my grandfather," Josh said.

"Actually, I sort of am," I answered.

It was possible Dad was hiding in a part of his life that Mom wouldn't know well. I needed to talk to someone who would have those insights. Sy Kaplan was that guy, but he wasn't here today.

Neither was Dad, at least not visibly. And it seemed Maxie was saying he wasn't here invisibly, either.

There were, however, two other ghosts hanging around: One was a woman in overalls who wasn't even looking at us, but was reading a newspaper that appeared to be vintage about 1955 or so; the other had the look of someone who had never had a good day in his life and was extending that streak into eternity. He was a man in his seventies or eighties, dressed in dark clothing that was of recent, if not current, vintage. If I hadn't been looking for my dad, I probably wouldn't have even noticed, either—it's gotten to a point where I expect to see spirits whenever I go out, so I didn't really pay much attention to these two.

"You see," I continued, giving Josh my hastily constructed cover story as Maxie seemed to size him up for some lascivious purpose, "I'm writing a memoir about my father, and this was one of his favorite places to hang out. So I was hoping to run into your grandfather for a few reminiscences, you know what I mean?"

He squinted at me, as if I were a long distance away or standing directly in the path of the sun. "Oh, Alison Kerby! Of course! You used to come here with your dad! I remember you from when we were kids."

Maxie got a really nasty grin on her face; she was trying

to figure out how this connection could best be used to humiliate me. But I was busy trying to think back. And I'm sure my face took on the same squint-through-time expression Josh's had just exhibited.

When it finally hit me, I actually went so far as to point at him, as if he wasn't sure he was there. "Joshie!" I shouted. "I remember! You used to crawl your way out of the bottom bins when Sy was stocking Spackle!"

Josh smiled. "You mean when *I* was stocking Spackle. It's so good to see you again." He reached out and took my hand, and Maxie's face went from gleeful anticipation to sour disappointment. "But no one's called me 'Joshie' for about twenty years."

"Sorry about that." Neither of us had let go of the other's hand yet. I wasn't rushing.

"It's okay." Josh finally let go, which wasn't as awkward as it should have been. "I could get Gramp on the phone for you if it's important."

Maxie seemed distracted now by the two other ghosts in the room, specifically by the grumpy-looking one. She tried to get between the grumpy ghost and me, but he simply shifted position to continue glaring at me as if I'd insulted him, badly, at some recent moment. "What are you looking at?" she demanded of him, but Grumpy simply glared and remained silent.

"No, that won't . . . be necessary," I said to Josh, remembering he'd just offered to call Sy for me. "I can come back sometime when he's here."

"That would be nice," Josh answered. "I mean, I'm sure he'd enjoy that. Your dad was a favorite of his. We were sorry to hear about his passing."

"Thank you," I said, because that's what you say when people tell you something like that. "Dad loved nothing better than hanging around here with Sy and the other painters. I never heard him laugh so much."

Maxie, waving her hands in front of Grumpy's face,

yelled, "Hey! Grim Reaper! What is your *problem*?" But the dour man never broke eye contact and never said a word.

"I remember a few things," Josh offered. "Maybe I could tell you a few stories about your dad from back then. Would that help your memoir?"

"My . . ." *Oh, yeah!* "Yes, oh yes, absolutely, that would be great! What can you tell me?"

The bells on the front door of the store jingled, indicating a customer was entering the place. Josh looked up and excused himself for a moment, then walked to the front of the store, where I saw a woman perusing the color sample cards for the shade she wanted.

Finally, as quietly and unobtrusively as I could, I looked up at Maxie and asked, "No Dad?"

"I'm not sure," she said. "I saw some shoes going through the roof, but by the time I got out there, whoever it was had gone. Nothing else."

The glare from the angry ghost was distracting me. I look up and asked, "Can I help you with something?"

Maxie got between us, but her movement did not distract the ghost from the staring contest he appeared to think we were having, as he could look through her. But I didn't get to ask him anything else because Josh had quickly returned from the front of the store.

"I'm sorry, but this is going to take some time," he said.

"Don't be sorry. This is your business. I'm taking up your time. I tell you what; I'll come back when your grandfather is here, during the week." I really just wanted to get out of the line of that ghost's hostile glare so I could think clearly. This guy was really spooking me out, and given my usual circumstances, that's saying something.

Maxie reached over and pulled off the grim ghost's black hat. Nothing; he didn't even try to reach for it back. "Geez!" she hollered.

I decided it was time to make a run for it. "Thanks," I said to Josh. "Should I call before I show up next time?"

He took hold of my arm gently as I walked by. "Wait," he said. "Maybe I could still tell you some of those stories about your dad. Like"—he looked away, in a shy sort of maneuver—"over dinner or something."

"Oh man!" Maxie hollered. "He's asking you out on a date!" She turned toward Grumpy. "Do you see this?" He, of course, did not respond. "I know!" Maxie answered.

I chose to ignore their antics. "I'd really like that," I told Josh, and he smiled at me. I picked up a business card from the desk with his name on it. "I'll text you my cell number and we can figure out a time and place."

"That's so twenty-first century," he said. "I like it." Then he went to attend to his customer, who was choosing among about seventeen shades of mauve.

As I turned to leave, I could sort of feel Maxie falling in behind me, muttering to herself about how a guy like that could ask me out. Like she'd had a chance.

But I decided to take one last parting glance at the angry-looking gentleman floating near the back window of the store. And sure enough, he was still there, still staring and still looking like I'd stolen his lunch money and called him a name. He narrowed his eyes as I moved away, and just as I was leaving the store, I heard him whisper: "Alison."

I ran. From the safest place I could think to have gone.

Eighteen

By the time I picked Melissa up from the bowling party, Maxie and I had hashed, argued, questioned, puzzled and dissected the idea of the grumpy ghost's knowing my name. She had said I was overemphasizing it (I believe her words included the phrase "drama queen"), and that the old spirit had simply heard Josh Kaplan use my name and repeated it for effect. But I knew how it felt, and it *felt* like he was threatening everything I held at all dear in my life, and possibly to all life everywhere.

Okay, maybe "drama duchess," but that was as far as I was willing to go.

Maxie was also appalled because after I'd texted Josh Kaplan my number, he'd called me almost immediately, and we'd made plans to go out the following evening (he closed the store early on Sundays). He'd pick me up at the guest-house and we'd "discuss my memoir," which I was starting to think could become code for something else.

The one thing Maxie and I had agreed upon was not to

mention the angry ghost to Melissa, who could put on quite a show of being self-possessed but was in reality still only ten years old. There had been no argument about that.

But I sure as hell was going to tell Paul the first chance I got.

Despite having complained about going to Justin Krenshaw's birthday bowling party, Melissa seemed reluctant to get into the Volvo to come home. This was partially understandable, as all her friends were standing in the frigid parking lot laughing and gabbing and also because the Volvo's heating system was roughly as efficient as the United States Congress, which is to say it made a lot of noise but got very little done.

But Liss's hesitation turned out to be less about hanging around and more about a possible sleepover at Janine's house that she hadn't known about until the sixth frame of the second game. "They asked me, but I'm not sure they really want me to go," she said. "Should I say no?" I should point out that at no time was permission to go to a sleepover that night with no prior notice an issue. I'm a fun mom.

"You have to go," Maxie suggested. "If you don't, they'll talk about you."

"Go, but only if you want to," I countered as quickly as I could. "Don't worry about why you were invited; the point is, you were invited. They wouldn't ask if they didn't want you to come."

"Hmmph," Maxie snorted.

In the end, of course, it was decided that Liss would spend the night at Janine's, which had been hastily arranged but okayed by Janine's mother, Kate. But first we had to go back to the house so that she could gather her sleepover equipment and I could check on my guests. I lit a fire in the fireplace in the den to try to heat the house a little and went to greet the Hendersons.

As advertised, now that I'd delivered Morgan's hearing

aids, he was a changed man. He still seemed to have to strain a little to hear conversation, but his demeanor was much less dour, and he could converse almost seamlessly. I wished I had known the devices had been on their way from the beginning, but Nan told me that Morgan was still vain about the hearing aids and hadn't wanted to mention what was in the box at all.

They had just returned from a long trip to the site of the Lindbergh baby kidnapping near Princeton, almost entirely on the other side of the state, and so were especially tired. I offered to order them in something to eat, but they said after a short rest stop, they intended to revisit one of the local restaurants they'd especially enjoyed. It was one that pays me a percentage for sending guests their way (with a ten percent discount for the diners), so I didn't argue too strenuously against their plan.

I did, however, resolve to ask Morgan for advice on my investigation into Lawrence's death as soon as there was a natural opening in our conversation. You can't rush these things when you're the innkeeper, I thought.

Melissa was upstairs assembling her overnight bag, with her "roommate" Maxie offering advice, when Paul bled through the kitchen wall (and the stove) for an update. I told him about the grumpy ghost first, and he looked especially concerned.

"You felt that he knew you somehow?" he asked, although I'd made that quite clear in the telling.

I nodded. "And I didn't like the way it felt. It wasn't like he was planning a surprise party for my next birthday."

Paul did something the ghosts do, which is similar to taking a deep breath but it sounds different because no air is actually involved in the process. It sounds more like a vacuum cleaner on a very low power setting.

"I think it's significant," he said. "But I don't under-stand it yet. Perhaps I can try to track down this spirit's consciousness. I don't have a name to work with, but I have an area to check. Let me try to contact someone later tonight, when things will be quiet."

I nodded my agreement. "In the meantime, what else can we do? I feel like I'm pulled in two directions here with the Lawrence thing and the search for my father. I don't know what to do first, and you're good at that." Always flatter a man; it brings out his best.

Once again, it did not fail. "You can divide your time. Obviously, your priority is finding out what is going on with your father," Paul began. "If I am unable to raise him or the spirit you saw at the paint store today, make sure that you keep in touch with the young man you met at the store."

I blushed but nodded coolly. All would have been fine if Maxie had not chosen that moment to slither down out of the ceiling. "Melissa says she'll be ready to go in five minutes," she told me in my role as chauffeur. Then she turned toward Paul. "So, she told you about the guy who asked her out today?"

I had, in fact, left that particular detail out of my investigation summary. Paul gets a trifle testy on those rare occasions I'm shown any interest by a man. He raised an eyebrow and his lip curled just a little.

"He asked you out?" he said, his Canadian cadence not exactly betraying upset so much as irritation. "Why didn't you mention that before?"

Maxie grinned at me. Lewis Carroll's Cheshire cat could not have done so with more enthusiasm. Unfortunately, the grin did not mean the rest of Maxie was disappearing. She existed, I thought, simply to watch me be uncomfortable.

"I didn't mention it because it didn't seem relevant," I told Paul. "I said I'd be seeing Josh again and that I would ask him about my father. Both those things are true. If we happen to be eating dinner while I'm seeing him and asking him about my father, I don't see what difference it makes."

"It clouds the report because you don't know what his

motivations will be now," Paul said, trying his very best to sound professional and professorial. "He might lie to you for reasons other than an involvement in your father's predicament, whatever that might be. And your judgment may be clouded emotionally."

I guess it was Maxie's grin, which widened, that finally got to me. Before I could think, I turned to Paul and said, "This is amazing. You haven't met Josh, and you've already decided not only that he's going to lie to me but that he'll do it because he wants to seduce me against my will. I have news for you, pal. I can tell when a man is lying to me, like when you tell me you don't get jealous." Paul looked astonished and then shot a glance behind me, but I was on a roll. "And my judgment is fine. If Josh seduces me, believe me, it'll be because I want him to."

Maxie make a coughing noise. She doesn't do that. For one thing, there's no way she can possibly catch a cold. So now I knew Melissa was probably behind me, but I had worked up a head of steam, and it was, for reasons that were completely and totally irrational, directed at Paul.

"You have to stop acting like you and I have a history," I said to him. "We have no history. The day I met you, you had already been dead for almost a year." Paul doesn't like to use the word *dead* in relation to himself, but then, who would?

I realized I'd probably gone too far when he evaporated before my eyes. The look on his face indicated pain and betrayal. I started to say, "Wait" as he vanished, but there was no time. So I turned to face my daughter.

"What did you just do?" she asked in her tiniest little-girl voice.

"It's okay, honey," I said, even though it wasn't. "I'll work it out with Paul later. Are you ready to go?"

Melissa looked at me with one of those expressions that flips our familial roles. "That didn't look okay," she said.

"Are you ready to go?" I repeated.

"I think so," she said quietly.

We drove to Janine's house mostly in silence. Luckily, Harbor Haven isn't a large town, and we were there in only a few minutes. I walked Melissa to the front door and forced her to let me give her a kiss on the cheek before I turned back toward the car, just to remind her that I was still her mother and we did still love each other. You have to do that every once in a while. Or at least I do.

Back at the house, Nan and Morgan had not yet returned from dinner, so I called to Paul loudly after I closed the front door and removed six or seven layers of outerwear. I figured it was time to clear the air.

But he didn't show up.

"Come on, Paul, I'm sorry," I said in a more conversational tone. "I've been upset and I said some stuff that I shouldn't have, and I apologize. We're going to be together in this house a long time. Let's not make it difficult."

Nothing. Not even Maxie.

I ended up spending the rest of the evening by myself. Once Nan and Morgan returned, they didn't want to sit up and talk, or have a cup of tea. Believe me, I asked. The sound of a human voice would have been helpful. I could have called my mother. I *should* have called my mother. I didn't call my mother. She'd want to know why I was calling.

Instead, I cleaned up as much as I could without making a lot of noise. It's a big job keeping such a large house looking good, and you have to work at it every day. I straightened things up in the library, the game room and a couple of the upstairs bedrooms, which didn't take long because we didn't have any guests staying upstairs.

When I finally gave into the inevitable and went to my bedroom, gratefully remembering that I had dusted the dresser so there could be no further unsolicited comments, I decided to take a shower. I thought some nice hot water after a day like this would feel soothing.

It did, and I spent an unusually long amount of time in

my en suite bathroom. Once I was out, I dried off, breathed a long sigh and came close to convincing myself things would be better in the morning.

That was, until I noticed the message written in the condensation that had built up on my bathroom mirror: "YOUR FATHER DIDN'T DIE THE WAY YOU THINK."

Somehow, petty arguments didn't seem important, and at the top of my lungs, I shouted, "PAUL!"

Nineteen

Paul Harrison is a very complicated being—he's sensitive, but masculine. He's funny while remaining serious. He is dead without actually being gone. But one thing he is definitely *not* is vindictive, so when he heard my bloodcurdling scream, he arrived in the bathroom in the blink of an eye. And then just as quickly covered his own.

"Alison!" he shouted. "Put on a robe or something!"

I'd forgotten that I'd just stepped out of the shower. I grabbed the terry-cloth robe I'd had hanging on a towel rack and threw it on. "It's okay," I reassured my proper Canadian dead friend. "I'm dressed." Sort of. It's amazing how someone else's panic can make you forget your own sometimes.

Paul unclasped his hand from his eyes. "What were you screaming about?" he said. "You scared me half . . ." He did not finish the sentence.

"That," I told him, pointing to the mirror. The words were still clearly visible, as Paul had not opened the door to come in, so the air was not losing its humidity very quickly. He hovered over to look at it more closely.

Then there was banging on my bedroom door. "Alison?" Nan called in quietly. "Are you all right?"

They were going to go back to thinking I was nuts. Swell. "I'm okay, Nan," I answered. "Sorry to scare you."

"Are you sure?" Morgan said, clearly after Nan had told him what she'd heard. "Can we come in and check?"

I beg your pardon? "Come in and check?" I said more to myself than anyone else.

"Of course," Paul said. "You said he's an ex-cop. He wants to come in and see that no one is holding you hostage and making you say everything's all right."

That made sense. "Just a second," I said, and stopped, once Paul had discreetly turned away, to at least throw on the pajamas I'd taken out and then got back into the robe. I walked to the bathroom door, then the bedroom door, unlatched it and let the Hendersons inside. "Sorry again. I didn't mean to worry you."

"Did something frighten you?" Nan asked. "You sounded terrified."

Paul, looking at the note on the mirror in the bathroom and stroking his goatee, seemed mesmerized. "Who could have gotten in?" I heard him ask himself. "Or what?"

"I found something in my bathroom that is . . . Well, I can't explain it." Maybe the time had come to tap Morgan's police expertise. "All the doors in the house are locked." I couldn't let them know I was perfectly capable of imagining something *flying* in and leaving a message. We were just getting past the point where my guests thought I was crazy.

Nan passed this along to Morgan, who had been cupping his ear standing behind her but clearly hadn't caught much of what was being said. And that's when I noticed he had only one hearing aid, in his right ear; he must have rushed to get here when Nan heard me shout. "Show me what it was you found," he said. Cops are cops. No niceties, just let's see the problem.

I led them into the bathroom, and for once, thanked fate that the words had not yet vanished off the mirror, which would have once again led my guests to the conclusion that they were giving their hard-earned vacation money to a madwoman. Morgan's eyebrows rose when he saw the message, and he examined the mirror very closely, opening the medicine cabinet door carefully with two fingers and touching as little of the surface as possible.

"Nan," he said, addressing his wife like he was directing another officer under his command, "go downstairs and get about a paper cup worth of ash from the fireplace. And some tape." Without so much as a blink, she was gone and headed downstairs.

I shot a glance at Paul, who was watching Morgan work, clearly with approval. Nan soon reappeared with one of the bathroom cups from the room she and Morgan were renting, filled about a third of the way with fireplace ash. Morgan reached out his hand and took it from her with a nod. Officer Nan was clearly acknowledged and took her place a few feet away to let the detective work.

Morgan looked at the sink where some of my makeup supplies were laid out and picked up a cosmetics brush. He held it out so I could see it. "Can I use this?" he asked. I had no idea what he was going to do, but I nodded.

He took the brush and very gently placed it into the cup, to get some ash in the bristles. Then he more or less painted the mirror with the ash, very lightly and just on the areas where the message had been scrawled.

"Hmmm . . ." Morgan sort of growled, a low sound in the back of his throat. It was almost like humming. I didn't dare say a word.

"He's looking for fingerprints," Paul explained. I nodded just enough for him to see I'd understood. We both knew he would find none.

Morgan repeated the procedure, smearing the fireplace ash on three separate areas of the mirror, each time looking very carefully at his work, then standing back to see it from another angle, all the while making that very low humming sound in his throat. I got caught up watching the procedure and actually forgot to be terrified for a few minutes.

When he was finished, Morgan put down the cup and the brush, moving his pursed lips back and forth, almost literally chewing over what he'd learned, which didn't seem to be much. "I don't see any prints," he said after a moment. "No need for the tape; I can't lift anything. My best guess is that whoever did this wore gloves, but not leather ones or anything with a seam. Maybe something knitted or cloth, but I didn't see any fibers or residue of any kind. Very careful work, probably with gloves."

I glanced at Paul, who was clearly thinking what I was thinking: *Ghosts wouldn't leave fingerprints.*

"Where does that leave us?" I asked Morgan.

"Without anything I can send to any of my friends to check," he responded. "Now. Why don't I get my other hearing aid and we sit down with something hot to drink, and you can tell us what, exactly, is going on? Maybe I can help."

Filling Nan and Morgan Henderson in on the situation with Dad and Lawrence Laurentz was, to put it mildly, tricky. With no mention of ghosts, the story had holes in it through which you could drive the Starship Enterprise. But if I'd mentioned ghosts, they clearly would have been calling various emergency numbers to have me sent somewhere I couldn't do any further damage to my impressionable daughter. So I went with the shakier no-ghost version of the scenario.

That one consisted of my fledgling private-investigator's license, the idea that Lawrence's sister had contacted me through Mom, some odd messages left for me when I was sure there was no one else in the house, and myriad suspects, a lot of whom had motive and one of whom could be placed at the scene of Lawrence's death. I said I had questions about my father's death, too, and believed there to be a connection.

I noticed that Morgan seemed to get happier with each minute I was explaining myself, to the point that he was almost giddy by the time he asked me to explain that last part. He didn't actually let out a satisfied laugh when he asked it, but he was wide-eyed and engaged in a way I'd never seen before.

His question, however, was spiked with difficulty for me. In the sans ghost version of the story, connecting the dots between Lawrence and Dad took some extra creativity. But I could rely on the one actual connection I had in real life, ghosts and all. I went back up to my bedroom and found my tote bag, where the business card Lawrence had given me after his disappearing act had drifted to the bottom, requiring a fairly serious spelunking expedition that took a few minutes after I got back downstairs with the bag.

I handed Morgan Dad's business card. "I found this at"—I had to decide which venue to implicate—"the Count Basie Theatre. It's my father's. I can't explain how it might have gotten there." That last part was true—I absolutely couldn't explain it.

Morgan took the card and examined it. Nan, watching him closely, seemed almost relieved, as if this unexpected turn in their vacation plans had brought her back the husband she remembered. Near the ceiling, Paul and Maxie were watching almost as intently; Paul seemed to be taking mental notes while Maxie, who had expressed disappointment at missing all the fun in the upstairs bathroom, was clearly hoping that something else deeply embarrassing to me might still happen and salvage her evening.

Morgan's bushy eyebrows were doing the merengue all over his forehead; he was clearly deep in thought. "What

would a handyman's business card be doing in a theater in
Red Bank five years after he died?" he asked, and then
before anyone could answer (which admittedly would have
been a while, since I had no idea), he added, "Did your
father ever do any work in the Basie theater?"

Realizing this wouldn't do any good since I *hadn't* found
the card at the Basie, I said, "I'm sure he didn't. I'd remember.
Besides, Penny, the box office manager, gave me a quick tour
and told me the theater had been remodeled and upgraded
just in the past year or two. It would have been too late."

"Interesting," Morgan said. "We have two situations that
seem unrelated, but seems much too big a coincidence to
be, you know, coincidental."

I needed to steer this back in the direction of the truth if
it was going to be any help. "What do you think I should
do, Morgan?"

He still needed a little help from Nan but finally answered, "I think this woman at the theater is the one I'd like
the most for the murder. But the first thing you have to do
is determine that there *was* a murder. Can you find the officer who reported Laurentz's death?"

I admitted I hadn't tried to do that yet.

"That would be first. See if he's on duty tomorrow. It's
Sunday, but cops don't care," Morgan said. His speech was
faster and more to the point in this conversation than it had
been in the five days he'd stayed in my house. Some men
love their work; others need it. Clearly Morgan was one of
the latter. "I'll see if I can drum up some information about
what a body looks like when it's been electrocuted, and
we'll talk after you get back tomorrow."

"Back?" I asked. "Back from where?"

Morgan looked at me with a combination of wonder and
pity. "From the Count Basie Theatre. You need to find out
from this Penny woman exactly how she explains her presence at Laurentz's house the night he died."

Twenty

Sunday

The box office at the Count Basie Theatre didn't open until noon on Sunday, so there were stops that Morgan suggested I make before I went to talk to Penny. First on the list was the *Chronicle* office, where Phyllis had texted to say she had some intelligence to convey. Even Phyllis texts these days.

"That must have been some musical," she chuckled. "Seven people got arrested, and two of them spent the night behind bars."

I almost spit out some of the Dunkin' Donuts coffee I'd bought for us both on the way over, to fend off her home-made brew. "A night in jail? Over a bunch of sixty-year-olds taking their clothes off for thirty seconds at the end of act one?" I'd done some research into *Hair* since I'd spoken to her last.

Phyllis nodded with a raised eyebrow while she sipped from her coffee. Black, of course. "I know it looks extreme, and it was, for the charges. Most of them paid a fine and left. But two"—she referred to notes written on the back of a W. B. Mason receipt—"a Frances Walters and a Jerome Rasmussen, were held overnight. I guess they were more naked than everybody else or something."

"Were the charges different for those two?" *The two New Old Thespians I already had questions about? Interesting coincidence. Or a disturbing one.*

Phyllis followed the chain of her notes from the office supply receipt to a brown paper bag with a grease stain on the bottom. "Nope. Lewdness, public indecency, disorderly conduct. No resisting arrest, nothing interesting out of context."

I chewed on the bagel I'd gotten with the coffee. Dunkin' Donuts does many things well, but bagels do not happen to fall into that category. This was a kaiser roll with a hole in the middle. "So why did those two have to stay in a cell overnight when the others didn't?" I wondered aloud.

"That's something to ask Officer . . . Robert P. Warrell," Phyllis answered, checking a second copy of an advertising invoice.

"Nothing to do with me. I don't sentence them," Officer Robert P. Warrell told me. "I arrest them and book them, and the judge decides who has to stay behind bars."

I'd driven directly to Monroe Township from Phyllis's office, and luckily, Warrell, who had been the arresting officer at the performance of *Hair*, was indeed on duty this Sunday morning. Even luckier, he wasn't out on patrol; he was finishing paperwork in the squad room and agreed to talk to me when I told the desk sergeant it was about the arrests at Cedar Crest a number of months ago. Clearly, that particular event has made an impression, since even now, mention of it provoked a decent amount of stifled laughter at police headquarters. But laughs or no, I figured it could be a motive in Lawrence Laurentz's death, so I was here as the private investigator asking Officer Warrell questions—or as the straight man (straight woman?) in a vaudeville act for which the officer was the unintentional comedian. It was all a question of perspective.

Officer Warrell, it turned out, was maybe twenty-five on a good day, very tall, very blond, and *very* serious about his work. He was the only cop in the room who didn't seem to find the—pardon the expression—bust funny.

"So they saw a judge?" I asked, doing my best to treat the matter with equal sobriety. "The people you arrested that night were arraigned right away?" I had the recorder on in my tote bag, but I was taking notes on a reporter's notebook, anyway, just to give the impression that I had an idea of what I was doing. The officer looked me straight in the eye without needing to consult an arrest report.

"It was a Thursday night. That's municipal court night. The judge was already here, so the arraignments were held immediately. None of the defendants had hired private counsel; most of them just wanted to go home, so they paid their fines and left."

"What alerted you to the . . . problem, anyway?" I asked. "You had to get there awfully quick to make arrests, no?"

Officer Warrell's gaze never wavered. "We had gotten advance warning that there might be an illegal element to the performance that evening," he said. "So I was positioned outside the clubhouse auditorium in case there was a problem."

"A problem," I echoed. At least Morgan Henderson had an excuse.

"The law is on the books," the officer said. "I'm paid to enforce it."

"Who gave the advance warning?" I asked. "Who ratted out the New Old Thespians for trying to be hippies?"

"The tip was anonymous," Warrell said. "I don't know who it might have been."

"Male or female?"

"I didn't take the call," he answered.

I was starting to think that it would take a graduate of dental school, some laughing gas and a pair of very strong pliers to get any information out of Officer Warrell, but I could hear Paul's voice in my conscience telling me not to give up. I backtracked a bit. "So you arrested seven people that night, and five of them paid their fines and left," I reminded him. "Two of them were detained overnight."

"Yes," he nodded. "Frances Walters and Jerome Rasmussen." Truly, his ability to recall the incident without so much as a Post-it note reminder was impressive.

"I don't understand. Why were some fined but others put in jail overnight?" I asked.

Officer Warrell did not blink. "As I said, Ms. Kerby, the arresting officer does not decide on the sentence. The judge decided they should be detained, and so they were."

"Were you in the courtroom when they were all arraigned?" I asked him. They say lawyers should never ask a question when they don't know the answer in advance. I would have made a lousy lawyer.

"Of course," the officer replied. "I was required in case I had to testify about the circumstances of the arrests."

"So did the judge say why he was keeping Ms. Walters and Mr. Rasmussen but not the others?"

For once, Officer Warrell hesitated before answering. But after a moment, he said, "Yes. He said there had been allegations made that there might be other charges pending against those two, and he did not want them to leave the county until that matter was resolved."

"Other charges?" What the hell did that mean? "What other charges?"

"The judge said an officer of the court had been advised those two might have had some connection with the distribution of a controlled substance."

There was a long moment that passed silently. "Drugs? Someone thought they were dealing drugs?" Retired septuagenarians Frances and Jerry as drug dealers? This thing just kept getting weirder.

"Prescription drugs. Specifically sildenafil."

That was a new one on me. "Sildenafil?" I repeated.

"Better known as Viagra."

"You're kidding," I blurted, before I remembered to whom I was talking.

"No, ma'am," Officer Warrell responded.

"And the tip about their dealing came from . . ."

"An anonymous source," he said.

"It's very simple," Penny Fields said. "I really don't understand what all the fuss is about."

I'd spent some time on the phone with Phyllis Coates trying to absorb what I'd just been told, but Phyllis was too busy laughing to be much help. Illegal Viagra? How much weirder was this case going to get? The only thing to do was push on, so I arrived just as the box office at the Count Basie Theatre opened at noon, figuring I'd have just enough time to talk to Penny and crack the case before I had to pick up Melissa at Janine's house at one. If I hit all the traffic lights.

That was the plan, anyway.

"You told me the last time I was here that you didn't know Lawrence Laurentz very well, that he wasn't too social and that he was condescending, but you were especially clear that you didn't know him very well," I reminded her. "Then I do the tiniest amount of digging and find out that *you* were the person who called EMS when *you* discovered his body, in his *bathtub*, at his *house*. If that's what you call not knowing someone, what's your definition of knowing someone well?"

(By the way, I had gotten Mom to ask Lawrence about that, and his comment—which I deciphered from one of

Mom's vowel-free texts—was, "How would I know who found my body?" A detective's dream client.)

Penny pivoted from her computer screen, which displayed a seating chart for an upcoming Micky Dolenz concert, and gave me her best intimidating glare. It was surprisingly effective for a woman about five inches shorter than I am. She had panache.

"And *you* told *me* you were here about some inheritance issue, that Larry had bequeathed someone here some money in his will," she pointed out. "Now you're here asking questions about how I found his body and that doesn't seem to have anything to do with an inheritance. What's *your* definition of the truth?"

She was good.

"I'm a private investigator and I'm looking for information about Lawrence Laurentz's death," I said. "That's all true. I'll show you the license again if you like. Now, please, what were you doing at his home the night he died?"

"It's embarrassing," she said. That I actually believed, based on the somewhat nauseated expression she was affecting. Had she thought she was the mysterious person who was mentioned in his (as far as I knew, nonexistent) will? (Come to think of it, I should ask Lawrence about his will.) Was that why she was so upset?

"It will be held in the strictest of confidence, assuming I'm not required to give information to the police," I assured her. I'd have to ask Paul when the law stated I might have to tell the cops something, but I did mean what I'd told Penny.

She turned back to the computer, ostensibly to check on the sales figures for the former Monkee, but I could see a little tightness around her mouth and she sniffed just a touch as she turned. "I was there to fire him," she said.

Well, that certainly wasn't what I'd expected. "You were firing him? Why?"

"He was causing problems with the part-time staff," Penny said, doing her best not to look at me. What was upsetting her so? Shame at having been about to fire a guy who died? Embarrassment over having seen him in the bathtub? Serious concern over Micky Dolenz's career? "He would . . . report other box office personnel to me for various infractions. People got nervous when he was around. He was creating a bad atmosphere in the office. I had to let him go."

All that was consistent with the mosaic I'd been building of Lawrence in my mind. "Any reason why that night in particular?" I asked.

"I didn't want to do it in front of the other employees," she answered. "And I felt I owed it to him to do it in person. That was the only night that month we were dark, with no show here, so that was the night I went."

"You had his address from employee records," I thought aloud.

Penny turned back toward me and nodded. "I went up and saw his car parked in the space marked for his unit," she said. "I rang the bell a few times, and he didn't answer. I tried calling his cell phone, but he didn't pick that up, either. I could see there were lights on in the house. So I went around to the back and walked up to the deck to see if he was in the kitchen. The French doors were open. I knocked on the glass, but again there was no answer. And I thought I heard water running."

"So you went in," I guessed.

"When I saw water dripping down from the kitchen ceiling. And knew that couldn't be good. So yeah, I went in. I probably should have called the police right away, but, you know, I was just thinking there was a faucet left on or something." Penny closed her eyes.

I really wanted to let her avoid the memory of what she found upstairs, but Paul would berate me later for not thinking like a detective and assuming that everything everyone tells you is a lie until you can prove it's not. So I fought the temptation to cut to the chase and instead said, "So you went inside and . . ." Sometimes you have to lead the witness into telling you the story.

She nodded, a little more violently than it seemed she'd intended. "I followed the sound of the water running. I called for Larry a couple of times, but of course there wasn't any answer." There would be no point in trying to confirm any of this with Lawrence later on; people don't become ghosts, at least not conscious, alert ghosts, immediately after they die. Paul has told me—and we've confirmed it a few other times—that it takes a few days before memory and cognition kick in. So Lawrence wouldn't know if Penny's story was true or not.

"What did you find?" I asked.

Penny shot me a look that indicated I was being cruel, and I felt like she was right. "You know perfectly well what I *found*," she said.

I couldn't apologize; for all I knew, this whole story was a lie and Penny had tossed the toaster in to French-fry Lawrence while he bathed. "Did you call the police immediately?" I asked instead.

"It was obvious he was . . . that I couldn't revive him myself," she exhaled. "I dialed nine-one-one on my cell phone. It felt like hours, but I'm sure they were there very quickly, really. I did do one thing while I was there, though."

My ears perked up. "What?" I asked.

"I turned off the water." Penny sniffed another time or two, and took a tissue from a box on her desk. She used it.

After a few moments of sniffling, I figured I'd exhausted the information I'd get from Penny about that night, so I figured I'd switch lines of question entirely: "How come Tyra Carter thinks you won't hire her back because of me?" I asked.

"I have no idea," Penny said. "Have you talked to Tyra?"

Does being threatened count? "Sort of," I said. "Do you want to hire her back?"

Penny looked like she hadn't considered the possibility

before. "I don't know," she said. "Tyra was moonlighting while she worked here."

I figured if I could help Tyra's employment picture, I could get her to stop calling me up and saying unsettling things. "I think she'd really like to come back," I suggested. "You might want to give it a thought."

"Maybe," Penny agreed. "I'll call her."

One less threatening figure to worry about, I thought.

On the way to pick up Melissa, I placed a call to Murray Feldner, who picked up on the first ring as if he'd been waiting by the phone. "Murray," was all he said. Clearly, a man of action.

"Murray, it's Alison Kerby." My Bluetooth made it sound like I was driving through a car wash in a convertible with the top down.

"Hi, Alison," Murray replied. "Do you need something? Is there gonna be snow tonight?"

"No. It's about the bill you sent me." The car in front of me was doing its best to break the record for slowest miles per hour in the passing lane. Pennsylvania plates. It figured.

"What about it? Did I add it up wrong?" Murray had not, if I recalled correctly, been an honors student in math. Or anything else, except maybe gym.

"Sort of," I told him. "You charged me for plowing my driveway and my walk."

This did not seem to make an impression on him. "Uh-huh."

Subtlety wasn't going to be a really powerful tool in this conversation. "It didn't snow Tuesday night, Murray. There was nothing to plow."

"What? What about a cow?" Clearly, the Bluetooth was working just as well on the other end. Terrific. And the slow car in front of me actually got slower.

"Not cow, Murray. *Plow*. There was nothing to *plow*."

"When?"

"Wednesday!" I considered passing on the right, which is not technically kosher, but there was a truck with Oklahoma plates there, big enough to be carrying all of New Jersey back home, and I was boxed in. I flashed my lights at the Pennsylvania car. It slowed down more.

"I came over to your house on Wednesday, Alison. Remember?" Great. Now Murray thought I was the one who hadn't been an honors student. Which, technically, I hadn't, but that wasn't the point. "Your daughter called me the night before. I have it right here in my book."

"I know you were there, Murray. But you didn't do anything; there was no snow. How can you charge me for plowing when there was no snow?"

Murray sounded honestly confused. "You wanted me to plow even though there was nothing on the ground?" he asked. "That would've damaged my plow, Alison."

"I know! I was the one who told you that!" I honked my horn, but I'm not sure what message I was sending at that point.

"Well, then, what did you want me to do?" Murray said.

"Exactly what you did," I answered. "You did everything right. Except then you sent me a bill for it, and that's the part I have a problem with." The Oklahoma truck had now passed me on the right, so I switched lanes to try to pass the Pennsylvanian.

And the second I moved, it picked up speed like a jackrabbit and disappeared ahead of me. Four more cars passed me on the left while I was stuck between Tom Joad and his load of whatever it is Oklahomans need imported.

"I'm in business, Alison. I always send a bill when I do work for somebody."

I wondered if this conversation was taking place in some alternate universe where what Murray said made sense and

I simply needed to adjust. "You *didn't* do any work for me, Murray. You came to my house, didn't do anything and left. How can you charge me two hundred dollars for that?"

Once there was finally room in the left lane, I switched back. And a guy in a blue Honda Civic immediately started tailgating me. Now I was the car going too slowly in the passing lane. This was the kind of week I was having. And it was only Sunday.

But at least I seemed to be making some headway with Murray. "Ooooooh," he said. "I see where you're going. Okay, I can fix that."

"Great. I knew I could count on you, Murray." I sped up to the New Jersey speed limit, and so did the Honda tailgating me. On my right, once again, the truck from where the wind comes sweeping down the plain.

"I'll cut it back to a hundred and fifty and send you a new bill," Murray said. "Thanks for calling, Alison." He hung up.

"Great. I . . . what?" But he was gone.

The only plus was that I was ready to pull off the highway. Of course, so was the truck from Oklahoma.

When I finally reached Janine's house, Melissa said good-bye to her friends as though they would be separated for years and not just until school began the next morning. Hugs were tight, tears were choked back and promises to call were made that, unlike similar ones in the adult world, would be kept.

Then she got into the car and switched conversational gears with the ease of an Indy 500 driver coasting down a suburban street. "What's new on the case?" she asked. "Have we found out anything about the ME's report?"

It was at that moment I decided I wanted my ten-year-old daughter—not my partner in detection—back. "Stop," I said. "Tell me about the party."

Melissa looked at me oddly but clearly decided to humor her mother, who was going senile before her very eyes. "Janine got an iPad for her birthday!" she began, and that was just scratching the surface. Apparently Kate, Janine's mother, was a closet heiress—the showering of gifts Melissa described would have set me back six months on my mortgage.

"That's some haul," I told her when she took a breath, no doubt anticipating her chance to describe more presents.

"Well, Janine's kind of sad," she answered. "Her grandpa died a few weeks ago."

"Oh, that's too bad," I said, thinking that expensive gifts probably weren't the best option when dealing with grief—but then again, they're fun to get. "Want me to go and see if he's hanging around her house?"

"I could do it myself if I knew where he was," Liss pointed out. "If he's a ghost now, that is." Not everyone who passes away goes through that stage, we'd discovered.

It had never occurred to me before. "Liss, how many of your friends know you can see ghosts?" Melissa's ability had become evident to some classmates right after we'd moved into the guesthouse, but Liss had some new friends now, and I didn't know how much of a reputation she'd developed. It could be a potential problem, if a bunch of fifth-graders started telling their parents how my daughter can communicate with the deceased. It's an icebreaker at PTA meetings, surely, but eventually the conversation would turn awkward.

"Just Wendy," Melissa said. "And she won't tell anybody. She likes it being a secret with me and her." Wendy was trustworthy, I knew, and her mother and father were easygoing. Not so easygoing that they'd understand talking to ghosts, probably, but it made me feel better, anyway.

"Janine said her grandpa knew Grampa," Liss added.

It was a major effort not to slam on the brakes. "What? He knew my father?" It was possible she was referring to The Swine's father, who was still alive and disapproving of me somewhere in Atlanta, I thought. We didn't hear from him much. Why get in touch with your own granddaughter, after all?

"Yeah," Liss answered casually. "She said he was Grampa's doctor. Does that make sense?"

"Possibly. He had lots of doctors, especially in the last few months," I thought out loud. "What kind of doctor was he?"

Melissa shrugged. "I don't know. A doctor." Kids think all doctors are the same and can treat anything. That's because even when they're ten, nobody stops them from watching *House*.

We were getting near the house. "What's Janine's last name?" I asked.

"Markowitz," she answered. "Did Grampa have a Dr. Markowitz?"

"I'm not sure, but I'll ask your grandmother," I told her. "I don't remember a Dr. Markowitz."

"How about Wells?" Liss said. "Her real name is Janine Wells-Markowitz, but she doesn't really use the part from her mom."

It took me a second to remember the name. Dr. Wells. My father's oncologist.

The one who was actually in his hospital room when he died.

Twenty-one

"You have a very specific problem," Tony Mandorisi said. "I don't think you realize how difficult this is."

Jeannie, Tony and Oliver had been waiting for us when Melissa and I arrived at the guesthouse. Jeannie claimed to have texted me that they were coming over, but my phone had helpfully delivered the text ten minutes after their arrival. Liss went upstairs to do homework she should have done before the sleepover.

While unpacking her child, Jeannie told me she had, as I'd asked, gotten in touch with the widow of Barney Lester, the New Old Thespian who had died a while before Lawrence. Mary Lester confirmed that Barney had died of heart failure (like Lawrence) after a long illness and two heart attacks. Unlike Lawrence, he did not die in a bathtub, and there didn't seem to be anything suspicious about it.

Tony knocked on the doorjamb of my library, lightly, with a hammer, not hard enough to make a mark, but enough to make a sound. The sound was solid, and did not indicate anything resembling space beyond the jamb.

"Hear that?" he said. Before I could answer, he added, "That means this side is a double stud. You can see that from the positioning of the electrical outlet here in the hall and the other one inside the library, too."

Jeannie was sitting in the den bouncing Oliver on her lap, within shouting distance but a little out of Tony's line of sight. I could see all three of them, as well as Maxie's lower half through the ceiling (she probably had the laptop resting on the floor in one of the upstairs bedrooms) and Paul, who was tapping his foot impatiently on the air, anxious to hear my investigative report and not Tony's evaluation of my library doorway. But since that was the price Tony had agreed to pay for my convincing Jeannie to help out in the Laurentz investigation, Paul had to endure it.

I sighed. "It's a load-bearing wall." The wall framing the library door was one that actually helped hold up the rest of the house. Which would restrict the amount of construction we could do (or more specifically, that Tony could do) on the doorway without incurring huge expenses compensating for the lack of support. It wasn't impossible to change—you could put a steel beam across the top of the wall from one end to the other—but that would cost thousands of dollars and be a huge construction project. I was not prepared to authorize that kind of work. "What about on the other side of the door?" I asked Tony.

He shook his head. "The other side is too close to the linen closet." He knocked on the wall with his knuckles this time, just for show. "We couldn't open it up more than an inch or two, and anyway, it wouldn't really do what you want it to, which is shed more light in that room and create the illusion of more space inside."

Paul rolled his eyes and spread his hands. "Can't this wait?" he asked me. "We have pressing business."

"Knock it off," I told him, quietly enough so Tony

couldn't hear. I tilted my head to the left toward the game room and muttered, "Meet me in my office." Paul followed me to the game room, where I filled him in on the interviews and what Melissa had told me about Janine's grandfather. He pursed his lips at that one.

"Why is this doctor significant?" he asked. "You've said before that your father had a team of physicians involved in his case."

It was a good question. There had been something bothering me since Liss had mentioned Dr. Wells, not long after Mom had said he'd passed away. But I couldn't put my finger on it. So I went on as if I'd had a workable theory. I'd have preferred to go on as if I'd had seventeen million dollars, but one does what one can.

"My mother mentioned him to me a couple of days ago, or I wouldn't have thought it was important, either," I admitted. "But think about it: He died at just about the exact moment my father went underground. That's an awfully big coincidence, don't you think?"

"Yes, but . . ."

"Haven't you told me never to trust really big coincidences?" I pressed on. "Don't you always say that there's got to be a reason behind them, that things aren't that random the great majority of the time?" My mind was sifting the possibilities: So Dr. Wells died. That was too bad, but it wasn't like we were friends. So Melissa's friend was his granddaughter. That was also a little sad, but again, not really close. What was nagging at me?

Paul sort of nodded the way guys do when you're proving a point they don't care for—shoulders up, mouth horizontal, eyebrow tilted. "Sure, but—"

"All this time we've been looking for something to investigate that would get me closer to my father, haven't we? What makes you think this isn't it?"

Paul waited a moment and watched my face. "Oh, is it my turn to get a word in edgewise?" he asked.

"A whole sentence, if you talk fast enough." I spread my hands to give him the floor, which he was not touching at all. It was a symbolic gesture.

"It's possible you're right. There could be some connection to Dr. Wells's death and your father's . . . disappearance. But I would caution you against getting your hopes up too high."

Well, of course he didn't want me to assume that Dr. Wells's death would lead me on an unobstructed path to Dad, but there was something in his voice that said there was more to it than that. "You think there is no connection?" I asked.

Paul shook his head. "You know how it works, Alison. I don't think one way or the other about things until I have some facts to apply to the question. What I'm saying is that you're focusing too much on the goal and not enough on the process. What's the motive? What about this doctor would force your father into hiding or seclusion or captivity? I asked this question about Lawrence Laurentz, and we still don't have an answer. I'll ask it about your father: What does he have to lose?"

It was an excellent question. And one for which I had no answer.

"But what about the message on the mirror? Maybe Dr. Wells knows something about the way my father really died. Maybe he's the one who left the messages." I wondered if there was any way Dr. Wells, living or dead, could know where I lived now; I hadn't seen him in five years, long before I'd bought 123 Seafront. By contrast, grasping at straws would have been decisive action.

"Let's take a step back," Paul said. "We don't know who left those messages or if they contain any truth at all. We both suspect it was a ghost, but Morgan could be correct in his assumption that it was someone wearing gloves."

"Someone who got in or out of the house, unseen, twice?" I countered. "Including into my locked bedroom and bathroom? No, I'm sure it was a ghost. The hard part will be explaining it to Morgan once we figure it out."

"We still have no proof," Paul insisted.

"What *about* Lawrence, then?" I asked as a way of avoiding the fact that he had a point. "Do you believe Penny's story about the way she discovered his body?"

Paul frowned. "Again, we have no facts other than the witness's own statement, which is suspect. I'm more interested in what the officer told you this morning. Officer Warrell told you that Frances and Jerry were suspected of distributing illegal Viagra, and that was why they were held overnight. But so far there has been no indication there were any charges filed against them other than the ones for public lewdness that all the New Old Thespians faced."

I giggled. "Lewdness," I repeated. It was the word more than the thought.

He looked at me disapprovingly, and I did my best to straighten my face into a serious expression. "When Morgan and Nan return, you might want to see if he can trace any further investigation of those charges or determine why they were not pursued."

On cue, there was the sound of the front door opening and people trundling into the guesthouse. Even back here, the rush of cold wind could be felt until the door was closed again.

But it wasn't Nan and Morgan at the door. From the den I heard Jeannie call, "Hi, Mrs. Kerby," and Melissa swooped in from somewhere to yell, "Grandma!"

I'd asked my mother to come watch Melissa tonight while I went out with Josh Kaplan. Whom she'd been thrilled to hear I was going out with, despite the fact that she'd never actually been to Madison Paint and didn't remember his name. The only problem was Mom had arrived four hours early.

Paul and I walked (well, I walked and Paul did whatever it is he does) into the den. Mom was removing a scarf with the Midas Muffler logo on it (mufflers, get it?) and a pair of gloves with the fingers cut off, like she was going to try to crack a safe.

The second she saw me, she said, "You've got to do something about this thing with Larry, Alison! That man is driving me crazy! I could kill him!"

"Who's Larry?" Jeannie asked while she changed Oliver into a new onesie. The woman never just let that baby be.

"The client," I jumped in.

"Funny. She has the same name as her brother, the victim." Honestly, I could ask Paul to float over and cut Jeannie's hair off—he'd never do it, but still—and she wouldn't allow that a ghost might be in the room.

"You don't miss a trick, Jeannie," Mom said. Jeannie was seated with her back to Mom, who exchanged an amused look with me, then chucked the baby under the chin and cooed at him a bit. Melissa, used to being the apple of her grandmother's eye, narrowed her own in a rare display of jealousy. It reminded me never to give her a sibling. "She called me because I'd told her my daughter is a detective."

"Oh. Sure." Jeannie had just wanted to hear Mom say I was a detective again. She loves that. And she loves watching other people be enthralled with her son.

But Melissa was not to be denied. "Come on up to my room, Grandma," she suggested. "I have a book I want you to see."

Mom hesitated. A trip to Melissa's attic lair meant either a creaky flight of pull-down stairs or a ride in the dumbwaiter Tony built to get there, which Mom will do but not happily because it makes her tired. "Why don't you get it and bring it back down here?" she suggested. "That's a lot of stairs for me today, honey."

Melissa glanced almost imperceptibly at the baby, her competition, and sighed just a touch. "Okay," she said, and headed for the stairs.

"What book does she want to show me?" my mother asked when she was gone.

"I'm sure she'll think of something," I said. "Just don't read it to Oliver, whatever you do."

Mom laughed. "Little green-eyed monster. She's so smart!" My mother could watch Melissa drop a priceless vase off a second-story landing and would comment on her granddaughter's good taste; that thing was so ugly. "Now, fill me in on the investigation." I told her all I knew, and she listened carefully throughout. "I think one of our main problems is that your pal Larry isn't telling us everything. There's something being held back, maybe a lot, and that's slowing us down," I finished.

Jeannie didn't look up. "If your client isn't telling you what you need to know, the only thing you have left to do is threaten to pull out of the case," she said.

"I've done that. She has . . . something I want, and if I stop investigating, I won't get it."

Jeannie picked Oliver up and tickled his belly, then started putting things back into her diaper bag. "If you need the money that badly, Alison, Tony and I can help you out for a little while."

How to explain this? "It's not money, Jean," I said. "It's more in the area of information."

Tony rescued me by walking in from the hallway. "So what do we do?" I asked.

He shrugged. "I'm stuck."

Just then Melissa came downstairs carrying a book called *Riley Mack and the Other Known Troublemakers.* I'm sure she'd taken it down off her bed stand because it was the one she was currently reading.

At the same moment, Nan and Morgan Henderson walked in the front door, bringing the inevitable frigid breeze with them. They were practically giddy; Morgan helped Nan off with her coat and hung it carefully on the antique coatrack

I have by the front door. It was without question the most affectionate I'd seen him act toward her.

He gave Nan a tiny peck on the cheek at something she'd said and they wandered into the den, where every eye (except Jeannie's, since Oliver still held all her attention) fixed on them. "Oh, hello!" Morgan baritoned into the room. "Nice to see everyone." Now that he was wearing effective hearing aids and able to converse normally, he was the very soul of conviviality.

Introductions to Mom, Tony and Jeannie (and Oliver) were made. Paul and Maxie both looked on, amused in characteristic ways: Paul had a wry expression on his face, and Maxie seemed like she'd just had her first beer and still thought burps were funny.

"Visit another famous New Jersey crime scene today?" I asked Morgan. You always have to show enthusiasm for the guest's interests, no matter how odd. I knew Paul loved the mental challenge of crime investigation, but Morgan seemed to revel more in being able to pass through the crime scene tape and take in the atmosphere without anyone stopping him.

"Actually, yes," he answered with a twinkle in his eye.

Clearly, he wanted someone to ask, so it was lucky that Mom filled the void. "Which one?" she said.

It was all Morgan could do to avoid breaking out in a grin that would undoubtedly meet at the back of his head.

"The place where Lawrence Laurentz died," he said. "And I think it's reasonably certain he didn't die from an electric shock in the bathtub."

Twenty-two

As you might expect, the reaction to Morgan's extraordinary statement was twofold: First, the idea that he and Nan had gone to Lawrence's town house was a little disconcerting and then the statement that our victim had in fact not been killed by a toaster thrown at him by an invisible assailant—outrageous though it was, that had been the working theory until now—was indeed a game changer. So at least three of us were barking questions, including Melissa and Paul, though the latter's contribution was not heard by the person at whom it was directed.

Jeannie was showing Oliver his own reflection in a plastic mirror shaped like a daisy.

"Easy, easy," Morgan said with a chuckle. The din from Melissa (and, I realized, me) died down. Tony stood in the doorway with a look on his face that indicated he'd reach for a ball-peen hammer if Morgan turned out to be dangerous. Tony is a good man but sometimes a tad overprotective of Melissa and me.

Once I could reclaim the floor, I asked, "How did you get into Lawrence Laurentz's town house?"

It was Nan, who had actually heard the question first, who answered with a grin. "It was so easy. There's still a 'For Sale' sign in front of the place. We just called the real estate agent and told her we might be interested in an active adult community in the area and had been driving by. She was there in fifteen minutes with a key."

"Nobody else had moved in yet?" Melissa asked. "It's been a long time since Mr. Laurentz died, hasn't it?"

"Actually, in today's real estate market, it's not unusual for something to be unsold for that long," Mom said. "And since Larry didn't have any family to come clean the place out, I guess it took some time to sort out all the details."

"But I want to know," I said, turning to Nan, who was clearly going to be the go-between for Morgan, "what makes Morgan so sure Lawrence didn't die the way he . . . the way our client suggested."

"I'll get to that," Morgan answered when Nan had relayed the message. "But first, let me tell you that the place is being offered furnished unless the new owner wants the stuff removed. I guess Laurentz's estate isn't interested in the town house or the furniture too much. Do you know who would benefit from the sale?"

"As far as I know," Mom said, "there isn't much money in his estate, and no relatives. I believe Larry willed everything after his burial expenses to the Count Basie Theatre. Even then, it won't be much after the mortgage is paid off and the real estate agents make their money." (She had no doubt gotten much of that information from the source himself; he was rarely anywhere but in her house now.)

"You're probably right," Morgan said. "Regardless, everything was still in place today, even though it had been cleaned up. Nan kept the agent busy while I checked out the scene of the crime in the bathroom. And that's how I found out he couldn't have died from electrocution in that bathtub. At least not the way you said, with a toaster thrown in."

"Why not?" I asked, although I saw Tony nodding as if he'd figured out the answer ahead of time.

Morgan raised his index finger like a professor who has been asked an especially precocious question. "Ah!" he said. "Because Laurentz's bathroom had GFCI outlets. The building is fairly new, and today's construction code mandates that all electrical outlets in bathrooms and kitchens—anywhere potentially near water—must only have outlets with GFCI, ground fault circuit interrupters. If water gets anywhere near electricity in those rooms, the built-in circuit breakers automatically prevent electrocution."

I should have realized that. I'd installed GFCI outlets myself, when I'd redone the bathrooms and kitchen. I reserved time later, when I was alone, for kicking myself.

"Also," Morgan said, "I checked with a medical examiner I know. He said the type of electrocution you're describing might leave burn marks, but it might not, either. A heart problem definitely wouldn't."

"That's really weird," I said, looking at Mom, who appeared to be equally confused. "Does this mean that Lawrence really did die of natural causes?"

Morgan thought about that as Paul stroked his goatee. "I wouldn't say it's definite," he said. "From what you told me, a lot of people didn't like this guy. If there's a question, you still have to proceed on the assumption that one of them didn't like him enough to kill him. Just because we don't know how doesn't mean it didn't happen. Maybe he was electrocuted somewhere else and the body was then moved to the tub."

That theory didn't fit with what Lawrence had told us, but then the ghost had told us a lot of things that turned out to be, let's say, questionable.

"Excuse me," Tony said. "Just because there were GFCIs

in the bathroom doesn't mean he wasn't electrocuted there."

At first the ex–police chief seemed taken aback that a building contractor was suggesting he was wrong, but it became clear that he just hadn't heard what Tony said. After Nan conferred Tony's statement, Morgan looked at him and put his fingertips to his lips in a sort of pyramid shape. "How?" he asked simply.

"It's the simplest thing possible," Tony said. "An extension cord. All the killer had to do was plug in the toaster or whatever through a wall outlet, maybe in the hallway, where there would be no GFCI, then attach it to an extension long enough to reach the bathtub. The charge wouldn't last quite as long, but if the guy had previous heart problems, it might be enough."

Morgan thought about that and nodded, then pointed at Tony. "Very good, young man," he said. Then he turned to me. "I think we have a lot of questions to answer."

"I wish I could at least get some of the suspects all in the same room," I said, sort of to myself. "All this driving around in a Volvo with an iffy heater is wearing me down."

"You can," Maxie said. I looked up at her, and I'm sure Nan and Morgan were wondering why I was staring at a spot just under one of the exposed beams near the ceiling. "At least some of the people you want to talk to will all be in a room together tomorrow night. I saw online that the New Old Thespians are giving a performance in Ocean Grove."

That was right. Jerry and Frances had both mentioned it. "So I'm going to the New Old Thespians performance tomorrow night in Ocean Grove," I said. I got a few odd looks, but no one said anything about my behavior. Just as well. "Maybe I'll be able to answer some of those questions." I looked at the clock. "But I'm not answering them now," I told the gathered assembly. "I have a date."

"Finally," Mom said. "Priorities."

*   *   *

"I can't believe you don't remember Color Quiz," Josh Kaplan said.

We had agreed that we needed to be able to talk at our dinner, but we didn't want it to be terribly expensive or fancy—that ups the tension for such a "dinner"—so we'd decided on Louie Ziana's, a Cajun restaurant in Avon-by-the-Sea, the most hyphenated town in the Garden State.

There was the usual Zydeco music playing, but not terribly loudly, and since I have an absolute aversion to seafood, I'd checked the menu online ahead of time to ensure there would be cuisine I could enjoy. No sense sweating over entrée choices when there was an attractive guy across the table. He was dressed a little less casually than at the paint store. That is, the clothes he had on were free of splats, bits of Spackle, and dust. Which was a nice improvement.

"What the heck is Color Quiz?" I asked.

He looked up at the ceiling and harrumphed, but smiling. "When we were kids and your dad and my grandfather used to spend all their time in the back of the store, you and I would go up front where the color cards were and we'd play a game we called Color Quiz. You don't remember? We'd pull out a color card and pretend each row was a different category. Then . . ."

It was rushing back into my head. "You'd ask me some crazy question that had nothing to do with paint at all!" I said. I started laughing. "You'd ask me about school or TV or something."

"That's right." Josh seemed either relieved, amused or both at my recollection. "And when you got a question right, I picked a color and you asked *me* a question. But yours were always about baseball or carpentry or something."

"I was sort of a tomboy," I said.

He looked into my eyes a little bit more deeply than was entirely comfortable. "Not now," he said. "I'm glad to see it."

"Don't kid yourself," I answered. "I still spend a lot of days with cordless drills and ball-peen hammers." Honesty. The best policy. Assuming you want guys to think of you wearing overalls and spitting a lot.

"A holdover from your misspent youth," Josh commented.

"Depends on how you look at it. My dad taught me a lot of things that have proven to be very helpful now that I'm legally an adult."

The waiter came to take our order (Josh got the blackened catfish, which put a serious crimp in his chances of getting kissed later, and I ordered the basil chicken). When the waiter retreated to the kitchen, Josh looked at me with a less playful expression. "Your dad," he said.

Oh, yeah. The pretense for this evening was that I wanted to hear stories about Dad. Not that I minded Josh telling me what he remembered about my father, but it wasn't necessarily the story line I was aiming at anymore.

"My dad," I parroted back. It sounded soulful without actually offering any information. "I have to tell you—I was lying about the memoir."

Josh looked surprised but amused. "Really," he said. "You were really just in the store for a gallon of semigloss?"

I could feel myself blush. I'm not proud of it. "No. I want to talk about my dad, but it's connected to a case I'm working on."

Surprised seemed to overtake amused, but just for a quick moment. "A case?" Josh said.

Other men—most of them my ex-husband—have reacted strangely to the news I was going to impart. "Besides running the guesthouse, I also have a private-investigator's license," I told him. Then I waited.

Josh broke into a broad smile. "Really? A private investigator? That's amazing!"

"It is?" Okay, he caught me by surprise.

"Yeah. Don't you think so?" He didn't wait for an answer. "So tell me, how can I help with your . . . case?"

"It's just"—I thought about how best to phrase this—"I have some suspicions about the way my father died. And knowing more about him from the people who knew him well can help me zone in."

Josh looked concerned. "You think there was something weird about the way your father died?"

"Well, I don't know. Not really. I'm not suggesting a crime was committed." I couldn't suggest that a grumpy ghost in Josh's store had made me suspicious or that my dad was now a ghost who was missing. When I thought about the grumpy ghost, something clenched in my stomach. I shook my head a bit to banish the thought and refocused.That kind of thing would have to at least wait until the second date. "I'm just sort of . . . practicing. I want to fill in some gaps, and I thought your grandfather—and you—could help."

Josh leaned back in his chair a little bit, never taking his eyes off me, though he managed to maintain eye contact without making it seem creepy. "It's just as well, since most of the things I remember are about you, not your dad," he said finally. "Mostly Color Quiz. But there were plenty of times in later years, when I was going to Rutgers and helping out in the store on weekends, that your dad would come in and we'd talk."

It wasn't going to help me find Dad or discover what had happened to Lawrence Laurentz, but I did want to hear the details. "What did you talk about?"

Josh grinned a little guiltily. "Mostly about you."

"Me! That couldn't have taken very long." The waiter came by with a pitcher of water and two bottles of beer. I grabbed mine and took a cold swig.

"You'd be surprised." Josh actually poured his beer into a glass—something I've always thought just made it warm when you drank it—but didn't drink any. "He could go on and on about you, how you were in college, what you were studying, how you were fixing up your dorm room until it was in better condition than when you moved in." He looked amused.

"I can't help it if the place needed spackling and painting," I mumbled.

"I thought that was great. Then once I was out of college and in the store part-time while I was getting the MBA, I heard all about you. When you dropped out of college, he was not happy."

I knew about that. Dad wasn't one to keep his feelings, good or bad, to himself. "He must have been just tickled to death when I got married," I said sarcastically. My dad had seen The Swine's true colors long before I had.

Josh, in the act of taking a sip of beer, almost lost it through his nose when he snorted a laugh. I chuckled as he mopped himself up. "That's your fault," he said. "I think the happiest I ever saw your father was the day he told me you were getting divorced."

I put a lot of attention into not rolling my eyes. "I'll bet. But not happier than when my daughter was born, I'll bet."

Josh shook his head. "No. Not happier than then. He was crazy about his granddaughter."

"And she was crazy about him." Liss was five when Dad died, and just old enough to understand what it meant. I remembered how, when I broke the news to her that morning, she looked angry and said, "I don't like this at all." That's all she said that whole day.

Out of nowhere, Josh got a funny look in his eye and said, "You know, there are days—and I wouldn't say this to anyone else—when I'm in the back of the store, and I'd swear I still could hear your father kibitzing with my grandfather and the other regulars by the coffeemaker."

That's just what I was hoping, I thought. My expression must have given something away, because Josh suddenly looked at me with concern. "Really?" I covered out loud. "You thought you heard him?"

"No, not really," he answered. "It's an expression, Alison. I mean, sometimes it just feels like he should be there, you know?"

Apparently it doesn't take long to blacken a catfish, because the server soon appeared by our tableside with the entrées, and conversation was once again interrupted while we ogled our dinners and tucked in just a bit—I'd realized I had barely eaten all day, and the chicken was wonderful.

When Josh and I came up for air, I had decided the best thing to do was downplay my previous lapse of control when he'd mentioned my father's presence—or perceived presence—in the paint store. Didn't want to alarm Josh, especially if he later had the good sense to eat a mint or four following that catfish.

"I sort of feel like Dad's around sometimes myself," I began, not getting into my desire to see him more often. "It's sort of a comfort mechanism, I guess."

"He was *so alive* when he was alive," Josh said. "I loved talking to him. But mostly, he loved talking about you, and I was happy to listen."

We gazed rather stupidly at each other for a few seconds. "You're not wealthy, are you?" I asked finally. "Because then you'd be too perfect, and that would ruin everything."

Josh smiled with the left side of his mouth. It approached adorable. I might have to push a couple of mints on him of my own volition. "I half own a paint store, Alison," he said. "The word 'wealthy' isn't even in my vocabulary. But I would like to see this guesthouse of yours. Sounds like you've made quite an investment there."

"Tell you what," I said. "What time do you close the store tomorrow?"

"Mondays we close at five."

"Perfect," I said. "I'll give you my address. Come pick me up at six thirty."

He looked quite pleased. "Where are we going?" he asked.

"To watch a bunch of senior citizens perform *Peter Pan*," I said.

Twenty-three

Josh and I parted in the parking lot at Louie Ziana's. We'd driven here separately, which I was starting to regret now that we were standing in a well-lit parking lot next to a county highway. Not exactly a secluded spot.

"I'm glad we did this," he said when we got to my car (the parking lot equivalent of dropping me off at my front door). "We were out of touch for too long."

I sort of wished he'd stopped at "I'm glad we did this," frankly, because now I wasn't sure if this was a date or a reunion of old friends. "I'm glad we did, too," I replied. I didn't add anything after that because I was afraid it would be as much a mood breaker as what Josh had tried.

"Tomorrow at *Peter Pan*, then," he said. He looked away, and it took me a moment to realize he was actually awkward. Which made him seem that much more engaging.

I decided to act rather than react and moved closer to him, opening my arms. He seemed to understand and spread his arms as well. We sort of walked into an embrace, which was nice.

But it was also somehow confusing. This was the kind of thing two old friends might do at the end of an evening. How could I define this, if only in my own mind?

We held the hug for a very enjoyably long moment. When I felt that he was going to let go first, I decided this was the time to establish what *I'd* thought we'd been doing. I'd been careful to hand him some mints the restaurant had in a cup on the way out, and he'd been smart enough to use them. So I closed my eyes and reached up just a bit to kiss him.

And ended up kissing him on the nose. Probably should have rethought that "closing my eyes" strategy.

Josh looked startled, then amused. Quietly, he said, "Want to try that again?" He didn't wait for an answer as he leaned over and kissed me.

Now, I'm not going to say that trumpets went off in my head or that I felt a tingle up my spine or any of the other clichés you might be accustomed to. Suffice it to say it was a very satisfactory (and nonfishy) kiss.

Until the moment that I heard a familiar voice behind me.

"Whoa!" Maxie said. "Must have been a good dinner!"

Josh probably thought I was insane. That's what any man would think of someone who broke up a very satisfactory kiss, blew out air like a drowning swimmer, whirled around to look at *nothing* and then, remembering what she must have looked like, turned back toward him, smiling an anemic smile and obviously trying to think of something to say.

"Are you all right?" he asked with real concern. "Did I overstep . . ."

"No!" I exhaled. "That was *so* not your fault!" I fought the urge to glare at Maxie, whom I'd spotted sitting on the roof of my Volvo. She was laughing hysterically, and now floated to a spot over Josh's shoulder where she could make eye contact with me. I had to fight the urge to glare at her even more. "I thought I heard something over my shoulder. I'm *so* sorry."

Josh proved he had great potential by looking, once again, less like someone about to call for security assistance and more like someone who was witnessing a very entertaining spectacle. "Don't worry about it. Maybe we'll give it another try after *Peter Pan* tomorrow night. How's that?"

I looked around the parking lot. "You mean you don't think this is a properly romantic spot?" I asked.

"It lacks a certain . . . ambience. And it's twelve degrees outside. Tomorrow." He touched me on the cheek and then turned as I unlocked the car door. Maybe if I pulled away fast enough I could leave Maxie stranded here. It'd probably take her a few days to walk back to Harbor Haven. Or if I were really lucky, she'd get lost.

Alas, she appeared in the seat next to me as I put the car into gear. "That was great!" she crowed. "Definitely worth sitting out here all evening."

"I'm surprised you showed that much restraint," I told her.

"I had work to do, but I didn't want to stay at the house," she said, producing my ancient laptop from her coat. "Luckily the restaurant's Wi-Fi extends to the parking lot." Maxie stretched her legs, which dropped her feet out of sight under the floorboards and gave the odd impression she was making the car move with her feet, like Fred Flintstone.

"What'd you find out?"

"I hacked into the files of your pal Lawrence's lawyer," she said. "Your mom gave me his name. Turns out the old guy really didn't have much to inherit. Nobody killed him for money."

"You could have done that at home. Did you just sit out here all night waiting to humiliate me?"

Maxie grinned. "That was just a perk."

"You are so lucky you're dead," I told her. "Because if you weren't, I'd kill you."

You've heard the expression "She laughed all the way home"? I'm here to tell you, it's not just an expression.

I did not utter another word to Maxie in the car, which didn't seem to bother her in the least. Even when I parked the car under the port behind the house, I got out without looking to see if she followed me. This whole new development about Maxie being mobile outside the property where she died was really getting to be a drag.

On the other hand, the thought of *Paul* being able to follow me on a date was somehow even less appealing.

It must have been at least eleven p.m. by the time I walked in through the kitchen. The lights were on and voices were audible in the den, so I headed that way. I swung the kitchen door open, and I could see Mom on the sofa and Liss on the floor. They weren't playing a board game or anything, just talking. That was unusual.

"I don't understand what it means," Melissa said.

"Neither do I," Mom answered. "Do you think we should—" She stopped when she saw me walk in. "Alison! How was dinner?"

But Melissa looked like she wanted to talk about something else. "Mom . . ." she began. She looked . . . scared would be too strong a word. More like unsettled.

"Fine, Mom." I turned toward Melissa. "What's the matter, baby?" I asked.

Melissa caught a glimpse of her grandmother, who gave her an expression that wasn't exactly disapproving—such a thing would be unthinkable—but slightly impatient. "We weren't going to say anything to you right away," Mom said a touch pointedly. "We wanted you to enjoy your evening."

A few hairs stood up on the back of my neck. "You weren't going to say anything about *what*?"

Mom stood up and Melissa followed her lead. "Come on," my mother said. "We'll show you."

I didn't like the way that sounded, but I followed them out of the den and into the hallway. Mom hit the light switch and turned in the direction of the library and the game room.

She waited. So did Melissa. For that matter, so did I.

"Okay," I said finally. "What am I looking at?"

"You don't see it?" Melissa asked.

"See what?"

"There!" she said.

To avoid shouting, "Where?" I scoured every inch of the hallway and finally saw a small mark on the crown molding near the ceiling by the library. It was red and looked like letters.

"What does it say?" I said. Moving closer, the letters were larger than I'd first thought, and the molding angled toward the floor, so they were easier to read when standing directly beneath them.

The message read, "STOP GO UP."

"What the hell does that mean?" I said.

"Hey," my mother scolded, shooting her glance toward Melissa.

"I've heard a lot worse, Grandma," my daughter said. Thanks for the help, Liss.

I took a step back when Paul's head stuck itself through the ceiling directly over the message. You never really get used to that.

"I've been trying to decipher it," he said, "but it's not as direct as the other messages."

"Other messages?" Mom asked. Oops.

"Um . . . yeah," I said. "There have been a couple others. But they weren't like this."

"There were?" Melissa said. Double oops.

"Over the past couple of days," I explained, giving Paul a dirty look. "But like Paul said, this one is different. I don't understand it." To avoid giving out any more details about the previous messages, since they'd only alarm Mom and Liss, I quickly said to Paul, "What do you suppose it means?"

He shrugged. "No idea. Did Maxie come back with you? I want her to run a search on the phrase 'stop go up,' and see what she gets."

"Yeah, Maxie came back," I said sourly. "Things were a lot easier when she couldn't get around so far, you know."

"Maybe for *you*." Maxie was right behind me, of course. "I'm thrilled to be out from these same four walls."

Paul ignored her remark, since she probably didn't realize how hurtful it was to him. "Can you run that search? I'm at a loss. I don't know what 'go up' might refer to. We looked all through the upper floors, the attic and the roof, and found nothing unusual."

Maxie seemed to fight the urge to say something mean, then shrugged one shoulder and disappeared into the ceiling. She'd be at work on the laptop in Melissa's room in no time. "Don't get too comfy," I called after her. "Melissa has to go to sleep soon." There was no answer from above. There so rarely is.

Melissa, having heard that part about going to sleep, made a show of thinking in order to delay the inevitable. "Maybe this is a theatrical ghost," she suggested. "When we did the school play last year, Mr. Lester said that 'go up' was something actors said happened when they forgot their lines."

That made an odd kind of sense, but it still didn't decode the message. "It's possible, sweetie," I told Melissa. "Do you understand what it means, then?"

She thought it over and shook her head. "But it doesn't make sense any other way, either."

She had me there. "I'm not going to worry about it any more tonight," I said. "I have a lot to do tomorrow and you, young lady, should have been in bed a half hour ago. Move it."

Melissa looked at me. "But I had to show you the words on the ceiling," she protested.

"I get it. You did. Say good night to your grandmother and get up there."

Mom had already packed up her backpack and gave Melissa a very enthusiastic hug. I kissed Melissa on the head, knowing I'd be upstairs before she was in bed, and gently nudged her toward the stairs. Children, who medical science insists need more sleep than adults, avoid going to bed with every fiber in their bodies. Adults would fall onto a mattress at three in the afternoon and sleep until Thursday. Nature is funny.

Once Liss was up the stairs, Mom gave me a meaningful glance. "Other messages?" she asked.

"Nothing to worry about," I lied. "Thanks for watching Liss. Drive home safely."

She clucked her tongue. "Of course I'll drive home safely. But that 'nothing to worry about' isn't fooling anyone." She left.

I looked up at Paul, who was at eye level with the words over the library door. "What do you think?" I asked.

"It's a little worrisome," he acknowledged. "What bothers me is that this doesn't look like it was written by the same person as the other two."

I let that sink in for a moment. Were there *two* ghosts sending me strange and unsettling messages instead of just showing up to speak their piece? "What do you mean?"

"The handwriting's different. The style is different. This is less neat but still carefully written to be legible."

"I can barely read it from here, anyway," I said.

That comment had the opposite effect of the one I was trying to induce. Where I'd been attempting to close down this line of inquiry, instead Paul swooped down, wrapped his arms around my waist, and lifted me up into the air to get closer to the ceiling, so I could get a better look. I managed to overcome the urge to yell, "Whoa!" when I realized what he was doing.

"You've come a long way," I told him instead. I remembered a time when Paul had trouble picking a quarter up off a radiator in the den.

He didn't respond. Even though the ghosts' strength seems . . . stronger than that of a living person, it was probably still an effort to lift a whole human, and he had to concentrate. "Look at the message," he said, making his best effort not to sound like he was straining. I gave some thought to cutting back on carbs and hitting the treadmill. As soon as I bought a treadmill.

Given a complete lack of options, I looked at the message close up. The words were still the same: "STOP GO UP." But I realized almost immediately what had been making me uneasy about getting this near the ceiling to read this. "Put me down," I said to Paul.

He returned me to the floor, which was a relief for both of us, I think. I made a point of not looking back up again. And he must have noticed that.

"I should have asked first before picking you up," Paul said. "Did I startle you?"

I shook my head. "It's not that. It's just that I had a strange feeling about this message, one that I didn't have with the other two. And I wasn't sure I wanted to see it that close."

"I'm sorry. I shouldn't have been so abrupt."

"No. It's good that you were. Otherwise, I wouldn't have seen what I saw up there."

"Cobwebs?" Paul joked, trying to lighten the mood. It didn't work.

I looked him straight in the eye, which must have meant that he was about ankle-deep in floor, because he's a few inches taller than me. "I recognized the handwriting on this one, Paul. You were right. The style was different."

Given a clue, Paul is as happy as a beagle given a chew toy. "You recognized it? Whose handwriting is it, Alison?"

"My father's," I said.

Twenty-four

Monday

Nan and Morgan Henderson were up early the next morning, so my usual six o'clock alarm was just barely in time for me to get myself presentable and start a pot of coffee before they came into the den. Morgan was still bordering on bubbly over the investigation, which he called "the Laurentz case," and Nan seemed very happy to have her husband in such a vital mood. I invited them into the kitchen, and they sat at the center island and drank coffee. I still had most of the breakfast feast I would have cooked had there been a blizzard last Tuesday, so I offered to cook them bacon and scrambled eggs. Yes, I *can* cook when I absolutely have to.

I did not mention the scrawl on the crown molding in the hallway. Explaining that it had been written by a ghost, and that it was, in my opinion, Dad's handwriting, would have simply been too bizarre and it wouldn't have advanced Morgan's ability to analyze the situation any better.

"What's on your agenda for today?" I asked. "More crime scenes?"

Morgan shook his head. "I think for our last full day here, we should concentrate on the Laurentz case," he said. "Check in with Chief Daniels of the Monroe PD. Maybe he can tell me something he wouldn't tell you. Daniels and I were in the academy together," Morgan said smiling.

"I hate to take up your vacation doing my work," I protested, but secretly, I was thrilled to have Morgan helping out.

Nan waved a hand at me. "Don't give it a thought," she said. "He hasn't been this happy since he retired."

"All right, then," I agreed. I wasn't about to try and dissuade them. "What do you think I should be doing?" I saw Paul slide in from the hallway through the stove. He was wearing a serious expression, though that wasn't the least bit unusual for Paul.

"You're going to the show with all Laurentz's buddies tonight?" Morgan asked. I nodded. "Okay. Would you get us tickets, too? And during the day, if you have the time, you need to try to trace the person who left you those two messages, the one on your mirror and the one on your dresser."

"I think I might have a lead on that," I told Morgan, although "lead" might have been overstating it by a factor of about 185. "What time will you be back? I'm thinking for your last evening here, maybe I'll actually make you dinner. It's the least I can do." Considering how poorly I cook, the very least.

"If the play begins at seven thirty, I think we should be back here at five the latest," Nan said. "Morgan can make his inquiries well before then. And then maybe *I* can get some shopping done." Morgan didn't react, not even by repeating "shopping done." He really was a changed man.

"Great. Let's plan on dinner at six," I said, thinking I'd ask Josh to come earlier so he could have dinner with us, too.

That would fit in nicely with the plan I was making for the day.

I heard Melissa starting to stir upstairs, getting ready for another inconvenient day of school. Then I suddenly remembered I'd been in the process of frying bacon and scrambling eggs. I looked at the stove.

"You guys like English muffins?" I asked.

The New Old Thespians performance of *Peter Pan* (who puts on *Peter Pan* for an audience of people over fifty-five?) this coming evening was already starting to be a hot ticket, if only because I was bringing just about everyone I knew. Besides Mom and Melissa, Jeannie was coming along as part of her new role as "operative" in the PI agency, Tony had insisted on coming as "protection," Oliver was coming in his continuing role as a baby, Morgan and Nan Henderson would attend to see if the retired cop could catch any clues I couldn't (which was a decent bet) and, oh, yeah, I was bringing Josh Kaplan as a date.

It was a good thing Jeannie and Tony had a minivan.

In preparation, I'd alerted Mom by text that I'd be dropping by her house this morning, and she had sent back an incomprehensible jumble of consonants that indicated after some deciphering that she'd try to contact Lawrence before I got there. I had some questions for my client, who until now had been anything but completely forthcoming with me.

Melissa was slightly more grumbly this morning than usual, but it *was* a Monday in January, the Christmas break rush had completely worn off, and the sky was the kind of steel gray we get here from roughly the end of November until sometime around the first of May.

This message has been brought to you by the New Jersey Tourism Board. You're welcome.

We didn't talk a lot in the car, but of course once

dropped off, Melissa rushed into a gaggle of her friends and there was much celebration. Parents are the people you don't have to notice. I tried to keep that in mind on the way to my mother's house, but I was really thinking about Josh Kaplan.

Lawrence had not yet materialized—literally—when I arrived, so Mom went about making coffee, and what do you know, she had some blueberry muffins available. Freshly baked. I'm hoping the cooking gene skipped a generation and will eventually manifest in Melissa. I sat down with a warm muffin and hot coffee and told Mom that I'd recognized the handwriting in the message over the door in the hallway.

"Your father?" Mom asked, seeming truly surprised. "Why didn't I notice that?"

"Because the downstairs has ten-foot ceilings and the message is maybe three inches in height," I pointed out. "It's not important that you didn't recognize it; what's important is that I did, and it was Dad's handwriting. I'd know it anywhere."

Mom's face got serious. "Tell me about the other two messages you say you've found in the house." There was no way around it, so I did. Mom listened carefully and expressed the requisite concern for my and Melissa's well-being, and for my privacy while showering, a sentiment with which I heartily concurred. When I'd finished, she sat for a few moments digesting the information.

"What does it mean, he didn't die the way we think?" she asked. "Your father had cancer for over a year. Of course that's the way he died. The death certificate lists cancer as the cause." She was dry-eyed, but I could hear a catch in her voice. Even though unlike me, she could see and talk to Dad, I guessed it wasn't the same as having him there alive.

"I have no idea what it could mean," I said. "I think whoever left the message was just trying to scare us."

"They're succeeding," Mom said drily.

Our conversation was cut short by a rumbling in the living room, which Mom said meant that my client had arrived. We went in to receive him and sure enough, there "stood" Lawrence Laurentz, in a theatrical cape and a black fedora. The only prop he was missing was an elegant walking stick. Maybe because he wasn't really walking.

"So, the *private investigator* returns," he said, his voice dripping haughty contempt. I saw Mom's lips tighten; nobody got to talk to her daughter like that. "I trust this time there is progress to be reported."

"There is," I informed him, "but I don't think you've earned the right to information."

Lawrence's face flattened out as if he'd been hit with a pie. Which would have been a nice touch, if I could have managed it. It's tough when the person you're trying to hit isn't actually there. "Young lady," he said, "do you have any idea—"

I didn't let him finish. "Here's the deal, *Mel*," I said. Lawrence went to raise a finger in warning, but I plowed through. Which reminded me to call Murray back about his bill and clarify. "You get absolutely nothing from me until you start to tell the truth, and I mean *all* of the truth when I ask you a question. So far, you've told me everything you wanted me to hear and nothing else. Well, I don't care about your ego and I don't care about your dignity. I care about finding out who killed you—if anybody did—and getting in touch with my father. The only way I'm going to be able to do that is if you start owning up. So I'm giving you this ultimatum, and then I'm going to ask you a question, which you will answer *completely*: I hear one more half-truth or I think you're not being totally honest, and you can find yourself some other PI who can see ghosts. Are we clear?"

Mom looked torn: On the one hand, the ghost had dared be rude to her daughter. On the other, her daughter had been blunt and disrespectful to a guest in her house. It was a tough choice, but she looked at me and managed a tiny smile.

Lawrence, however, was not in a cheery mood. "How dare you?" he demanded. "The idea that I have been anything less than candid with you—"

I cut him off again. "Are. We. Clear?" I repeated.

"Must I remind you that I hold the key to your father's whereabouts?" the old specter asked, playing his hole card.

But this time I was ready. "What you hold, Mr. Brookman, is a very poor hand indeed," I told him. "I think I can find my father without you. In fact, I believe my father came and found *me* just yesterday. So I'm going to say this one last time: You tell me everything you know, or I walk and you spend the rest of eternity with the image of a toaster flying into your bathtub. Now. What's it going to be?"

The puffed-up old actor seemed to deflate like a Macy's balloon on Thanksgiving afternoon. He got smaller. He got thinner. He actually looked like he got older, which was not the least bit possible. His eyes took on a sad quality that replaced the arrogance they usually displayed. It was not an improvement.

"You're right," he said. "I have been holding back. I don't like people to know the real me; that's why I loved the theater. I could pretend to be someone—anyone—else. But you're doing a favor for me and I have not been helping. For that, I apologize."

But I was sticking with the tough-chick approach. "That's all well and good," I said. "But it doesn't tell me anything I don't already know. Spill." I sat down on Mom's overstuffed easy chair and crossed my arms.

"Everything I've told you is true." Lawrence did his best to compose himself after that emotional scene, which I believed since he wasn't that good an actor. "With one exception."

"You really don't have a clue where my father is, do you?" I challenged him.

"No."

Behind me, Mom gasped, but I'd had my doubts about

Lawrence's story from the beginning. He'd never been able to provide any details at all.

"I have tried to contact him," he went on, "but I have been unsuccessful. He doesn't appear to be staying anywhere I'd know to look."

"How did you know to use him as incentive?" I asked him.

"Your mother mentioned she hadn't seen your father in a few weeks and that it was odd," Lawrence answered. "I assumed that would be sufficient to motivate you."

"Why did you need to motivate Alison?" Mom jumped in. "Why didn't you just ask?"

Lawrence stared at the floor, which was about eighteen inches below his feet. "It never occurred to me that she would help," he said.

"Where did you get that business card?" I asked him. "The one from my father's business?"

Lawrence pointed at the side table next to the sofa, which had a drawer where Mom kept some odds and ends in addition to coasters she might need while entertaining. "There," he said. "One day when you weren't in the room, Loretta, I found it. And I kept it in my pocket to use if you demanded proof. And you did, so I left for a few seconds to make it appear I was traveling to see Jack, and then I came back and handed you the card I had already gotten ready. Please forgive me."

Silence. I looked behind me. Mom was standing at the entrance to her kitchen, backed against the pass-through. Her face was pale and her eyes were wide. For a moment, I was worried about her health.

"You looked through my things?" she gasped.

The old ghost hung his head. "I am sorry. I needed something that could solidify my story. You don't understand. Not knowing what happened to me, or why, it's made me do things I would never have considered when I was alive. I can't go on not knowing why I am this way. But I was very, very wrong, Loretta. I am so sorry."

I breathed out, knowing Mom would understand. Lawrence was a guest; she'd give him a good deal of leeway.

"Get out of my house," Mom said.

I reacted so fast I think I was facing her even before I could stand. As I spun, I saw Lawrence's eyes widen and his mouth drop open. But before I could absorb that sight, I was staring at my mother, who was pointing at the ghost floating in her living room over the coffee table.

"Get out of my house," Mom repeated. "And don't ever come back."

"Mom," I began. If Lawrence left and couldn't be contacted, I would never be able to find out what else he knew about his case that he'd been concealing. Lawrence was the only one who could answer the questions that might come up after tonight's performance of the New Old Thespians. The whole case was gone if he was gone. "You can't just—"

Mom shook her head slowly. And she pointed behind me. I turned back to face into the living room.

Lawrence Laurentz had left the building.

It wasn't until I was halfway to Asbury Park that I realized I wasn't sure whether I still had a client or a case to investigate. Somehow it felt odd to consider not finding out what had actually happened to Lawrence; on the other hand, if I were to find out and still never see him again to tell him, what would I have accomplished?

Mom had been immediately apologetic about the way she'd reacted to Lawrence's confession and had even tried (through gritted teeth, but still) to summon the ghost and forgive him, but he had not responded, and we were left with no client, no source of information on his death, and no forwarding address.

It was only nine in the morning, and already I had lost ground to yesterday.

Route 33 was not cooperating this morning, which was

typical, and I was stuck in traffic, frustrated, and cranky. This was not the proper attitude for a woman about to drop in unexpectedly on a guy she'd had a first date with only the night before.

I decided to call Jerry Rasmussen, whose number was luckily programmed into my cell phone since he had once called me to apologize. He answered on the first ring, and I asked him if I needed to buy tickets in advance for tonight's performance of *Peter Pan*.

He sounded just a little startled. "You want to come to Brookside Manor to see *Peter Pan*?" he asked. "You sure?"

"Is there a reason I shouldn't?" I said. "Does the play need more rehearsal or something?" I'll admit it; I threw that in because I knew it would annoy him. I wanted to get a reaction out of him.

"Of course not," he huffed. "We are professionals." They weren't, really, but there was no use quibbling—I didn't want to alienate him entirely. "The show will go off exactly as planned. My concern is the venue." He said that last word with a real sense of heady condescension in the pronunciation.

"The venue?" I realized it was a straight line, but it was the only way to get to the next piece of information. I'd been sitting with my foot on the brake here for five minutes. There was no sense that any of us would ever move again, so I needed at least the illusion of progress.

"Yes," Jerry answered, having been properly primed. "It is an assisted-living facility. Many of the residents will be in some way incapacitated, so it will not be exactly the best showcase for our troupe. The stage is simply a raised platform. I'm not sure it will be large enough for all the scenery."

Like I cared whether it was the best showcase. "I'm sure it'll be fine," I said. "But again, do I need to buy tickets in advance?"

"There are no tickets," Jerry admitted. "But if you like,

I will leave your name at the front gate. Brookside is fastidious about security. How many will be in your party?"

I decided to go with the best case scenario. "Eight," I said.

Jerry sounded astonished. "Eight?"

I counted again: me, Mom, Melissa (how could I leave her behind, even on a school night?), Jeannie and Tony, Nan and Morgan and Josh. "Yup, eight," I confirmed. "Unless babies count. Then nine."

"Excellent!" he shouted. "We will look forward to seeing you there!" He hung up before I could return his enthusiasm, which was just as well since I was feeling particularly unenthusiastic as it became obvious that the three lanes on the highway were being condensed into one, and some of my fellow drivers were doing their very best to ignore the alternate feed rules that most Jersey drivers are usually pretty good with, at least in comparison to those assassins from New York and Pennsylvania.

I checked in with Mom again, ostensibly to confirm the time for the play but really to find out if Lawrence had reappeared; he had not. Mom said she'd considered baking cookies to lure him, then realized that would not do much good. Ghosts don't eat. Which takes a lot of the allure out of the afterlife for me.

Mom and I ended the conversation, and I mused on my latest theory, that Dr. Wells and/or the grumpy ghost had left the first two messages in my house. This was based strictly on the timing of his death and of Dad's vanishing (and the complete lack of other ghostly suspects), but it was all I had to go on. Assuming he had been the intruder, how could the doctor have gotten my address?

There were enough crazy threads to this case that I could have knitted a sweater out of it. If I knew how to knit. If Dad wasn't being held captive and was free to move about, why wouldn't he come to Mom at least? Did he *know* all that was going on?

Once the merging was done, traffic started to move fairly well again, and I was in Asbury Park in about a half hour. I parked across the street from Madison Paint, took a deep breath, wrapped my scarf back around my mouth and got out of the car.

The plan was this: First of all, I hoped to see Sy Kaplan. But Morgan's pep talk about finding the source of the messages in my house had hit home in ways he hadn't expected—I knew the perpetrator of the first two little shockers was a ghost, and the grumpy ghost had known my name. Could he have known my address, too?

If I could go in without showing the old lemon sucker I was afraid of him, maybe I could get up the same kind of attitude I'd used this morning against Lawrence. While that situation hadn't worked out in exactly the way I would have liked, it had gotten Lawrence to fess up about what he'd done, and he'd seemed on the verge of telling me some truths before Mom had rashly banished him. This time, I'd have to seize any moment I had when Sy and Josh were dealing with customers. I hoped business would be brisk.

So screwing up my courage was a definite need here, since I wanted to work that same kind of magic on the grumpy ghost. The only problem was—he creeped me out.

Before entering a scenario like this, I usually get myself amped up by thinking about The Swine. Preferably with his "significant other" of the moment, although right at this second I was unable to remember which one might be most significant. The last time I'd seen him, he'd been planning to move in with a woman from the San Diego area; I'd heard now that the arrangement "hadn't worked out" and he was living with an aspiring actress who worked at Starbucks. That sort of thing usually gets me irritated to a point that I can confront my quarry with exactly the right amount of attitude.

I made a grumbling sound in the back of my throat to remind myself I was fierce and got out of the car. The frigid wind hit me smack in the face, and effectively blew the sum total of my fierceness away. Still, I was determined, so I crossed the street and headed for Madison Paint.

But as I crossed, I couldn't help but notice that a blue Hyundai had parked directly behind my car despite there being plenty of empty spaces on both sides of the street. I also noticed that the driver bore a certain resemblance to Tyra Carter. But the driver was wearing sunglasses despite this overcast day, and a hat that obscured part of her face, so it was difficult to tell.

It was so cold, however, that my brain simply said, *I can't wait to be inside!* It's a question of priorities. I'd worry about being followed by a six-foot former man later. Plus, once I was inside the store, the relief of the heating system—so much more efficient than the one in my Volvo—removed all anxiety. Which was bad, because anxiety was what would motivate me if I ran into the grumpy ghost. On the other hand, here came Josh, and . . . emotionally, this was getting complicated.

"Alison! I wasn't expecting to see you until tonight!" Josh didn't look disappointed and gave me a quick hug.

"I know," I said when we unclenched, "but I wanted to see if your grandfather was around. It's been forever since I've seen him."

"Yeah, I told him I saw you, and he was really disappointed to have missed you. Come on, he's in the back." Josh led me to the back of the store, less an "office" than an area with a desk and a couple of chairs. I thought I glimpsed a ghostly leg disappear into the ceiling as we approached, but there were no other spirits visible. The modern laptop computer sitting on the desk was a jarring reminder that it was no longer the 1990s, but the man sitting behind the desk was not.

Sy Kaplan, at ninety-one, looked like the Sy I remembered, only smaller. It was like he'd spent too much time in a clothes dryer—he was the same man, but if you tried him on again, he wouldn't fit. His eyes lit up when I approached, which for a guy that old, was something of a pleasant surprise. I didn't expect him to be able to see me from ten feet away.

"Ally" he shouted. "How are you, sweetie?"

I walked over as Sy stood up, which took longer than it used to and didn't get him as far, a strange incongruity, and gave him a hug and a kiss on the cheek while Josh beamed in the corner. "I'm good, Mr. Kaplan," I said. "You look terrific."

He waved a hand and in doing so, called me a liar. "I look like I should have died ten years ago," he said. "And call me 'Sy.' You're not nine years old anymore."

He might have been smaller, but he hadn't changed. "I wasn't kidding. You look good, Sy."

Sy made a "yeah, sure" face but let it go. "I heard you went for dinner with Josh last night," he sort of half sang. "Something going on?" You have to love old people; they figure the regular rules of polite conversation don't apply to them, and they're right.

"Give us a few more days to decide, would you?" Josh laughed from the corner.

"Well, hurry up. There's no telling how much time I have left."

"You'll outlive all of us," his grandson told him.

"I hope not."

The banter was everything I remembered from my days here with Dad, and once again, it was strange not having him present when it was going on; it was like he'd gone next door to the deli to get me an orange juice or a bagel, and he'd be back in just a minute.

But I hadn't forgotten why I was there, and instead of my father, I had indeed found the grumpy ghost, who rose from the basement looking just as displeased and threatening as he had when I'd been here on Saturday. I swallowed my dread and tried to think of The Swine. It was working but not as well as usual.

Sy excused himself to use the adjacent restroom at just about the same time a customer entered the store through the front door and Josh headed off to assist her.

And that left me in the room with this disapproving, vaguely dangerous presence, as I'd planned. I spent a moment concentrating on my ex-husband in Malibu, no doubt sitting by a pool instead of freezing his butt off in an ancient Volvo, and then I looked up at the grumpy ghost and didn't give him time to stare me down. I spoke quietly but firmly in his direction.

"All right, you've gotten my attention. Now drop the silent act and tell me what this is all about."

If anything, the grumpy ghost stared at me more intently. But I stared back, put my hands on my hips and waited.

Nothing. Okay. I could wait him out (well, until Sy and Josh came back, but why think about that now?). It took a while, but I finally got the grumpy ghost in my gaze and held him there, and eventually he cracked.

"Your father did not die as you think he did," he intoned, probably wishing his voice were echoey and spooky, like ghosts in the movies. So it *was* him!

"Yeah, I got your messages. How did you find me?"

His grumpy expression changed to one of condescending pity. "They do have a phone book here," he said.

Okay, so I was an idiot, but one with a mission, and somehow his comment made him less scary. "I'm here to tell you, I don't appreciate your sneaking into my house and playing your little games," I said. "If you have something to tell me, let's hear it. But you don't come back into my bedroom without an invitation. Is that clear?" I wasn't as confident as I hoped I sounded, and I did indeed check that neither Sy nor Josh was anywhere near when I made that comment about being invited into my bedroom.

"You needed to be told," he said in the old monotone. The guy was out of a Vincent Price movie.

"Yeah, but so far you haven't actually told me anything. What do you mean, my father didn't die the way I thought? How did he die?"

"Badly," the old gasbag let out.

There was a familiar sound from the direction of the bathroom, then water running, indicating that Sy would be back in the room in a few moments.

"I don't have time for this, pal. Tell me straight up: Did you kill my father?"

Sy opened the bathroom door, smoothing his hair with his left hand. Frankly, at ninety-one, it was amazing the man had hair to smooth, even if he had the receipt for it in a drawer at home. "Ally," he breathed. "It's been such a long time. There are days I still expect your father to come walking in, and then I remember."

"I know what you mean, Sy," I said, and looked up for Grumpy.

He was gone.

I reminisced for about an hour with Sy and Josh, hoping the old ghost might come back, but to no avail. Today was turning out to be my day to make ghosts disappear. A trick that might come in handy with Maxie; I'd have to remember it.

Sy had some great stories about Dad; I actually turned on my recorder to preserve them. One, which involved a particularly difficult wallpaper customer who insisted on hanging the paper horizontally, was especially precious, very Dad, and something I'd have to tell Mom about when I got the chance.

When it got to be about lunchtime, I mentioned something about having guests in my house, invited Josh to drop by for dinner around six (Sy, twinkling, said he'd make sure

Josh was out of the store "in plenty of time to spiff up"), then wrapped myself back up in my costume from *Dr. Zhivago* and headed across the street to the Volvo.

The royal blue Hyundai was still there, but there was no driver sitting in it. So I climbed into my Swedish Model T and turned the key as fast as I could, hoping the heater might have remembered that "heat" was part of its name while I was in the store.

Luckily, I had not yet put the car into gear when I heard the voice in the seat behind me.

"So, what are you doing about my employment situation?" Tyra Carter demanded.

I spun, shouting, and felt my heart leap up into my throat. It's not pleasant.

"What the hell are you doing back there?" I yelled. "How did you get into my car?"

"You left the back door unlocked and the wind was cold," Tyra said, shaking her head. "What did you want me to do, freeze to death?"

I caught my breath and tried very hard not to audibly hyperventilate. It's so embarrassing to pass out when your life is being threatened. Or something. *Was* my life being threatened?

"I *wanted* you not to follow me here," I said in the best indignant voice I could muster. "If you're so cold, why not stay in your own car?"

"I didn't know you were going to be in there for an *hour*," she answered. "How long does it take to buy some paint?" The fact that I hadn't been carrying anything when I left the store seemed to have been lost on her. Tyra was imposing, but she was no genius.

"What do you want?" I asked Tyra.

"What I said—I want to know what you're doing about my employment situation. I need to get back at the Basie. This tire thing isn't paying enough to cover my rent."

The thing about adrenaline is that it isn't specifically

purposed. If the stuff starts flowing through your veins because you're terrified (let's say, for example, that an unusually large woman who supposedly used to be a violent man was discovered in the backseat of your car when you weren't expecting her) and it transpires that maybe you don't need to be terrified, the adrenaline doesn't simply say, "Oh well, false alarm," and vanish from your system. It stays, and your brain decides what to do with it. In this case, my brain shifted from terrified to angry faster than I could shift from park into drive.

"Are you out of your *mind*?" I demanded. I'll admit, it wasn't my most original or well-purposed question; has anyone ever answered in the affirmative to that one? "What makes you think you can jump into my car and tell me to find you a job? Besides, you told me not to call Penny about your job! When did I become your employment service?"

"When you talked to Penny Fields about me and stopped me from getting my job back," Tyra explained, as if the answer were so obvious it was a waste of her time to even address it.

It should be noted that it is, if not impossible, extremely difficult to grind your teeth into a fine powder in a few short seconds. I can tell you that from personal experience. "I *didn't* talk to Penny," I reiterated, impressed that I could talk with my jaw clenched like that. It was possible I had a future in ventriloquism. "That didn't happen. I never mentioned your name to Penny. Penny mentioned your name to *me*. Why is it difficult for you to understand that?" If I mentioned now that I actually *had* asked Penny to give Tyra her job back (since Penny clearly had not made an offer), Tyra would find a way to blame me for that, too. I decided not to bring it up.

Tyra's eyebrows lowered. So did her voice, to near-Tyrone levels. "Are you calling me stupid?" she asked.

Once again, adrenaline is not a thoughtful hormone. "Are you calling me a liar?" I shot back.

She rolled her eyes. "Penny Fields fired me because of your pal Larry. Now he's dead and she won't hire me back. What should I think?"

That sounded disturbingly like motive to me, but there was something strange about it. "That doesn't make any sense, but okay. Let's say Larry Laurentz snitched on you to Penny. Why would she listen to him?"

"Boy, you are a really lousy detective, aren't you?" Tyra asked, I assumed rhetorically. "Because you always listen first to the guy you're sleeping with."

Right. And . . . whoa! "What? Penny Fields and Lawrence Laurentz were . . ."

"Now you got it," she said. "So what are you going to do to get my job back?"

"Wait. No. You have to tell me—"

"I don't have to tell you *nothing*, lady." I didn't like the tone in Tyra's voice. It was too Tyrone.

There was a knock on my window, and once again I spun with a great amount of panic. Who *else* was chasing after me today?

Josh Kaplan was standing next to the car in his jeans and sweatshirt, arms wrapped around himself in an charmingly futile attempt to keep warm. I lowered the window. "Is everything okay, Alison?" he asked, looking more at Tyra than at me.

Catching my breath was becoming a hobby. "Sure," I managed. "Tyra was just . . ."

"Leaving," she said, and stepped out of the car, letting even more subzero air into it. Not that I was complaining; anything that got her out of my backseat was a resounding success in my book. She looked Josh up and down. "You provide a lot of service to your customers," she said.

"This one's special," Josh told her. He looked at me, making his point. "What time am I picking you up for *Peter Pan* tonight?" he asked.

Oops.

Tyra's eyes registered the information. "So I'll see you at the show tonight," she said, looking directly at me with something in mind other than adding my name to her Christmas card list.

"You'll be there? At the show tonight?" Josh asked Tyra.

"Of course," she said. "I do the special effects. And there are a *lot* in this one." She turned toward me, so Josh couldn't see her face, and glared into my eyes. "So we'll talk *later,*" she said. Then she turned and walked back to her Hyundai, which probably had a working heater and would have been a better venue for this conversation.

Josh leaned over into my window a little to talk more privately as Tyra drove away. "Better to let her get a head start," he said. "Now what was that all about?"

"It's a long story, and you're freezing," I told him. "I'll explain it all when you come for dinner tonight. Just not in front of my mother or daughter, okay? I don't want them to worry."

"I'm starting to think *I* should worry."

He was just figuring that out *now*? "Go back inside with your grandfather and sell paint," I said. "I'll be all right."

Josh looked like he was going to say something, then decided against it. He leaned into the window and kissed me quite casually, just a good-bye thing, which was sort of interesting. "I'll see you later," he said. "It's cold outside. Couldn't you tell?"

"Hadn't noticed," I said.

He ran back across the street and into the store, and I got my GPS out from the glove compartment. I knew how to get to Whispering Lakes, but I wasn't going to see Mom, and those places are so similar that it's best to get your directions clear. Better to give the little box time to line up its satellites.

I had a ghost to track down.

On the drive to Manalapan, I tried to sort out the facts as I knew them: Lawrence Laurentz, amateur theater buff and

colossal irritant, had died about six months earlier, a death
the medical examiner of Monmouth County had determined
to be from natural causes. Except that Lawrence, whose
real name was Melvin Brookman, was convinced that he'd
been murdered by way of an electric toaster thrown into
his bath.

It was true that Lawrence had annoyed a great many
people: Penny Fields, his boss, had all but said he was a
snitch and a pariah among the staff at his job. Although
according to Tyra, a former fellow employee who was for-
merly a fellow, Penny was sleeping with Lawrence. Tyra
believed Lawrence had gotten her fired. She had also
belonged to a community theater group with Lawrence, as
had Frances Walters, who didn't have a grudge with him
(except maybe that he'd informed on the group to the cops
and gotten them all hauled in for public nudity) but had
been ostracized a bit by her colleagues for bringing such a
pain in the butt into the troupe. The group's director, Jerry
Rasmussen, admitted he didn't like Lawrence, had thought
he was a bad actor and a poor sport and had seen to it that
Lawrence was drummed out of the group.

Not long after he was, the troupe was raided during an
overly reverent performance of *Hair* and a number of its
members arrested, all because of an anonymous tip, presumably from Lawrence. The only ones held overnight,
though, were Frances and Jerry, on suspicion that they
were running some sort of illegal Viagra ring. No charges
had been filed, but it seemed odd that the cops had dropped
it so quickly.

And now Lawrence had banished himself from Mom's
house and I was probably no longer officially (although
with a dead client, that's always a little fuzzy) hired to
investigate his death. So why was I still investigating?

The truth was, I felt bad for the guy. Yeah, Lawrence was
a pompous blowhard and possibly a tattletale, but underneath it you could see the kid who'd always been picked last

for the team, the man who was just hoping to find his niche all his life and who never did. Someone had to be his champion. And that left . . . me. If that's not a reason to feel sorry for the old guy, I can't imagine one.

So now I was on my way to the scene of his death because I was fairly sure I'd find him there. Where else did he have to go?

His town home was on the other side of the complex from Mom's. The GPS got into a funny mood for a minute, insisting I had "reached my destination" when I was actually at the community's clubhouse (they all have clubhouses) but found its bearings and eventually deposited me at the address Mom had given me. A quick check of the mailboxes showed that the name "Laurentz" had been painted over but not entirely obliterated. This was definitely the place.

Lawrence's unit was the usual brick front, small deck in the back with French doors leading into the kitchen. The house wasn't really any different from a few thousand others in this community alone, and surely hundreds of thousands elsewhere, though it was a different model from Mom's, an "up and down" town home, meaning it had an upstairs unlike Mom's single-level, better for those who have difficulty with stairs (not that Mom does, but she likes having everything on one floor).

Having worked for some months in the door and lock department of a home improvement store, I know a little bit more about picking a lock than, let's say, almost everybody. It would have been easy for me to get into the house as Nan and Morgan did, by calling the real estate agent showing Lawrence's home. But I didn't want to disrupt her working day on a sham (I certainly wasn't interested in buying this or any other place while I was still paying the guesthouse's mortgage). And I really didn't relish the idea of trying to locate Lawrence's ghost while hiding my intentions, and what would have seemed like my insanity, from an unsuspecting stranger. Not to mention it would take longer.

Still, I didn't want to attract attention if my skills were a little rusty, so I walked around to the back—which was a real eye-opener, literally, with the frigid wind blowing in my face—and went to work on the lock to the French doors, the same way Penny Fields said she'd entered the night Lawrence died, which was probably a lie.

It took me about ten minutes to gain entry using a tiny screwdriver made to fix eyeglass frames, mostly because it's hard to pick a lock when you're wearing mittens and are being stubborn about taking them off. Once I finally admitted defeat and removed them, the lock picking itself took only a minute or two. But my fingers got really cold. Life is full of trade-offs.

There was no reason for this to feel eerie, but it did. There was nothing especially different or noteworthy about the place—it was clean and neat, having been more or less "staged" by a real estate agent, no doubt—with the matching white appliances, faux-granite countertop and laminate flooring that was supposed to look like ceramic tile. Whatever water damage might have been visible on the ceiling after Lawrence's demise had been repaired.

But it was creeping me out, and I couldn't explain why.

For one thing, it was quiet. "Maybe *too* quiet," they'd say in the movies. There's a feeling you get when you're in someone else's home in their absence—when a relative is on vacation, perhaps, and asks you to water their plants—that casts a strange pall over the place, and that's part of what I was feeling in this case.

The town homes were really row houses; they were attached in groups of three. Lawrence's was a corner unit, so he had only shared a wall on one side, but it still meant that I had to be wary of calling too loudly for him; I'd noticed a car in a spot designated for neighbors and so assumed someone was home next door. They'd know the unit adjacent to theirs was supposed to be empty, and I'd end up explaining my purely honorable intentions to the Manalapan police, no doubt while my mother, who would have been strolling by in the Antarctic-style weather on a whim, watched in horror.

Yes, that's how my mind works, and no, I'm not proud of it.

I started out calling in a conversational tone, the way I do when there are civilians in the guesthouse and I need to talk to Paul. "Mr. Laurentz," I said, as if asking if the mail had been delivered yet or the coffee was brewed. There was no answer.

The living room was no less unsettling in its complete averageness. The plush furniture looked to have been recently vacuumed along with the generic beige wall-to-wall carpet, not the kind of décor I'd have expected from as flamboyant a soul as Lawrence Laurentz. There were no books on shelves, no music in cases, no DVDs visible. Clearly the real estate agent had come through here, too, and had eradicated pretty much any lingering remnant of a particular taste.

"Mr. Laurentz?" I tried, just a little bit more boldly, as I got to the foot of the staircase. There was no escaping it; I'd have to go upstairs. I did notice the lack of creaking, something I could not brag about at the guesthouse. Of course, my stairs were over a hundred years old, so I couldn't really complain. Because then I'd have to fix them.

There were two bedrooms upstairs, one of which Lawrence had obviously used as a den or office, with a desk that must have at one time held a computer in one corner. The only decorations that indicated Lawrence had ever lived here were theatrical posters framed on each wall. One of them, announcing the opening of *Gypsy*—the original cast, from 1959—was signed by Ethel Merman, Jack Klugman and Jerome Robbins. If the toaster hadn't gotten Lawrence, the fact that Stephen Sondheim had not signed it had probably killed him.

It also occurred to me that he'd likely taken his "stage name" as an homage to Arthur Laurents, who had written the book for that musical as well as for *West Side Story* and a great many others.

I called his name a few more times in the den, then advanced to the bedroom, which was the next–to-last place that I wanted to look (the last was the bathroom, but I was fairly sure that having died there, Lawrence would not want to revisit that particular spot). But again, it had been homogenized to a beige, bland sort of place. The den was the only room with a hint of personality left.

"Mr. Laurentz, it's okay. I talked to my mom, and she's not mad at you anymore. Please come talk to me."

Nothing.

Well, I'd gotten an idea when I was in the den, though I hadn't wanted to try it for fear of alerting any neighbors in the area. But if Lawrence was going to be stubborn about it, though, I'd have no choice.

I walked into the den, looked around and called his name out one more time, still with no response. Might as well give it a shot, and if local security showed up, I could always run like hell.

I took a deep breath and, completely cold, started belting out a tune from *Gypsy*.

"'You'll be swell! You'll be great! Gonna have the whole world on the plate!'"

Lawrence materialized over the desk almost immediately, looking downright nauseated. "Stop!" he shouted. "You're butchering it!"

I grinned and stopped singing. "So. You were here all along, weren't you?"

"Yes. Please, just don't sing anymore." Lawrence wiped his brow as if there were sweat on it, with a cloth handkerchief he produced from his inside pocket. He was no longer wearing the cape but was still in a suit and tie. Just in case Cole Porter came by later for a few cocktails. Which, let's face it, was possible. "Why, *why* have you come looking for me? Why couldn't you just leave me alone?"

"Because you still haven't told me the whole truth, have you? What was the story with you and Penny Fields? She didn't just come by to deal with job issues that night. She was *here* because you two were having a relationship. Why didn't you tell me?"

Lawrence looked profoundly embarrassed and stared at the ceiling, which was only a few inches from his head. "There are some things one simply doesn't disclose," he said with a sniff. "But your insinuation that Penny might have had a hand in . . . what happened to me . . . is incorrect. She would never hurt me. She didn't like me, but she wouldn't hurt me."

"She had a funny way of showing she didn't like you," I suggested. "And your feeling that she wouldn't throw a toaster in your tub is very touching, but not what I'd call 'evidence.' Where was she when you were taking a bath?"

"She went out to get us some tea," he said, adding, "I refuse to discuss this matter with you any further," he said. And he looked away, which led me to believe he might be planning on vanishing again.

I sat down in his office chair and looked up at him. "We still don't really know what happened to you," I said. "That's why I didn't just leave you alone."

Lawrence wrinkled his nose and looked away. "Why? Nobody ever truly liked me when I was alive. I lied to you about your father. I asked you for help but then withheld information about Penny and the Thespians. I went through your mother's furniture to find ways to further deceive the two of you. What makes you care?"

I'd had to think about that one myself, so I had an answer ready. "Because every human being deserves to live. Because that was taken away from you and it's not right." Then I looked up at him. "And because I disagree that nobody ever liked you. I think it was more a question of *you* not much liking most other people. But you came to my mom after you died, you sought her out. She enjoyed your company; you're the one who didn't want to admit that she considered you a friend. Penny, clearly, liked you. I think you were so afraid that nobody would like you that you beat them to it. You need to loosen up a bit, Lawrence."

He didn't speak for a while. Finally, he said, "I think it might be too late for that."

"You are . . . existing proof that it's never too late," I told him.

He hovered in a sitting position, as if standing was too much of an effort. It had the added effect of bringing us closer to eye level with each other. "Then let me try," he said. "I apologize for the way I treated you and your mother. I was thinking of myself and no one else, which I believe has been a fault of mine roughly since kindergarten. I'm very touched by your persistence. What can I do to help?"

"You can tell me where to get illegal Viagra," I said.

Twenty-five

The records office at Freehold Area Memorial Hospital (a name which doesn't make sense to me at all—What's it memorializing? Are we supposed to remember the Freehold area?) was the same kind of bureaucratic room you'll find in government buildings, impersonal to a maddening degree and bland almost to the point of a style statement.

That blandness made it even weirder that I was so on edge I thought my head would explode.

Granted, this was the first time I'd been to the hospital since Dad died, and shockingly enough, the place did not hold pleasant memories.

The overall effect was not improved by the fact that the hospital was crawling with ghosts. Many spirits, I've discovered, are at least semiconfined to the physical space in which they died. And a hospital, no matter how well its staff and physicians perform, is by definition a place where a good number of people pass away. Even the room I was standing in, behind the inevitable counter separating the in crowd (staff) from the uncool types (patients or, in this case, me), had at least twenty ghosts hovering about its ceiling, passing through its workstations and just generally hanging around like in a cosmic waiting room without any good magazines. One ghost in particular, with slicked-back hair and a gunshot wound in his chest, was giving me the same grin I remembered from when The Swine and I were dating.

It made me wonder how Mom, who's been seeing ghosts all her life, must have felt when Dad was a patient here. Did she start looking for him in the ceilings as soon as Dr. Wells gave her the worst news she'd ever gotten?

It was, I'll admit, a little unnerving. I found myself tapping my right foot in what appeared to be impatience but was really anxiety.

Roberta, the middle-aged woman standing behind the counter and in front of the workstations, who was indeed alive, misread my unease. "It's been a busy morning," she said as an excuse even before I asked for anything.

I smiled to show camaraderie. "I'm sure," I said. "I'm wondering if you can help me find the records from a few years ago. My father passed away here, and I need to see some of the paperwork."

Without changing facial expression, she said, "I'm sorry for your loss." It was probably something she would say if the phone rang at three in the morning. "What do you need?"

"I'd like to see the records of his stay here and the death certificate," I answered. I gave her the date Dad died, and his name. "Would you still have those?"

"Oh, we have them, all right," Roberta said. "But I'd have to pull them up and make copies. And you'll have to pay for the copies, a dollar a page." That seemed pretty pricey for something run off on an office copier, but the hospital, as they often do, had me over a barrel.

"Not a problem," I said. "How long will it take?"

"Give me a half hour," Roberta said. "Busy morning." I

didn't tell her that was quicker than I'd expected. Somehow it seemed she would have been disappointed if I was actually impressed by the hospital's efficiency. Since I didn't want to damage her worldview, I nodded grudgingly and headed through the maze that is the modern palace of healing to the food court, which is an odd concept for a hospital. It was next to the gift shop, which is an even odder one.

Once there, I texted Mom. After my consultation with Lawrence, I'd alerted her that he was in a more reasonable mood and might venture by. But I'd also asked if she would go to the guesthouse and find Paul, so she could text back his replies. Ghosts can't be heard over the phone. Hey, I don't make up the rules. Frankly, I'm not clear on who does, but whoever it is has an odd sense of order. At times I think the afterlife is run by an eight-year-old with ADHD.

After ordering a hot chocolate and a small salad, I texted Mom, "Ask Paul if Maxie's found anything about the Viagra ring yet."

Lawrence Laurentz had been oddly reluctant to tell stories out of school, but after insisting that he'd never even looked into the possibility of a pipeline to Viagra pills because he had suffered a heart attack ten years earlier and was not a candidate for the drug, he admitted he'd heard rumors that they were obtainable through people in the New Old Thespians.

"I wasn't asking about it because I couldn't use it, but I heard about it from Jerry and from Barney Lester at the Thespians," he'd told me.

"Was Jerry asking like he had some prescriptions and was offering them to you?" I'd asked. That was the implication I'd gotten from Officer Warrell.

Lawrence shook his head. "No, it was more like he knew about this great thing and he wanted to show off how in-the-know he was," he said. "The man is a moronic boor."

Barney Lester, I recalled, had passed away before Lawrence, of natural causes, his wife had said. "Did something happen with the Viagra that caused his heart problem?" I'd asked Lawrence.

He shrugged. "I was out of the group when he died."

"But not when he got sick," I'd reminded him.

"He was one of the ones not talking to me. But I don't remember anyone who *was* talking to me saying it was anything but his heart."

That hadn't been much help. Sitting now at a table with my salad and warm chocolate ("hot" would have been an overstatement), I was considering my options when my phone buzzed, and I read the text from Mom: "nthng n vgr bt pl wnts rprt."

Of course.

Muttering to myself about reintroducing my mother to vowels, I texted back a very clear "WHAT?" and waited.

I recalled a time when people could simply talk to each other over items we called "telephones" and get our answers almost immediately. It took me a moment to ponder this, after which the phone buzzed again, and I got Mom's latest missive: "Nothing on Viagra, but Paul wants a report."

Now, was that so hard, really?

I really would have given in and called Mom myself, but the idea of the interminable delays during which Paul would relay a message to Mom, then me to Mom, then Mom to Paul, then Paul to Mom . . . was more than my brain could handle this afternoon, and the room was noisy, which would have necessitated my shouting questions about Viagra and murder into my phone. I sighed and texted back as much as I'd learned from Lawrence. By the time I'd deciphered four or five more of Mom's texts, which appeared to be in Estonian even when she deigned to throw in the occasional vowel, I'd eaten half the salad, finished all the tepid chocolate and was heading back to the records department, where my buddy Roberta was plying her trade with a gentleman ahead of me and the leering gunshot victim had apparently left the room.

Roberta's client moved on, and she waved me over. "I got the records," she said. She handed me an envelope on which had been printed, "NO CHARGE" in block letters. I looked at her. She pursed her lips a little and chewed on her gum a bit. "You shouldn't have to pay for that," she said, and turned back toward her computer screen.

You can't ever figure people.

I took the envelope and walked into the corridor. There was a waiting room a few doors down, so I ducked inside to sit and examine the records. An older woman, transparent and dressed from the 1970s, was hovering over the only available seat in the room. I walked over to her and waited, but she didn't move.

Putting my hand over my mouth as if to stifle a cough, I said quietly, "May I?" The ghost looked displeased but rose up out of the way and through the ceiling. Two other ghosts in the room, noticing, glanced disapprovingly in my direction. Apparently I was being rude. Ghost etiquette. I suppose I could have sat down in the middle of the older lady, but that did not seem a considerably more polite alternative.

The envelope contained many documents I vaguely recalled having seen before. Much of it was medical mumbo jumbo I couldn't possibly decode, but there were a few things that came from Dr. Peter Wells, which was what I was looking for right now. There were orders for various tests and medications, MRI and CAT scans, which told me nothing, and the certificate of death itself. I'd probably gotten a copy five years before, or Mom had, but I'd never had the strength to really look at it.

Knowing that Dad was potentially at the other end of this search, I took in a deep breath and steeled myself. It wasn't like I wasn't aware he was dead; it was more the idea of mentally bringing back those last days that I dreaded. But this was necessary.

I promise I'll try as hard as I can, but you have to promise to take care of Mom. Okay?

The document, really the copy of the document, was not nearly as official and final a piece of paper as you'd expect. It looked very much like an innkeeper's license (my own point of reference) or a certificate of divorce (see above). At the bottom was the signature of the attending physician, Dr. P. Wells. The cause of death was listed as cancer. That plain and that simple.

I could have saved myself the trouble; there wasn't anything especially helpful here. I searched through the envelope again, saw nothing else, then got up and walked back to the records department and to Roberta's station. She glanced up, looking puzzled.

"I really appreciate your help," I said. "Just one thing: There's no autopsy report in the folder."

She looked at me for a moment, trying to assess exactly how stupid this woman in front of her might be. "That's right," she said. "There was no autopsy."

"No?"

Roberta shook her head. "Of course not. The attending physician was present in the hospital room at the time of death. There was no sign of foul play. The police weren't called. The cause of death was known. Unless you or another family member had requested it, there was no reason for an autopsy."

I thanked Roberta again, mentally rejecting the idea of trying to give her a tip, and left the hospital, once again wrapping myself up in the nineteen layers of clothing that felt like they added a half ton to my overall weight. I walked to the parking lot and got into the Volvo, which was probably thrilled with the weather, a reminder of its childhood in Sweden.

But before I drove away, I texted Mom, "Get Maxie to check up on Dr. Wells."

Twenty-six

I picked Melissa up at school and drove home, a place I felt like I hadn't been in a very long time. We found Mom there with Paul and Maxie in the kitchen. My mother was already cooking, despite my having said I'd make dinner tonight for the large contingency coming to the show. Mom had seen me struggle with cooking before and was making a preemptive strike.

I had spent the drive home on the phone with Murray Feldner, who once again seemed not to understand why he shouldn't be paid for something he hadn't done. When I suggested I would be happy to pay him for not plowing my sidewalk if he would agree not to charge me when he did, he did not find the humor in my suggestion.

"I don't get it, Alison. We agreed on the rate when you called me the first time."

"That's for plowing, Murray. You're charging me for *not* plowing."

"Look," he said, clearly on the road himself because

there was a police siren in my phone and not in my vicinity, "if you don't want to honor our agreement, I don't see how we can honor your contract."

Melissa saw the look on my face and become very engrossed in her science notebook. It was the wonders of the Milky Way galaxy all the way home.

Once there, Melissa stood by the stove and observed my mother closely. She loved watching Mom cook, probably because it was such a novel sight for her. Again, I hoped for Melissa's sake that she'd inherit some of Mom's skills in that area.

Mom asked if there had been any further progress since we'd spoken. I didn't want to mention my suspicion that Dr. Wells had had more to do with Dad's death than simply signing the paperwork. The fact that Dr. Wells had been the only one in the room when Dad died, and that neither Mom nor I had requested an autopsy, would have made Mom feel guilty, and that wasn't necessary. Whatever had happened to Dad, it certainly hadn't been her fault.

"Nothing we didn't already know," I said, which was technically true. Paul gave me a look that indicated he didn't believe me, but he inclined his head toward Mom, who was concentrating on the stove, and I nodded back. We'd talk later.

"Did you find anything on Dr. Wells?" I asked Maxie. Mom's brow wrinkled a little, but I couldn't completely hide my questions. She seemed to understand; she said nothing.

"Haven't had much time to look," Maxie answered, a green visor appearing on her head, her hair moving back to form a bun. "But he wasn't ever sued for malpractice or anything like that. What is it you want me to find?"

I was saved from having to tell her I didn't know the answer to the question because Nan and Morgan Henderson arrived, and from the canary-eating grin on Morgan's face, had clearly unearthed some new information. As always when there was a police officer (or former police officer) around, Paul paid extra attention and Maxie looked bored.

"Okay, out with it," I told Morgan. "I take it you had a good day?"

"Better than good," Morgan said. "I think we have some stuff that will help. You'll probably be able to make an arrest in a day or two."

"I'm private, Morgan. I couldn't make an arrest if the killer showed up in my living room and confessed." (Not that it had never happened . . .) "But I get what you mean."

Nan and Morgan took stools by the center island. I put out a plate of celery, carrots and slices of apple with a savory dip (it said it was savory on the package I'd picked up at the convenience store on the way home) and gave them drinks. Nan nibbled, but Morgan was too excited to eat, it seemed.

"I spoke to Chief Daniels in Monroe," he began. "He was more open with me than Officer Warrell was with you. The fact is, this group of actors has something of a reputation. It seems all the active adult communities like to book them, and it's not because they put on such a great show."

"It's because someone in the New Old Thespians has a connection to illegal blue pills," I said. "The question was who snitched about the Viagra."

Morgan pointed at me and nodded his head, acknowledging my guess. Mom turned and gave Melissa a worried glance. Mom sometimes thinks I let Liss sit in on conversations I shouldn't, but since Mom's code of never thinking I do anything wrong is ingrained in her cerebral cortex, she can't admit that, so she never says anything.

"Not just Viagra," Morgan said. "A number of different prescriptions. The word is that *someone* can acquire a number of different drugs, not necessarily prescribed for the seniors in the communities, and when the actors come to put on their show, whoever it is can deliver the goods. So to speak."

"Did the Monroe cops find out who the connection is?"

I asked. Paul nodded approvingly at the question; it was what he wanted to know, too. We both figured it was Frances or Jerry, but you had to be able to prove such things.

But Morgan frowned and he shook his head. "They'd gotten this tip it was either Frances Walters or Jerry Rasmussen"—bingo!—"but they didn't find any pills on them or anything else on any of the company members."

"Ask him if they searched the residents who attended the show," Paul suggested, so I passed it along.

Morgan looked impressed with my—that is, Paul's—question. "No, and that was interesting," he said. "I asked Chief Daniels about that, and he seemed embarrassed. They couldn't arrest someone for possession of Viagra without finding the stash, so it's possible the cops looking for a bust didn't bother because they didn't think it would do them any good."

"If they were looking for a bust, they were in the right place," Maxie grinned. Everyone (who could see her) glared at her, and she put a hand to her mouth. "I mean, hey, they *were* all naked," she added. We all went back to looking at Morgan, who didn't appear to have noticed.

"I also did some checking on some of the other people you mentioned, through the state police databases," Morgan said. "Penny—not Penelope, mind you—Fields has never been arrested but was fingerprinted once when she was teaching a class at a public school in Westfield, which requires it. She didn't appear to have a record of any kind."

"Wait," I said, and told him that I'd discovered (through my diligent detective work, of course, and not from a ghost) that Penny and Lawrence had been involved romantically but that Lawrence was not a candidate for Viagra use because of his previous heart condition.

"I'm not blaming anybody for the investigation," I said. "I'm looking for someone to blame for Lawrence Laurentz's death."

"Then you might want to take a look at this Tyra Carter,"

Morgan suggested. And then he told me everything I already knew about Tyra, which he'd managed to get through use of the police computers in Monroe, and added, "When he was a guy, he was a pretty bad guy. Six arrests, no jail time, but he did break a guy's jaw once."

"What about Jerry Rasmussen and Frances Walters?" I asked.

"Rasmussen worked for thirty years for Johnson & Johnson in New Brunswick," Morgan said, referring to a notepad he took out of his back pocket. "Something to do with marketing for the consumer products division. They don't make Viagra, by the way. Married once, divorced after three years, has a son, no arrest records on him and no fingerprints before the arrest for public nudity. Joined this theater group six years ago, became its manager and"— here he mimed quotes— 'artistic director' two years ago. Not really a guy you like for the crime, if there was a crime. Same with Ms. Walters. Born Frances Nussbaum, married Philip Walters, who died a few years back, and Frances moved where she is now. Two sons: Barry, a pharmacist and Mark, an accountant. Barry lives in Livingston, Mark in Flagstaff, Arizona. Again, no prints on Frances; no record, and she never worked in a public school or other profession that would require it.

"They've both been as close to off the radar as you can get, just by not misbehaving."

Mom checked her pot roast one last time and walked to the island, wiping her hands on a dish towel. "So there's really no evidence that anyone killed Larry." Mom apparently had now appointed herself a member of the detective agency I had been striving not to create.

"That's right," Morgan agreed. "We might have some suspects, but we have no proof at all."

That was hardly encouraging.

Jeannie and Tony arrived a few minutes later, carrying Oliver in the requisite car seat, just as Melissa was helping me set the kitchen table, the only one in the house large enough to accommodate all of us. We got them up to speed on the Laurentz investigation, leaving out the odd messages left in my house. Once Oliver was happily ensconced in a baby swing I'd discovered in my basement among the toys I'd never gotten rid of (although Jeannie seemed slightly less happy, presumably counting ways this contraption could somehow be harmful to her son), Tony went back to contemplate the library doorway, looking for inspiration.

The kitchen was quiet for a while, everyone was in one way or another lost in thought. Okay, Maxie was changing her toenail color every few seconds, but each of us has his or her unique method of thinking.

Tony walked back in, shaking his head. "I just don't see any way around those beams in your doorway," he said. "I mean, it could be done, but not within your budget."

"You're just trying to get out of our deal," I teased him.

He raised an eyebrow. "Never."

Just then the doorbell rang. It was the moment I'd been anticipating and in some ways dreading—Josh's arrival and introduction to my motley crew—and my stomach turned around a couple of times as I walked to the door, having let Melissa know I'd handle this one myself (kids love to open the front door and will let absolutely anyone in).

Josh stood on the doorstep holding two bottles of wine, one white, one red.

"I didn't know what we were eating," he said. "So I brought both."

"You should have drunk them both," I told him. "You don't know what you're in for." He grinned and we walked inside. He must have thought I was kidding.

Josh didn't even look all that overwhelmed when the throng, which had moved into the den, descended upon us like teenage girls around the Beatles in *A Hard Day's Night*. There was slightly less screaming but only because Jeannie was busy changing Oliver as a ploy to get him out of the "dangerous" swing. Melissa waited until Josh's attention was elsewhere and gave me a thumbs-up, which was befitting someone of her age but not her maturity level. Mom winked, which I won't even discuss.

Introductions were made all around, except for the ghosts, for obvious reasons—though Maxie continued to look at Josh the way she might have looked at a juicy steak when she was alive (I'm assuming).

Paul, who has had jealousy issues whenever I have shown even passing interest in a breathing man, hovered in a corner and stroked his goatee, but he did not look particularly peeved, which was really all I'd have asked.

Nan and Morgan were cordial. Morgan was probably catching every other sentence, since ambient noise is a problem even with hearing aids, and stood there with a fake smile plastered on his face while Nan exchanged the requisite pleasantries. Tony assessed Josh coolly. He tends to act like a father figure when I least require one, but he smiled and shook Josh's hand, apparently deeming his grip acceptable. I'm not sure, but I think Josh probably expected someone to check his teeth by now. So far, things were going fine. Being me, I expected to hear an entire Payless store drop shoes any second.

We grow sunny dispositions in New Jersey.

Mom had timed the dinner perfectly, and we sat down to pot roast, sautéed onions, asparagus, salad (I had contributed by putting baby carrots on top, the one thing Mom trusted me to do), rice pilaf and sourdough bread. Still, she apologized for, as she put it, "the rushed dinner."

"It's delicious, Mrs. Kerby," Josh volunteered. "I can't imagine anything being better prepared." His parents were right; he was wasting his talents in the paint store. He should have been involved somehow in diplomacy.

Mom blushed.

"What version of *Peter Pan* is the one they're doing?"

Melissa wanted to know, perhaps trying to give Josh a break from the constant scrutiny. She's a sensitive girl.

"It's one Jerry Rasmussen wrote himself," I told her, omitting the eye-rolling that Lawrence had performed when passing the information on to me. "Apparently he writes music and lyrics, too." Okay, so it was hard not to eye-roll.

"Uh-oh," Jeannie intoned. She was letting Tony feed Oliver, because Jeannie eats first. That's the deal. You don't get between Jeannie and her dinner. I've been there when some have tried; it wasn't pretty. That's all I'm saying.

"Keep an open mind," Mom said, sounding close to sincere. "You never know."

I would have joined in, but as good as Mom's cooking is, my stomach was still a little nervous while I watched Josh take in the scene.

"I can't imagine what this one sees in you," Maxie helpfully told me from her perch just to Josh's right. "He cleans up nice."

"Are you a big *Peter Pan* fan, Melissa?" Josh asked. Rule number one of dating a single mom: Show interest in the child. Well played.

"Not really," Liss told him. "I'm more of a Star Trek fan. Or Harry Potter."

Josh nodded. "Both good."

Morgan, who had complimented Mom's dinner (as had everyone else), found his way back into the conversation, clearly having missed much of what was being said. "Here's what we should be looking for tonight," he said out of the blue. "Any signs of tension between the group members would be interesting. But we also want to see if any of them tries to get some residents aside and talk privately."

I immediately looked to Josh. You never know how a guy will react to talk of cases and suspects. Some might be, let's say, a little put off by the idea of a woman they're dating being involved with violence and crime. They might feel the need to be the "protector" or to feel threatened that the woman is more macho than they might be.

He was intent and hanging on every word, like it was the best movie he'd ever seen.

"That would mean they were probably trying to sell some drugs, right?" Melissa asked. Criticize my parenting. I dare you. She's intelligent and interested. Hasn't had a nightmare in three years. Go ahead.

Morgan nodded. He didn't seem at all fazed that the question had come from a ten-year-old. To him, everybody thought like a cop, or should. "But I don't want you anywhere near that, Melissa. You tell me or Nan or your mom if that happens, and we'll deal with it, okay?" Liss nodded earnestly; she was going to follow Morgan's orders because he commanded respect, and because she really was a smart kid who knew enough to be wary of anything shady.

"Also," Morgan continued, "I want you, Alison, to talk to Rasmussen and Tyra Carter, just so I can see their faces when you do."

"I'm not sure I want to ask Tyra anything even a little bit touchy," I said, having cleaned my plate and noting that others had done the same. I nodded to Melissa, and we began to clear the table. We'd decided on no dessert right now, with the possibility of something after the play if it wasn't too late.

Josh asked no questions. He hadn't heard some of these names before, but he was taking it all in. I assumed he'd ask me later what he needed to know.

"You don't have to ask her anything about Laurentz," Morgan told me. "I just want to see her manner when you approach." Paul, wanting as always to learn from a more experienced professional, pursed his lips—this was something he hadn't thought of before.

"Anything I should do, Morgan?" Jeannie asked. She was getting a little bit too into this detective sideline, I was starting to think.

"Watch your baby," Morgan answered. Shockingly, Jeannie looked a little disappointed. "If a situation arises, I'll be sure to let you know what to do. That goes for everybody else here." Josh looked a touch surprised, but he didn't say anything and helped, over objections from Mom and myself, to clear the table and load the dishwasher. "You should all be watching for anything unusual, and let Alison or me know about it," Morgan concluded.

"Should we get going?" Mom asked.

Many coats, sweaters and other garments were donned, and the party headed for my Volvo and Tony and Jeannie's minivan. Paul stopped me as we were starting out, and called me over toward him.

"One last thing you need to watch," he said quietly. "Try to keep Melissa with Jeannie and Tony, and away from the others. Make the seating seem as if it's a coincidence these people are all together."

That sounded ominous. "Why?" I asked.

Paul looked just as ominous as he sounded. "Because none of the Thespians have ever seen you with anyone except your mother or Jeannie before. If someone there is a killer, and they think you're getting too close, they'll look to see who means something to you. Those are your weak spots, and they can be exploited."

I quickly tried to think of a way to dissuade Melissa from going, but there was no way she'd be talked out of it. I'd make sure she stayed close to Mom and away from me. "Gee, Paul, thanks a heap for that one," I told the ghost.

"Enjoy the show," he said.

Twenty-seven

It had gotten dark sometime around five that afternoon, and the sky was now that combination of gray and pink that makes you think snow is on the way, though there was none in the forecast. The front gate at Brookside Assisted Living Facility was less of a wrought-iron cliché and more like the tollbooth at a rather sedate theme park. I gave my name to the young man in a polo shirt sitting in the little structure, he pushed a button and the gate in front of us rose up to let me drive through. The same thing had happened a moment before with Jeannie's minivan, and she was waiting for me to go through to push on ahead, having gotten directions from the polo shirt guy.

"Why do they call this place Brookside?" Melissa wanted to know as I drove the Volvo through the gate. "I don't see a brook."

"Well, my development is called Whispering Lakes," Mom pointed out. "There are no lakes there, either."

"It's just a name, Liss," I said. "It sounds nice, that's

all." I had lost the argument in which Liss was to ride in Jeannie's van in case anyone was watching when we got out. She wanted to stay with me, Mom and Josh, mostly because she wanted a less crowded venue to vet Josh. My daughter doesn't miss a trick.

For his part, Josh had kept up the conversation, but it was clear he saw I was on edge and was waiting until we were alone to ask what was wrong. I had to put on a better show to convince him that it had nothing to do with him, which it didn't.

"Maybe there's a brook in the back," Mom suggested. We drove on.

Melissa thought it strange that I kept standing in front of her as we got out of the van, and then seemed to abandon her into the custody of Jeannie and Tony (Frances and Jerry knew Mom) once we walked into the clubhouse, a large, more or less octagonal building at the front of the facility. A sign directly out of someone's home printer was taped to the door—"*Peter Pan* by the New Old Thespians"—and listed the date and time.

Inside, I strode rapidly ahead, to put distance between me and Liss and Mom. Josh kept pace with me but took the opportunity to ask, "Should I not have come? Am I going to be in the way?"

"No!" I said a little too loud. "I was afraid you were thinking that. No. It just . . . occurred to me that if the killer is here tonight . . ."

"You don't want to be seen too close to Melissa. Very smart. Do you think Lawrence really was murdered?" Josh had increased his pace when I'd explained, and now I was having just a little trouble keeping up with him through the corridor to the auditorium.

"The only thing I know for sure on this one is that I don't know anything for sure on this one," I said. Josh grinned. I was starting to really like that grin.

"This sounds like fun," he said.

Frances Walters was the first familiar face I saw when we got to the auditorium, which appeared to have doubled as the dining room. A stage of sorts, really, as Jerry had said, risers put up at one end of the room, stood in front of a good number of folding chairs, most of which were empty at the moment. The residents appeared to have left the front three rows almost empty, perhaps so they could leave more quickly if the show turned out to be a stinker. I gestured—surreptitiously, I hoped—to Jeannie for her to find seats for Melissa and herself, then walked to Frances. Mom walked over, having seen that Frances's face showed recognition. Josh walked to one side of the room and leaned against a post, looking casual.

"I'd heard you were bringing some people," Frances told me. She assessed the crowd, which consisted mostly of Brookside residents, many in wheelchairs and not a few with oxygen tanks. "I didn't realize your mother would be one of them."

Mom smiled and nodded at Frances. "It's nice to see you again," she said. "I never knew you were a star."

Frances laughed. "Oh, don't be silly. I'm just an aging chorine." But she looked just a tad annoyed when neither of us contradicted her on the point. "I'm glad you came with so many people," she went on finally. "My son was going to fly in for this, but he had an emergency."

"Which son?" Mom asked. "The accountant or the pharmacist?"

"The accountant, can you believe it?" Frances answered. "Who knew there could be an accounting emergency?"

"It's too bad he couldn't make it," I said. "But I'm sure he's seen you perform before, no?"

"Oh yes," Frances responded. "He's seen us many times. Both of my boys have been here for shows."

"It's an interesting idea for a show," Mom noted. "*Peter Pan* for senior citizens?"

"Oh, you'll love it," she said. "Jerry's written a great

show. He took the original story of *Peter Pan* and adapted it for a more mature audience." She must have seen the look on my face as I fought the urge to glance at Melissa and laughed. "Oh, not *that* kind of mature! You'll see; it's more appropriate for the audiences we usually get. How is your investigation of Larry's death going?"

I told her that I'd made some progress—let her pass *that* around the company—but wasn't specific. "A lot of it has to do with the setup of his apartment," I lied, thinking of the only thing that would make it sound technical. "Were you ever there?"

"Never. Not even sure where it was." Frances shook her head. "But I'm certainly familiar with the units in our development." she said. "Except I guess now there's no toaster in the kitchen." She shivered at the thought.

"The poor man," Mom said.

I had to give Frances something to spread around the crew, particularly Jerry. "I think I'll be able to make a definite statement about what happened very soon," I responded, although I thought the exact opposite of that. I had pegged Frances as the source of information (aka gossip) for the New Old Thespians; I figured a few bits of misinformation placed just so might spur a little reaction. She appeared to take the bait, eyes widening just a touch.

"That's really exciting," she said. "Care to give me a sneak peak?"

"Play nice, Frances. You'll get the skinny when I can give it. Just keep it quiet. I promise you'll be the first, okay?"

She seemed pleased with that, then "remembered" something she had to do (which was probably to pass my "secrets" along to the rest of the troupe), excused herself and went backstage.

"Please don't stand near me or Melissa," I said to Mom once she was gone. "I don't know who's dangerous here."

"You're not letting me help," Mom protested.

"Getting one of us—especially Liss—in the sights of a

killer isn't going to help," I countered. Mom pouted but went to a seat at the far end of Tony. Melissa looked a little puzzled that her grandmother wasn't sitting next to her but did not protest, since Mom wasn't making a fuss over Oliver, either.

Josh walked over, not too casually, and pretended to introduce himself in case anyone was watching. He shook my hand.

"Nice to meet you," he said. "Which one was that?"

"Frances Walters. And she's backstage right now passing on everything I told her was in confidence, just as I planned."

"You're very smart," he said. It seemed I was fooling everyone I needed to tonight. Looking just over my left shoulder, Josh smiled again and said loudly, "Really! I could have sworn I met you at the Steam Fitters Convention in Atlantic City!"

I turned and saw Jerry Rasmussen was approaching. Behind him, Jeannie, Tony, Oliver, Nan and Morgan were settling into front-row seats, probably to accommodate Morgan's hearing, although he was hardly the only one in the room with such difficulties. Jerry held out his hand and took mine as if we were old friends.

"Alison!" he gushed. "I'm so pleased to see you!" He gave Josh a look that was something other than adoring. "Who's your friend?"

Josh missed a beat, then chuckled. "Oh, we just met!" he said, extending his hand so Jerry would have to let go of mine. "I'm Michael Ellis. Stanhope Pipe Fitting. And you are?"

Jerry straightened like a soldier brought to attention. "Jerome K. Rasmussen," he said.

"The one who wrote tonight's production?" Josh said, looking as awed as if being introduced to Abraham Lincoln. "It's an honor, sir."

"Wrote *and* directed," Jerry corrected, but he was smiling

broadly. "So nice of you to say, Mr. Ellis." He gestured toward me. "Might I have just a word with Alison?"

"Of course!" Josh held up his hands in contrition. "I should take my seat, anyway, shouldn't I? Again, a great pleasure to meet you!" He backed away. I thought it a small triumph that he didn't salaam as he went. "Nice to meet you, too, Ms. Kerby." He went to a seat two rows behind Mom and Melissa and put his coat down on the one next to him, no doubt saving it for me.

"What a nice young man," Jerry said. "Now, may I ask about your investigation?"

What, you haven't gotten the six thirty news from Frances yet? "I can't tell you much," I said, and then proceeded to tell him everything I had told Frances, adding, "I think it was clearly not a simple heart attack." That covered my bases, since it would be true even if Lawrence had died of natural causes; an arrhythmia is not a heart attack. But it gave Jerry that little extra nugget of information that might make him feel he'd gotten something out of me more than I might have entrusted to Frances. I wasn't sure this was getting me anywhere, but it was a strategy Paul had endorsed, so I was playing it through to the end.

And suddenly it seemed to pay off a dividend. "Oh, my," Jerry said. "That's very distressing." But he didn't look the least bit distressed until he spotted Penny Fields, whom I wasn't even aware would be here tonight, entering the auditorium. Interesting; I hadn't realized these two knew each other. "I really must go backstage. We go on in five minutes." Jerry nodded at me, then turned to walk away. Suddenly, as if getting an idea on the spot, he turned back and asked, "Would you like to watch from the wings? You might get a more 'inside' look from back there." I got a very strong vibe that he wouldn't mind getting me away from Penny, either.

I thought it over, noting that it would help keep me from being seen with Melissa and would also get me closer to some of the other suspects, so I said, "That would be exciting! May I meet you back there in a minute? I'd like to get a bottle of water first."

Jerry looked quickly at Penny, who hadn't seen him yet, and nodded. "Certainly," he said, wiping his forehead. He was gone backstage before I could blink twice.

I walked near where Josh was sitting and dropped my glove next to him. While bending over to pick it up, I told him I would be going backstage for the performance, then added, "Michael Ellis?"

"It's from a Monty Python sketch," he said. "It's a man who is never seen."

"I know what it's from. I'm impressed." I stood up with the glove in my hand and casually added, still not looking at Josh, "Keep an eye on Mom and Melissa, would you?"

"Sure." He barely opened his mouth saying it. No questions, no arguments.

I thanked him with my eyes and walked down to the front row, where Jeannie was bouncing Oliver on her knee, Tony was going through the diaper bag and Nan and Morgan were watching opposite sides of the stage, occasionally turning to scan the crowd. The couple that surveils together stays together.

"See anything interesting?" I asked Morgan, who did not break his pattern to look me in the eye. "Break the case wide open yet?"

"Not yet," he answered. "But I am wondering who the younger woman in the red and white striped top is in the back."

"That's Penny Fields," I told him. "Strange that she's here, don't you think?"

He tilted his head: "Maybe, maybe not. Could just be because one of her employees is in the cast and one of her ex-employees is working backstage. Show some support." Then he finally looked me in the eyes. "But I doubt it."

I told them I'd be in the wings for the performance.

Jeannie held Oliver close to her, probably hoping he'd be asleep soon.

"Do you want me to come with you?" Tony asked. "In case something happens?"

"Nice try," Jeannie told him, "but you're staying out here with me and your son."

"I really don't think it's necessary," I answered him. Oliver's eyelids were dropping, and he put his head down on Jeannie's chest, fading. "But I asked Josh to keep an eye on Mom and Melissa. Would you look out for them, too?"

Jeannie grinned. "Yeah. Josh."

"Stop it," I told her.

"Uh-huh." The woman could squeeze more innuendo out of a nonword than most could find in five paragraphs. It's an art.

"He seems like a very nice young man," Nan said, still scanning the crowd.

"Ten o'clock," Morgan told her. I was about to tell him it was much earlier than that when I saw Nan turn her head to that vantage point, and my eye followed. Tyra Carter had stuck her head out of the stage right wings. "Is that . . . ?"

"Yeah, that's Tyra," I said. "Probably looking to see if I'm talking to Penny and convincing her to give Tyra her job back."

"Maybe you should go talk to Penny," Morgan said quietly.

"What?"

"Let's kick the beehive a little. See what happens."

I wasn't sure I wanted to know what would happen. "Easy for you to say," I answered.

"You've got enough backup here," Morgan nudged.

I didn't say anything, but I walked back—past Josh, who looked perplexed—to Penny and said hello. I fought the urge to look at Tyra, but Penny, standing next to her last-row-on-the-aisle seat, was clearly looking over my shoulder.

"What brings you to the show tonight?" I asked her.

"Well, Frances has been talking about it. But mostly I'm here because of what you said," Penny answered, and if that hadn't already thrown me off, what she said next definitely would have. "I'm giving Tyra her job back like you suggested, and I knew she'd be here tonight, so I came to give her the good news."

"Can I sit down?" I asked. Penny gestured to go ahead, and we took the two last seats in the house. Literally. "Why did you decide to do that?"

"She called me after she talked to you. For some reason, she thought it was your fault I hadn't rehired her."

"Imagine," I said.

"I told her you had nothing to do with it. I hadn't even realized she wanted to come back before you said something," Penny went on, possibly not noticing my comment. "And once we spoke, I understood how badly she wanted it. I told her I'd think about it, and now that I have, I'm going to hire her back on a trial basis and see if things have changed."

Having digested that piece of information, I was ready to press on. "That's not the only reason you're here," I told Penny. Matter-of-fact. As if I were sure. "This isn't your first time here; you're a regular at the troupe's performances, aren't you?"

Penny blushed a little and looked toward the stage. "How did you know that?"

"The way Jerry Rasmussen looked at you when you came in. He knew you well. Was it because of Lawrence Laurentz?"

She nodded. "I think Larry would want me to see what the group was up to. He really loved the theater, you know, and even after they . . . after he had to leave the group, he kept tabs on what they were doing. I'm just keeping up for him. How did you know about Larry and me?"

I didn't want to risk Tyra's impending reemployment and I couldn't tell her that Lawrence had confirmed it for me himself. "I can't divulge my sources," I said. That's really more true of reporters than detectives, but people don't know that. "But that whole story about going to fire him was a lie, wasn't it?"

From the corner of my eye, I saw Frances and Jerry standing in the aisle, talking to Mom, who had separated from the group, perhaps to avoid sitting next to Melissa while the lights were up. The three of them were laughing about something.

Penny looked up at the stage. "No, that was real, but I'd fired him three nights before. Larry really could be a very dear man when he wanted to be, you know," she said. "He was older than me, but we bonded. I really did have some very warm feelings for him. We had two relationships, a professional one and a . . . personal one, and they were separate. I miss him." She looked like she might cry.

"I'm sure he was very nice," I said, since I was never supposed to have met Lawrence. I spotted Jerry looking out from the wings—the side opposite where Tyra had been a few minutes earlier, and I stood up. "I think I'd better get back there," I said. "Thanks for getting Tyra off my back."

Penny smiled. "No problem."

I walked down the aisle to the foot of the stage, then up a few stairs to the stage itself and immediately to the right to get back to the wings. Sure enough, Jerry Rasmussen was standing there waiting for me.

"That must have been some water bottle," he said.

Twenty-eight

🗝

The play began almost immediately upon my arrival backstage. I'd scarcely gotten my bearings and was still trying to find a place that wouldn't be in someone's way, when the "orchestra"—a lovely little man who must have been in his eighties playing a spinet piano to one side of the stage—struck up what I'm sure Jerry would have called "the overture."

Jerry was so busy giving orders to cast and crew that I don't think he heard a note of the music. He was one of the lucky ones. It was, in a word, awful.

The scene backstage was just short of chaos: It was a small cast, consisting of Frances as Wendy, a guy named Morris as Peter Pan, a flashlight as Tinker Bell, Jerry himself as Captain Hook, a woman called Marjorie as Mr. (?) Smee, and assorted chorus members. When I say "assorted," I mean three.

The only stage crew member was Tyra, but when you had Tyra, you didn't really need anyone else. She was holding a ladder with one arm and what appeared to be a doghouse with the other. I decided to approach her with the good news from Penny, since having a happy Tyra backstage with me was greatly preferable to an angry Trya.

I sidled over to her. "Do you have a second?" I said softly.

"I have a cue coming up," she hissed back, watching the stage. "What do you want?"

"Penny's giving you your job back," I said. "It wasn't my . . ."

"*Seriously?*" Tyra said in a louder, excited tone, drawing a glare from Jerry. "How did you do that?"

"I didn't," I explained. "She just told me when I saw her, and I thought you'd want to know. So we're good, right?"

The piano playing stopped and the curtain (some window treatments raised on PVC piping the Thespians appeared to have brought with them) started to rise (Jerry pulled the string on one side). "Gotta go," Tyra said, and ran onto the stage with the ladder and the doghouse, which she placed strategically where the curtain had met the stage. She exited to the other side of the stage, so we couldn't continue the conversation.

That forced me to watch the show. Talking to Angry Tyra would have been preferable.

From my vantage point in the wings, I could see the stage right side of the audience, the left side if you were facing the stage. I had learned this during the Harbor Haven High School production of *Pippin* some twenty years earlier. From here I could see Mom, Melissa and Josh, but not the Hendersons or Jeannie and Tony. I assumed Oliver was asleep, since I heard no crying from the front of the house.

The dialogue was audible but not decipherable. Apparently Jerry had "adapted" the classic tale of the boy who wouldn't grow up by turning it into the story of a woman named Wendy who was born a senior citizen, decided it was fabulous and refused to "grow down." When she meets

Peter Pan, who is—elbow in the ribs, nudge nudge—a never-aging peanut butter tycoon (I am not making a word of this up), Wendy, dressed in an "old lady" dress slit up the side and tights to "show off the gams," Frances had told me, tries to convince him that "it's way cool to be old" via a series of sketches and songs that had nothing to do with each other, aside from the fact that they were all terrible. Mr. Pan, I could only assume, would learn his lesson and wrinkle up stat to join in the fun.

The songs—because there is no other word for them—were on a par with the rest of the production, sad to say. But every time I looked over at Jerry when he wasn't onstage in the role of Captain Hook, a Somali pirate—I'll give you a moment—he was beaming. Clearly, the production was exactly what he'd envisioned when he sat down to write this catastrophe.

I gave a glance to the crowd of about fifty. (Well, actually about a hundred, if you counted the ghosts floating around the room.) Melissa seemed to be stifling a good number of laughs, and Mom appeared more horrified by some of the script's more blatant land mines. One, describing Neverland as "a place where everyone is on Medicare," was especially unnerving.

Josh had his hand shading his eyes, either trying not to see what was going on in front of him or attempting to conceal the fact that he was dozing off.

At one point in the first act, Wendy tried to convince Peter Pan to come with her to Managed Care Heaven and burst into a song that must have been called "In Flight" only because previous versions had used up "You Can Fly" and "I'm Flyin'." Frances warbled:

> *We can soar*
> *Don't be a bore*
> *Come along with me*
> *To maturi—ty!*

I'll spare you the rest; suffice it to say, the point of the song was that they could take to the skies and blow this Popsicle stand for a better place where the grandchildren really do call and persimmons are always on sale at the Stop & Shop. I saw Tyra shift into high gear, indicating that a "special effect" was about to take place. She picked up a fishing rod—no kidding—and headed to the edge of the wings just this side of where she might be seen by the audience.

Frances did a couple of Rockettes kicks, having been handed a top hat and cane by Tyra on her last pass, and sang about the exciting trip she and Morris were about to take. As the piano pounded away, she led him around the back of a stage flat painted with a window full of starry skies.

From the wings, Tyra cast the fishing rod. Attached to the end was a heavy cutout, perhaps made of sheet metal because it didn't flutter or fold and seemed to have weight, of "Wendy" and "Peter Pan" flying off toward Neverland, where the early bird special is offered all night. With practiced precision—Jerry had told me this was the third time they'd performed this particular theatrical gem—Tyra manipulated the cutout into the space where the stage flat's window showed the moon, and the dark cutout set against the "glowing" moon actually made for an effect that was sort of neat. If Frances hadn't been offstage, singing, "We can be back in time for canasta," it might have been a nice little moment.

The act ended when the song was put out of its misery, so the "curtain" came down and the audience's sparse applause indicated there were people in the auditorium who actually liked the show. I guessed we'd see a smaller crowd when the curtain rose for act 2.

The intermission was going to be exactly fifteen minutes, Jerry told me in no uncertain terms, so I had to do a good deal of detecting quickly. It would have been better if Paul had been there, because I wasn't really all that sure of what to ask or to whom I should be putting the questions. "Just observe as much as you can," he'd say. "You'll learn more when people don't think you're trying to learn anything."

Taking this imaginary advice, I looked out past the end of the curtain to check on my entourage first; Mom had walked down to Jeannie and the others, and they were clearly quite amused by the production. Liss especially was laughing as they no doubt relived some of the particularly excruciating elements of act 1. Morgan had stood and was pretending to stretch for the intermission, but I knew he was scanning the crowd. He seemed interested at one point in something near the back of the house, which I couldn't see from my vantage point. Josh hadn't joined them but was instead standing near the rear of the auditorium, leaning in a corner opposite where Morgan was watching, observing. I could bet he would be reporting back to me later.

Mostly, it looked like Josh was watching Penny Fields, who was sitting quietly in her seat, doing something with a smartphone in her hand. I hadn't pegged Penny as a heavy app user, but you never could figure people.

Given the short time I had, I figured it was best to let my operatives (I had decided to think of them that way) do their work and concentrate on my own backstage. Before I could head for Frances or Jerry, though, Tyra came bounding over and stopped me in my tracks.

"Penny texted me!" she crowed. "You were right—I get my job back." Then her face darkened a bit. "But only on a trial basis."

Uh-oh. "So what does that mean?" I asked as if I didn't understand the term.

"If they don't like what I'm doing, they'll fire me again," Tyra said with a moan. She could go from exultant to miserable in a nanosecond.

I didn't like Tyra when she was miserable. "Well, you do good work. They won't have any reason to fire you," I encouraged her.

She looked skeptical. "They didn't like it when I was doing the tire thing at the same time."

"So you won't do that again."

"I *have* to," Tyra said. "I need the extra money."

I looked behind her. "Oh, there's Frances. I should go tell her how much I'm enjoying her performance." And I bolted past Tyra before she could find a way to blame me again.

Frances, in costume already for the second act (since she wore the same thing throughout), had a bottle of water in her hand and was talking to herself when I reached her. I debated addressing her, since she seemed engrossed in preparation for the second act, but she spotted me and approached.

"Alison! What do you think?"

I was afraid people would ask me that, so I'd prepared an answer. "Oh, you're marvelous, Frances!" I said. "Your professional experience is really showing."

"Thank you," she agreed. "Jerry gives us such wonderful material. You know, we haven't deviated one word from his text. He's so creative."

That was one way to put it. "The effects are very interesting," I said, moving off the subject of "the text." "Did Tyra create them herself?"

"Oh no, that's Jerry again," Frances said. "On nights that Tyra's not here . . ." She lowered her voice. "You know, she doesn't have the commitment some of us do; but, anyway, when she's not here, Jerry works most of the effects himself."

Now that *was* interesting, because that fishing-rod thing had given me an idea about how Lawrence's "invisible" person might have dropped a toaster on him. "No kidding," I said. It was a placeholder.

"Oh yes. He practices all of them over and over until he knows they'll work."

"So you don't have to be as strong as Tyra to handle them," I said.

Frances shook her head. "Oh no. Even I can do them if I have to, but I've never done it in performance."

I thanked her and moved on to where Jerry was addressing the chorus. "Don't drop your consonants!" he scolded. "This audience probably can't hear half of what you're singing, so you have to enunciate even more severely!" The group of performers, mostly in their sixties and seventies, looked properly chastised.

There was no time to react when Jerry suddenly turned toward me. "So! What do you think of the experience, Alison?"

That was going to be tough to dodge. "Being backstage is very exciting!" I tried. "I love seeing how everything works."

Jerry's eyes sharpened. "What do you think of the *show*?" he asked. Being blunt and to the point; how was that fair?

My mind raced, and the best I could come up with was, "I've been so busy watching all the excitement back here, it's been hard for me to concentrate." Yeah, you try it sometime.

He scowled. "That bad, is it?"

"I'm not a critic," I said. My mother always said, when you can't say something nice, stall.

"How can you say that in the middle of a performance?" Jerry demanded.

"How could you *ask* in the middle of a performance?" I countered. The best defense and all that.

"Do you understand the dynamic of a theatrical troupe?" Jerry went on, loudly enough to turn some heads backstage. "It is a delicate thing, a china cup." He started to advance on me like an invading Visigoth. "One tiny flaw, one scratch, and the *whole thing* can come crashing down!"

Jerry was so incensed that I backed away from him as he walked toward me. We must have looked as awkward as the dances he had no doubt choreographed himself for the production. He actually looked like one of those murderers in the 1940s movie noirs, coming at the camera with hands raised, about to strike (usually by strangulation). I was seriously unnerved.

"You're trying to ruin my play!" Jerry snarled.

"I'm really not," I tried to say, but it came out as a squeak. I was actually thinking, *It doesn't need my help*, but that wouldn't have done much good out loud, either.

I kept backing up, and he kept coming. Vaguely, I became aware of some noise behind me that sounded like people talking and some gasping all of a sudden. I might have heard Jeannie yell, "Hey!" Jerry actually stopped and shouted, "Look out!" And then something weird happened.

There was suddenly no floor under my feet. That came as something of a surprise for the feet in question, I have to tell you, and they didn't take kindly to it. They flailed about for a second while my head seemed to develop an overwhelming interest to inspect the auditorium's ceiling, and I fell backward.

Right into Josh Kaplan's arms.

I don't know where he came from, but suddenly Josh was holding me up, and not a nanosecond too soon. He looked me in the eye with an expression of some perplexity, and said, "What was that about?"

"What . . . where . . . ?" I wasn't at my most coherent. I looked around for Jerry, who was standing at the skirt of the stage, staring down at me. He looked absolutely horrified. "Are you all right?" he asked. Hardly the tone of a man who had been doing his best Hannibal Lecter impression only a moment before.

My posse—that is, the Hendersons, Mom, Melissa, Jeannie and Tony (and Oliver, if you want to count him sleeping in the sling around Jeannie's neck)—swarmed around me. Josh put me down, and my feet were mostly solid on the floor. Mostly. I told them all (including my feet) I was okay, and physically at least, that was true.

From where I was (thankfully) standing, it was obvious

many of the audience members had indeed left (including the deceased ones, as I saw only ten or eleven floating around, and none of them was looking toward the stage). Penny Fields was nowhere to be seen. Back up on the stage, the company had all come out to see what had happened. A chastised Jerry knelt down on the stage and kept asking if I was all right. He apologized a few times, too.

I looked up at Josh. "I'm thinking maybe we can skip the second act," I said.

"Works for me," he answered.

Twenty-nine

As it was getting cold and an actual flurry was beginning to fall, we decided to skip going out for dessert and drive back to the guesthouse in the two vehicles, (I told Melissa I was too shaken up, which was about thirty percent true) and instead stopped at a drive-through Dunkin' Donuts on the way.

Jeannie and Tony dropped off the Hendersons and left to take Oliver home—they said they hadn't seen anything in the auditorium that would help the investigation. I think they just wanted to go home.

The rest of us converged at the front door to the guesthouse. I fumbled for the key, and after a few bone-chilling moments, we were in my front room removing layers and swapping basic reconnaissance. Paul, clearly having been waiting, had started watching through the door (literally—he'd had his front half on the outside and his back half on the inside) before we'd made it inside. Maxie (who had luckily not wanted to go to the show), he told me, was upstairs doing further research on Dr. Wells and said she'd have something soon. I did not impart that information to the Hendersons, and Melissa and Mom had heard it for themselves.

Josh, unaware of the extra participant in the conversation, did what he had done at the performance: He found a spot in the den that was a little detached from the group, stood and observed with a wry expression on his face. He appeared fascinated.

"I didn't see any of the patients there coming up to the performers for drugs," Morgan said, sounding disappointed. "Of course, a lot of them are a little less active than in the communities these people usually play."

"Something was wrong," I said. "I can't put my finger on it, but there was something just off about the whole thing."

"I think it was the show," Melissa suggested, stifling a yawn. She took a bite of the chocolate-frosted doughnut she'd chosen. Eating that doughnut would be the last thing she did before going up to bed, I'd decided, though she didn't know it yet. Best not to provoke the argument too early; it just gives her time to come up with logical ammunition. "It was terrible!" Everyone had a chuckle at that.

"I don't get why Penny Fields was there," I said, giving voice to one of the many things that had been bothering me. "If she really wanted to give Tyra her job back, she could easily have called; she didn't have to show up in person to do it. In fact, when she finally did it, it was by text, anyway."

"There's a bigger picture," Mom suggested. She eschewed the doughnuts but was sipping on a decaf tea I'd brewed. Morgan and Nan had coffee from the Dunkin' Donuts, and Melissa had a white hot chocolate. Yes, I was indulging my daughter. "But I don't think I'm seeing it."

"I'm most interested in the fishing-rod contraption you told us about, Alison," Josh said. "I've seen that kind of equipment used for a lot of different purposes, and some of the fishing line you can buy in sporting goods stores can stand up to very large fish fighting a hook. Does it occur to you that . . ."

"That someone could hook an electric toaster on one and cast it into a bathtub, thus making the person doing the casting 'invisible' to the person in the tub?" I said. Yeah, it had occurred to me. "But if that's the case, why bother? Whoever wanted to kill Lawrence could have just thrown it into the tub or walked in and dropped it. He was going to die, anyway. Why bother to hide yourself from the victim?"

Morgan, who had been eyeing the vanilla crème doughnut but had not partaken, stood from the sofa and raised a finger in contemplation. "Because electrocution is a very tricky way to kill somebody," he said. "You can't be sure it's going to work, even in someone who had a history of minor heart problems like Laurentz did. If it didn't work, and Laurentz had lived, he'd know who tried to kill him and could put them behind bars."

Melissa finished her doughnut and hot chocolate, and I immediately sent her to bed—with a sugar high that potent, suffice it to say the argument was short and to the point, but after her grandmother offered a bribe in the form of another home-cooked dinner the following night, she finally was convinced. I felt properly chastised and resolved to ask my mother for cooking lessons.

Putting my maternal shame aside, I came back down from Melissa's room after giving her a good-night hug and looked at Paul, which was convenient because he was hovering just over Morgan's head, and this way I could get the opinion of both professionals. "So, we have all the conflicting words everybody said and we think we know how somebody killed Lawrence Laurentz," I said. "Now how do we figure out which one did it?"

"It's not the figuring out," Morgan mused. "It's the proving it."

Paul nodded. "We have a lot of testimony and some

good guesswork but absolutely no evidence at all. Even if the ME had done a really thorough autopsy, he would've only had a small chance of finding any evidence of electrocution."

Morgan hadn't heard that, hearing aids or no, but he added, "The fact is, Laurentz really did die of a heart issue. The only question is whether it was caused by someone tossing an electric toaster into his bathtub."

"So?" I reiterated. "What's next?"

There was a long pause. Morgan looked me directly in the face and said, "I honestly don't know. There's nothing else to look into. Penny Fields was a witness, but there's no proof she was actually there when he died. Nobody was reported as acting suspicious near the building at the time, according to Chief Daniels in Monroe, who checked with Manalapan. There was no sign that any drug deals were going on while we were there tonight or that anyone was even interested in doing some. I've got nothing left to suggest. I wish I could help more, but Nan and I need to go home tomorrow. I'm sorry."

"Don't be," I said. "I appreciate all you've done for me when you were supposed to be on vacation. I'm sorry you didn't get to enjoy yourself more."

Morgan brightened. "Are you kidding? Best vacation of my life."

Nan chuckled and nodded. "I'm going to tell all the cop wives I know that if you keep your private-investigator's license, there's always going to be something for their husbands to do here."

I suppose I could have taken that in a negative way, but I chose not to. I gave her a hug. "I'll be sorry to see you go," I said honestly.

Nan sniffed a little. "You'll have to let us know how it all works out."

I shook my head. "I think you're seeing that now. I'm out of ideas." I looked up at Paul, but he was gone, which was odd. This was the moment he'd usually give me a pep talk about how you can't give up. Maybe even he thought we were beaten.

Nan and Morgan said their good-nights and went up to their room to pack. I looked over at Mom and Josh and shrugged. "I guess that's it," I said.

"I guess," Mom agreed. "I'm sorry, Alison. If Larry"— she looked at Josh—"were able to hear me, I'd tell him I'm sorry, too."

"I'm sure he knows, Mrs. Kerby," Josh volunteered.

Or will, once you get home, I thought.

She shot me a look that said, "Don't let this one get away," and patted him on the hand. "You call me, Loretta," she said. Then she pulled on her coat and her backpack and walked to the door, saying she was tired. Josh stayed back, letting Mom and me have our moment. Then Mom added casually that, Jerry Rasmussen was coming to her house for brunch the next morning.

"Mom!" I exploded. "How could you not mention that until now? He's a suspect in what might be a murder! He almost strangled me tonight!"

"I know," Mom assured me, "but I don't think he's actually violent, just crazy like an artist." She threw me a look. "Not a *good* artist."

"Mom, Lawrence hasn't come back to your house yet; he won't even be there to protect you. What are you thinking?" I demanded.

Mom looked into my eyes. "I'm thinking I can help. Look. Maybe I can do a little detecting myself," she said. "Don't worry. I'll text if there's trouble."

You can't argue with Mom when she decides something. "Call," I said. "By the time I figure out what your text means, Jerry could be out on parole."

Mom laughed, as if I was kidding, bid Josh and me goodbye, and went out without so much as a look back. My head was clogged with thoughts, none of them good.

"She's crazy," I said, mostly to myself.

"Alone at last," Josh said when Mom closed the door behind her, and I chuckled a little. Okay, maybe one of those thoughts was good.

"I really know how to show a guy a good time, huh?" I said.

He walked over to me and smiled. "Maybe not as great as Color Quiz, but you've still got it," he said. And he leaned down and kissed me very nicely for a good long moment. I felt his arms closing around me, too, something I did not attempt to stop at all.

Until we heard the crash.

It was clear the sound, a good loud one, had come from the area of the hallway near where the "STOP GO OUT" message was scrawled near the ceiling. Without exchanging a word, we ran to the spot, and sure enough, a huge chunk of the plaster above the door to the library had been knocked out. The mallet that had been used to do it lay on the floor, along with a bunch of smashed plaster and some insulation.

Paul and Maxie appeared from somewhere upstairs just as we reached the hallway. I could hear footsteps on the stairs, too, meaning Nan and Morgan were on their way.

"Not again," I said without thinking.

"Again?" Josh asked. "This has happened before?"

"It wasn't me!" Maxie insisted. "I have an alibi this time!" I looked up, and Paul nodded—this wasn't Maxie's handiwork.

"This is a really interesting house," Josh said.

It took a while to convince everyone it was okay to quit for the evening, especially Melissa, who rushed down but was sent immediately back to bed. Nan and Morgan checked through the house looking for the intruder they assumed had broken in, and Josh had stayed by my side throughout, which was more than I probably would have done for some crazy person who'd just ambled back into my life for the first time since middle school.

I knew that there was no intruder, at least not a living, breathing one, so I must have seemed unnaturally calm to the others. In truth, I was hoping everyone would clear out so I could plot strategy with my two nonbreathing squatters.

Satisfied that there was no further danger in the house, and stocked with yet another great story to tell the gang at home, Nan and Morgan went back upstairs, assuming again that this was it for the night. And Josh, who was improbably not rushing for the nearest exit, had to be reassured that I would be all right, so he kissed me a few more times to be sure. Which would have been lovely but for the ghoulish Greek chorus I had in the room. Paul stuck his head up through the ceiling so he wouldn't see anything, but Maxie's sarcastic cries of "You go, girl!" and "Hubba hubba" somehow killed the mood for me.

Josh must have felt me holding back, because he stepped away. "Too soon?" he asked.

"No!" I stressed. Maxie laughed. "How could it be too soon? I've known you since I was eleven."

"Still."

"I'm tired," I said. "Believe me, that's all it is."

He studied me for a moment, then nodded once. "Okay. I'm going to go so you can stop being tired. Thanks for dinner."

"Thank my mother."

"I'll thank you for the rest of the evening, then. It's been completely unexpected."

I didn't ask what that meant, which I consider a sign of maturity.

Josh scuffled out into the night, which was somehow not as cold as before. And I looked up for my two ghostly sidekicks, who were now drifting back down to eye level.

Maxie tried to get the first word in, but I knew what it would be, so I blazed past her and talked directly to Paul. "Are we really done with this investigation?" I asked him.

His eyebrows rose and he made a sheepish face. "I honestly don't know," he said.

I walked into the den and lay down on the sofa. I threw my left arm across my eyes. It all seemed so exhausting. "I think I'm done," I said. "I can't help Lawrence Laurentz. I can't find my father. I can't even stop some crazy ghost from punching holes in my walls."

The voice that came back to me wasn't the one I expected. "I think I can help." That couldn't be Maxie, could it?

I took my arm off my eyes, and there she was, hovering almost directly over me, wearing a black T-shirt with the slogan "Rhymes with Rich" emblazoned on the front and a blue denim miniskirt—it was sort of like what a skirt would be, anyway, if it had been left in the dryer for a week—and holding my prehistoric MacBook in one hand.

"What?" I asked. I was confused by what she'd said; those words just sounded so incongruous coming from her.

"I can help you. I found some stuff out about your Dr. Wells, and maybe that can help you find your dad." She said this with a straight face and not the least inflection of irony.

"Who are you, and what have you done with Maxie Malone?" I asked this impostor.

Maxie's lip curled. She let out a sound similar to a whoopee cushion and said, "Do you want to hear it, or not?" I nodded my assent. "Well, Wells's . . . that sounds funny: 'well, Wells's.' I like that."

"Maxie," I said.

"Yeah. See, he had pretty much a spotless record both as a doctor and as a guy. No hint of any problems with the family, no divorce, two kids, five grandchildren, blah, blah, blah. Never sued for malpractice. Never reprimanded by the hospital or any medical board. Never called in question for a diagnosis or a treatment. The guy was just about as good as you could get."

"I don't see how this is helping."

"I'm *getting* to that," she said. "Here's the thing: One time, out of the blue, he decides to take a break from being a doctor. Just takes six months off, doesn't go anywhere, doesn't travel, doesn't write a book, just stops." She waited.

"And?" I asked.

"And nothing. After the six months are over, he goes back to what he was doing and never has a hiccup again. Weird, huh?" Maxie grinned broadly and gave an emphatic nod like Stan Laurel proving a point.

"Yeah. A revelation," I told her. "I'll be sure to act on that first thing." I put my arm back across my eyes. Maybe I'd just sleep here on the sofa tonight. It seemed so much easier than actually standing up and walking up all those stairs to my bedroom.

"You want to hear when this happened?" Maxie's voice asked.

"You mean what day of the week? I'm betting it was a Wednesday. I hate Wednesdays." But I needed to take off my makeup and brush my teeth, and all that stuff was upstairs. Life was so hard.

"I mean the date." Maxie read off the date that Wells had taken his sudden sabbatical from the medical profession.

Suddenly, I didn't need to sleep anymore. I sat straight up and stared at her, no doubt giving her exactly the response she'd been hoping for. But the information had flooded over me like cold water, and now I was wide awake.

"That's the day after my father died," I said.

"Interesting," Paul said.

"Do you have a picture of Dr. Wells?" I asked her. It had been five years since I'd seen him, and I had to wonder . . .

Maxie clicked some keys and a photograph of Dr. Peter Wells appeared, attached to a recent obituary. I shook my head.

"He's not the grumpy ghost," I said, although I'd always pretty much known that to be true.

We debated the significance of Maxie's finding for over an hour. I suggested it was simply the doctor reacting to losing a bout with an awful disease, but Paul pointed out that such things happen to doctors on a regular basis, and that it could hardly have been the first time Wells had lost a patient. Paul can be annoyingly logical.

I said that it had been a particularly grueling and difficult case, and Paul said pretty much the same thing he did to shoot down my previous argument. So I advocated the theory that Wells had liked my father and the loss had especially devastated him, and Paul didn't even have to point out what a stupid argument that was.

Maxie, throughout, fought valiantly for her point, which was that she had done a really awesome job of research and should be given lots of credit.

The initial rush of adrenaline finally wore off, and I admitted that I had no reasonable explanation for what Dr. Wells had done, and that it was now past midnight and I was exhausted. So I bid the two ghosts good night, mumbled thanks to Maxie for her help—which she seemed to think was sarcastic—and went upstairs, past the hole in my plaster wall that would need repairing, to go to bed.

At three in the morning I woke up straight out of the recurring dream about finding a tool and sat up in bed. You see people do that in the movies for dramatic effect, but this was, I'm pretty sure, the first time I'd ever done it in real life. Because sometimes when your mind isn't actively attacking a problem, it will come around to the solution that you've been searching for all along.

"Frances killed Lawrence Laurentz," I said aloud to no one. I could have explained how I knew, but no one was there, and I didn't have a plan of action yet. That could wait until morning.

For fear of forgetting, I wrote a note on the back of a bank receipt I'd left on the bed stand, rolled over and went back to sleep. I knew exactly what to do in the morning.

But I wasn't counting on the two and a half feet of snow outside my door.

Thirty

Tuesday

"This was not in the forecast at all," I told Morgan Henderson the next morning at seven.

"I heard the governor's declared a state of emergency," Morgan said. "All the major highways are closed. I'm afraid we're going to be here with you at least another day."

I'd risen that morning to a wall of snow accumulated up and over my front porch—which meant it was more than covering the four steps up and then some—and nobody in sight of my front windows was even attempting to shovel out from under yet.

Not even Murray, who wasn't answering my calls.

Morgan and I were the only ones awake in the house. You can't really count the ghosts, who were loitering about the room, Paul more attentively than Maxie. In fact, Maxie was playing a harmonica, which she concealed from Morgan by wearing gloves on her hands, which had the same effect as if she'd kept it in her pocket. She could be really clever when she wanted to irritate me, which was about ninety percent of the time.

It was working like a charm.

"I'm happy to have you," I told Morgan, "but I'm sorry to keep you here after you meant to leave."

He waved a hand dismissively. "Now. Tell me what you figured out about Frances Walters." I'd told him about my revelation in the middle of the night.

I'd been waiting to tell him and Paul, but Maxie's tooting on the harmonica was making a racket that drove me nuts and was inaudible to Morgan. I glanced at Paul, who said, "Maxie, please."

She took that to mean she should play louder. I wasn't sure what I'd done to annoy her, but she was clearly taking her revenge.

I turned toward Morgan so he could read my lips if necessary (although his hearing aids appeared to be working perfectly) and did my best to ignore the cacophony from above while Paul tried unsuccessfully to wrest the harmonica from Maxie's hands. "It's simple," I said. "It was one thing that she said to me when we first met."

I let that sink in. Maxie stopped playing the harmonica to ask Paul, "Which one is Frances Walters?" He refused to answer her but took the opportunity to yank the harmonica from her and put it in the pocket of his jeans.

"When I first went to interview Frances, she made a remark that didn't seem like a big deal. She said it was a shame that Lawrence had died upstairs in his bathroom like that."

Morgan's eyes narrowed. "Well, that is how he died. I'm trying to follow you."

Paul snapped his fingers, which made a sound only I could hear. Yeah, it's weird. "Of course!" he said.

"Of course what?" Maxie demanded. "And give me back my harmonica." Paul turned away from her.

I had to explain to Morgan. "She said 'upstairs' in his bathroom. But last night at the show, when I asked Frances if she'd ever been to Larry's place, she said she'd never been there and didn't even know where it was located in the complex. One side, where Mom and Frances live, has units that are all one floor. The other side, where Lawrence had his place, is all town houses with two stories. They're a little less expensive in communities like that because a lot of people don't want to have to climb stairs."

Morgan nodded slowly. "So if Frances didn't know where Lawrence's house was, she would assume it was like hers and wouldn't know he was upstairs when he died, because she wouldn't have known he had an upstairs."

"Exactly," I said.

"I see what you're saying," Morgan acknowledged. "But in the police business, that's what we call 'really skimpy stuff we know that won't hold up in court.'"

"Frances was also one of only three people who knew how to operate the special effects apparatus that could have been used to drop the toaster into Lawrence's tub," I said, eschewing the impulse to add "ha!" to my sentence.

"It's a fishing rod," Morgan said. "Millions of people know how to use them."

Probably best I'd left the "ha!" off, I realized now. I thought of the "bird" Lawrence said he'd seen in his last living second that could have been the prop Wendy and Peter attached to the fishing line, but that didn't eliminate Tyra or Jerry from the mix, either.

"There's one other thing," I said. "Frances made another comment last night."

"You're grasping at straws," Paul suggested.

"What?" Morgan asked. He really hadn't heard me.

I spoke a little louder but didn't shout; apparently it only irritated Morgan when people did that. "Last night. Frances said she guessed Lawrence's apartment didn't have a working toaster anymore."

Morgan shrugged. "She's probably right. Didn't the cops say there was no toaster in the kitchen, but there were crumbs? The killer took the toaster after the sparks stopped flying and Laurentz was dead. So what?"

"So," I said, playing my trump card, "I never told Frances—or any of the other suspects—about the chances that Lawrence was electrocuted by a toaster in his bathtub. I just said that there were suspicions his death wasn't from an arrhythmia."

Morgan and Paul had similar responses. They stopped, tilted their heads to the side and did a few half-nods. It was interesting, like watching two very large, odd bobblehead dolls.

"You might have something there." Paul spoke first.

"Maybe," Morgan chimed in a second later. "Still not enough to go to a prosecutor with, but something."

"So you agree it was Frances," I said.

"I don't know," he answered. "What's her motive?"

"Lawrence snitched on the troupe for being naked in public and on her and Jerry Rasmussen for the illegal Viagra business," I said, having anticipated the question. "They hadn't gotten charged, but it had been close, and she was either terrified of going to jail or just mad enough to get revenge."

Morgan puffed out his lips, thinking. "You don't have any evidence," he said. "You just have guesses."

"I've been thinking about it," I said. The fact was I hadn't slept much after coming to this conclusion. "It's something about the way her mouth tightens when she talks about Lawrence, even when she says nice stuff. It's like she wants to bite her tongue."

"Again, not much to tell the judge," Morgan pointed out.

"No. But I know it, and that makes me feel better about Jerry coming to my mother's for brunch today, because I think Frances is the killer."

"They'll probably cancel that because of the snow anyway, won't they?" Morgan asked.

I shrugged. "Mom will cook up a storm whether Jerry shows up or not."

Melissa came down a few minutes later. I'd snuck into her room and turned off her alarm clock once I'd seen the wall of snow outside, but she always set her cell phone alarm, too, and I'd forgotten to get to that. Liss was so thrilled with the idea of a snow day (or two, as it looked at the moment) that she was happy not to have missed too much by sleeping in.

I decided I'd start my new life—the one where I cook for my daughter and maybe occasionally guests—this morning, and got a box of Bisquick out of the cabinet to start making pancakes. I didn't let anyone see that I had to read the ingredients from the side of the box. Who knew there were eggs in pancakes?

By the time my cell phone buzzed indicating a text, I was more than ready for the interruption. Maxie had been offering cooking tips, and I was gullible enough that Paul had to tell me she was "kidding" when she suggested adding Tabasco. I pulled the phone from my pocket and was surprised to see a text from Mom. I'd planned to at least let her sleep until nine before I called to see how she was holding up with the snow.

Naturally, when I opened the phone and read the text, just as Melissa wandered into the kitchen, it was indecipherable.

It read: "frncs n jrr r hr fr brnch wnn sy hll."

Luckily, this time I had my daughter nearby, and simply handed her the phone to translate. "Easy," Melissa said. "It says, 'Frances and Jerry are here for brunch. Wanna say hello?"

Frances and Jerry!

I grabbed the phone from Melissa's hand as she asked what was wrong. I ignored her and immediately called Mom.

"Hello, Alison," she said when she answered. "Isn't this

snow something? Our power went out a little while ago—
I think the snow brought down a wire—and when Jerry
came for brunch, Frances had decided to come along. Isn't
that nice?"

I didn't feel better about Jerry coming over anymore.

"How did they get there?" I asked. "The snow must be
up to their waists."

"Please, Alison," my mother scoffed. "This is an *active*
adult community. They had cross-country skis."

Now, I had no reason to think that Mom was in any
immediate danger. Even if Frances had been the one who
killed Lawrence, she was not aware I knew that. And I
hadn't seen any evidence that Jerry was involved, despite
his rather menacing move toward me at the show the night
before.

On the other hand, I was scared to pieces for my mother,
but I knew if I said something straight out to her about it,
she'd react badly and Frances, then, would know.

And I couldn't get to Mom to help.

"Mom, listen. Don't react to what I'm going to say."

"Don't react?" she said out loud. "What do you mean,
don't react?"

This wasn't going well. "I'm saying, after I tell you what
I'm going to tell you, say nothing. No. Say, 'That's nice,
dear.' Can you do that?"

"That's nice, dear."

Paul floated down toward me. He looked concerned.

"No, Mom. I wasn't . . . Okay, listen. I'm going to say
one more thing. And after that thing, I want you to say,
'Okay, Alison.' *Don't say it now.* Here's the thing I want to
tell you: I think Frances might have had something to do
with . . ."

Suddenly there was that silence you get when the other
end of a cell phone call has been disrupted. It was as if
Mom had driven into a tunnel. I stared at the phone. I don't

know why people do that. It's not like the phone is responsible for what just happened; it's just that you can't see the other person, and you have to stare at *something*.

And I still couldn't say anything upsetting in front of Melissa. But she was no fool and had sat down and put her hand to her mouth based strictly on my tone of voice.

"What is it, Alison?" Morgan asked. "Is your Mom all right?"

"Yes," I answered. "She's fine. The connection just gave out." I looked toward Paul. He was glowering with concern. Even Maxie looked worried; she adores Mom. "Can you excuse me for just one second?" I asked Nan and Morgan.

They nodded. Neither said anything. I looked at Melissa; she appeared to be holding back tears.

I wasn't fooling anybody.

I spent much of the next hour on the phone. After trying to reach Mom six more times, my next call was to Lieutenant McElone, who would surely have forgiven my trespass under the circumstances, but I got put straight through to her voice mail. I left a message. Then I called the Manalapan police, under Morgan's tutelage, to ask for a "status check" on a senior citizen. The dispatcher who took the call wrote down all the information but mentioned something about there being thirty inches of snow on the ground and suggested it might be awhile before they managed to get out to the complex, which also probably had not been plowed just yet.

Saying that I knew a murderer was in the house with my mother would probably have been construed as hysteria, leading to someone being sent to my house instead of Mom's, so I refrained from making that statement. Again, as per Morgan's instructions.

Nan and Morgan began trying to get in touch with some

of his statewide connections to see if there was some reason Mom's cell phone wouldn't be answering other than the one I was trying not to think about. But the state police had been mobilized to deal with the unexpected blizzard, and his friends were hard to reach. I told the Hendersons I was going upstairs to think, but Melissa and I both knew why we were heading to her room. We never questioned it, never said a word; we just both got into the dumbwaiter and pulled our way up.

Paul and Maxie were already waiting when we got there. Paul was pacing in thin air and Maxie, galvanized by anger when someone she cared about was in danger, flew about the room like she'd had too much Ritalin and helium at the same time.

"We don't know it was Frances," Paul reminded me.

"Yes, we do. And Jerry may be in on it."

"If it's either of them, whoever it is has no reason to cause your mother any harm and won't do anything with the other one there, anyway," Paul insisted

"Do you think . . ." Melissa was trying hard to come up with an alternative way to ask her question. "Is Grandma all right?"

"I don't know yet, Liss, but we're going to find out." I looked up at Paul. "I've got to get out there. I don't care about the snow."

He shook his head. "You'll never make it. The highways are closed. There's no safe way to . . ." He stopped. And looked up at Maxie.

"What?" I asked.

Paul chewed on his lower lip a moment, then nodded, as if he'd won an argument with himself. "If you can't make it *through* the snow, maybe you can get there *over* the snow," he said.

Clearly, he was ranting. "I don't own a pair of skis or snowshoes, Paul," I told him gently. "I live at the beach."

Paul's tight smile was one-sided. "No. I'm saying maybe

you can travel over the snow. By air." And he looked at Maxie again. "Do you think you could?" he asked her.

Maxie stopped bouncing off the walls—literally—and sized me up. She shrugged. "I don't see why not," she said. She turned to me. "Let's go."

Their plan was starting to dawn on me, and it was not the kind of dawn one generally welcomes in. "You're not suggesting that Maxie carry me all the way to Mom's, in the . . . by the . . ."

"Out the window," Maxie said. "Let's go."

"Are you nuts?" I asked. "How do you even know you could—" Before I could get out "lift me," Maxie had scooped me up and I was coming into close proximity with the ceiling. She helpfully stopped a few inches short of full-on collision.

"Any questions?" she asked. "Let's go. Your mom's in trouble."

This was sounding disturbingly realistic. "People will see us," I said. "They'll see *me*, anyway. How could I explain flying all over Monmouth County?"

Maxie planted me back on the floor and changed her clothing in a blink, like always. Except now she was wearing a huge trench coat, much too large for her, and she wrapped it around me. "Can you see your mom, Melissa?" she asked.

"Just her shoes and the top of her head," I heard my daughter say. It's amazing how little you can see and hear when engulfed by a trench coat. "Scrunch down, Mom." I did. "Yeah, that's better. It's just her feet now."

"We can handle it," Maxie said. "Let's go."

"Will you stop with the 'let's go'?" I demanded. "Nothing happens to *you* if you drop me. I have to think about this."

"I don't," Liss said. "I'll go." She started reaching for her snow boots.

I disentangled myself from the trench coat and faced

her. "You most certainly will not," I said firmly. "I'm not letting you fly anyplace. Besides, what are you going to do when you get there?"

"Save Grandma," my daughter insisted.

"You're staying here. Man your cell phone." I looked at Maxie. "Well, what are you waiting for? Let's go."

Thirty-one

I put on as much outerwear as would fit inside Maxie's Harpo Marx trench coat but insisted on facing out. I wasn't going to fly to Manalapan with my eyes closed. Not all the way, anyhow.

"If someone sees a flash of eyes flying around, they'll think they had the sun in their face or something," I said by way of justification. Maxie didn't care which way I faced as long as we left immediately.

Paul gave me a few last-minute instructions on what to do once we arrived at Mom's and told me he'd stay with Melissa and her cell phone if texting was necessary. I told Liss for the millionth time about 911, like she hadn't known that since she was four. Then I told her to stay in her room until she heard from me and to tell Nan and Morgan that I'd decided to brave the drive in the Volvo. I didn't tell her how to explain to them that I'd managed to get to the car without going past them, which wasn't technically possible. It wasn't much, but it was all I had.

I knelt down to talk to her, although that's not really necessary anymore. "Don't you worry about your grandma," I told her. "She's one resilient lady."

"What's resilient?"

"Tough," I said. Then I gave my daughter a very tight hug, sucked on my teeth to force back any tears that might have the audacity to try and appear in my eye and stood. I nodded to Maxie. Paul opened the window and the storm window on the rear side of the house, where I was less likely to be spotted from the ground.

Maxie wrapped her arms around me. As I held the trench coat tight, I felt my feet leave the floor. I no longer had control over the direction in which my body was traveling, because out the window surely wouldn't have been my first choice.

But that's the way we went.

For those who have never flown thirty feet in the air over central New Jersey while being held by a ghost, let me try to describe the experience for you: The first thing that struck me was *COLD*! That lasted a full minute, and I realized that under the trench coat, Maxie was still in a T-shirt and short denim skirt.

"Aren't you freezing?" I shouted at her. The wind was brutal up there. Maxie laughed.

"One of the advantages of being dead," she said.

We traveled toward Route 33, which was the way I would normally go to Mom's. It would be about twenty miles as the ghost flies. It didn't look like the real central Jersey I knew, anyway. Everything was covered in unexpected snow and a lot of it, and only the most hearty of homeowners was already out and shoveling or snow blowing. The rest were probably sitting at their breakfast tables, stunned and trying to shift into action mode. The empty streets were better for me, so I was glad for the laziness of my fellow shore denizens. We were up high enough to be above regular houses and power wires but not office buildings and the like. So far this was not a problem, but Maxie would have to dodge some buildings when we got as far as Red Bank or so.

After I got over my initial vertigo, the trip was sort of enjoyable in a touristy sort of way, but I was anxious about Mom, frustrated by our snail-like pace and also freezing off various parts of my body. Our progress was very slow. "I've never tried it without a car before," Maxie said. "This is the best I can do." We were traveling about as fast as if we were running to Mom's, which would take hours.

But then the otherwise-empty streets offered up something that was as welcome a sight as I've ever seen: a plow. I pointed down, and Maxie saw the plow pushing its way through the streets, covering people's parked cars with even more snow to shovel off later.

"I have an idea," I told her.

Maxie started to descend, and as we got lower, I could see the plow more clearly and started to laugh. "What the hell is so funny?" Maxie asked.

"It's too perfect," I told her.

We set down about twenty yards from the plow, and I waved my arms as it approached. Sure enough, it stopped, and Murray got out of the driver's seat.

"I've got to plow all these streets, Alison," he said. "Don't have time for nonpaying customers." Murray was really good at being single-minded, but then he couldn't possibly have handled more.

"Murray, my mom is in danger. Drive me to Manalapan and I'll pay you double for my plowing."

He didn't skip a beat. "Won't matter. You don't pay, anyway."

I didn't have time for this. "Look. I don't have my wallet with me. But this is a matter of life and death. I'm telling you straight out that I'll pay you twice what you usually get, and you can have the money as soon as we get back."

"I have to get all these streets done, and the parking lot at the Foodtown." This wasn't a bargaining tactic; Murray was trying to avoid doing something he was being asked. It was a reflex with him.

"You can put my house off until tomorrow. Just please, Murray, I have no other way to get there, and she's really in trouble." I told him the whole story—well, a condensed version of it, anyway—and it seemed to work. Murray looked determined as he pulled on his Phillies cap. "Climb in," he said. Indiana Jones and the Snowplow of Doom.

Before Murray could rethink his decision, I was in the warm cab of the plow and Maxie was standing—yes, standing—in front of me. "That's easier," she said. "You could stand to drop a couple of pounds, you know." I couldn't even answer.

As we drove away, Murray asked, "Hey, Alison, how'd you get here, anyway?"

"I flew," I told him.

He nodded. That's Murray.

Even with the plow attached to the front of his truck, Murray had to stop occasionally to get through especially heavy drifts. "We're lucky," he said. "It's a dry snow. Powdery. If it was slushy, it'd be harder to move."

Not that this wasn't fascinating, but I was anxious about Mom. "Just keep going, Murray," I said. "Don't stop." He looked determined and plowed on through.

I pretended I was talking to Murray but looked directly into Maxie's eyes. "I don't understand why you were upset with me," I said.

Murray droned on again about how unreasonable I was for not wanting to pay him for doing nothing, but I was really listening for Maxie's explanation: "I did all this great work to find out about Dr. Wells and your dad and everything, and you were getting all the credit," she said. "I want people to notice."

"Credit isn't the issue," I said, and Murray began talking about how he was a cash business, but he'd take a check if he had to.

"I know," Maxie answered. "But I don't have that much I can do these days. When I help, I want to get recognized for it."

I mulled that over. Sometimes I act like Maxie doesn't have feelings because she acts like mine are unreasonable. I could make an effort. "That's fair," I said.

"Good," Murray agreed. "I'll bill you when I get back to my office tonight." That didn't sound good, but I was in no position to argue now.

Maxie, meanwhile, smiled and held out a hand, which I touched when I was pretending to brace myself on the dashboard. My hand went through hers, of course, but it was the gesture that counted.

Then we both went back to staring worriedly through the windshield, waiting for the entrance to Whispering Lakes to show up.

It did, finally, and I guided Murray and his plow—which was helpful, since indeed, the community's service clearly hadn't arrived yet—to the front of Mom's unit. We passed a utility truck along the way and saw two technicians working on a power distributor. In front of Mom's house, I thanked Murray again and got out of the truck, leaving behind Maxie, who didn't have to worry about trifles like solid objects in her travels.

"I'll come with you," Murray said. "I've got a gun in the glove compartment."

A gun? Would it come to that? My mind went through about fifty scenarios in a second, and some of them were pretty grim. I nodded. "We'd appreciate it," I said. Maxie nodded her agreement.

"Who's 'we'?" Murray said.

"My mom and me," I answered. "Thanks." Murray and I trudged through the heavy snow and made it to Mom's front door. There were two other sets of boot prints leading to the threshold and two pairs of cross-country skis leaning against the outside wall.

Frances and Jerry.

I took a breath but not a long one because I was in a hurry. Murray stuck the pistol into his coat pocket and grunted. Manhood at its finest.

"Let's brace ourselves for what we might see," I told Maxie. But she was gone. Again, doors and such things don't stand in her way. I didn't hear anything from inside when she got there and chose to take that as a good sign.

"I'll be fine," Murray said.

I worked the lock quietly in case someone was inside and tried hard to open the door with very little sound. It swung into the living room, and I looked inside. There were no lights on, which made sense given the power outage.

Sitting on the couch were Frances and Jerry, drinking coffee. The rats! How could they just sit there and smile at each other after what they must have done? And where was Maxie? I had expected to see her taking the place apart in her fury.

"Rough," Murray said.

Frances and Jerry looked up at the sound. "Alison!" Frances crowed. "What are you doing here?" She stood up.

I was about to comment on the gall she had to sip a hot beverage in her victim's home when Maxie floated in from the kitchen, smiling. And then Mom ambled in from the same direction.

Mom!

She was carrying a tray of muffins and humming. "Alison!" she said. "How did you get here? You're so silly."

I was starting to subscribe to that opinion myself.

"What happened?" I asked.

"Nothing happened," Mom told me. "What are you doing here?"

"You . . . I couldn't talk to you . . . your phone . . ." Even I didn't think I sounded coherent. What was going on?

"My phone died and I couldn't charge it because the power's out," she explained. "That's hardly an emergency."

She looked behind me. "Oh, hello, Murray," she said. "How did she talk you into this?"

"Hello, Mrs. Kerby," Murray answered. "Alison said it was an emergency."

Mom waved her hand after she put the tray of muffins on the coffee table. "That's ridiculous. Jerry and Frances were here. There was no danger. It's just some snow."

She avoided looking at Maxie, who said, "Yeah, well. You had to be there."

Murray shot me a disdainful look. "Well, I guess there's no emergency. I have places to plow. Do you want a ride back, Alison?"

And worry about my mother in a room with these two? Hell, no! "I think I'll stick around for a while, Murray. Thanks again." Mom looked puzzled; how would I get home?

He scowled a little and walked to the door, which he opened. Then he turned back and nodded at the assembled group. "Well, I'm glad it turned out there wasn't a killer here, after all," he said. The door closed behind him.

Jerry looked stunned and confused. "A killer?" he repeated.

But Frances Walters's face didn't look all that surprised and not a bit confused. She looked furious.

No, I wasn't at all happy to be right.

Thirty-two

I tried to come up with something I could say that would placate Frances, but by an hour later the only thing I'd thought of was, "What's he talking about, a killer? That Murray!" In all honesty, though, that probably wouldn't have helped even in the moment.

In any event, there wasn't enough time. Frances reached into the pocket of her jacket and pulled out a handgun. And for the first time in my life, I was sorry Murray wasn't in the room.

Mom gasped. You have to love that woman. Here I had all but faxed her a "Wanted" poster with Frances's picture on it, yet she was still astonished that such a nice woman could be violent.

Maxie started looking around the room, no doubt for a decent weapon that could be used against Frances. I tried to get her attention and push my glance toward the wall connecting the house to the garage, where some of Dad's old tools and other useful paraphernalia might be found.

Maxie, out of sync with me as ever, first avoided my glance, then looked at me and said, "What?"

"Frances, what are you doing?" Jerry demanded. "What is this all about?"

Frances did a perfect high-school-junior eye roll and heaved a sigh of exasperation. "Oh, seriously, Jerry," she said. "They know I killed Larry Laurentz."

Jerry's mouth opened and closed. Five times. But no sound came out. Maybe he was trying to figure out what rhymed with *toaster* for his musical on the subject. Wait. He didn't know Lawrence had died of toaster-inflicted electrocution. Frances did.

Mom gritted her teeth. It was one thing to kill a man in his bathtub. It was another to ruin her brunch.

I reached into my tote bag, drawing a quick turn with the gun from Frances, but all I held when I dropped the tote on the floor was my voice recorder, not a weapon. I held it out toward Frances.

"Would you mind repeating that?" I asked.

Frances clearly found that amusing; she smiled broadly, leaned in toward the recorder and said, enunciating perfectly, "I killed Larry Laurentz. Dropped an electric toaster into his bathtub and gave him a heart attack."

"Arrhythmia," I corrected out of reflex. "So let me get it straight. You were just passing by Larry's house with your fishing rod and a toaster and decided to see what happened if you cast it into his tub? Why? Just because he snitched to the cops that you guys were going to get naked in a production of *Hair* after you kicked him out of the group?" A confession is better if you don't get the subject just to say yes, so I was deliberately professing the wrong theory. I was pretty sure.

Jerry's hand went to his mouth, which was still flapping soundlessly.

Frances scoffed. "Don't be ridiculous. The nude scene is a perfect depiction of the innocence of idealism." She turned toward Jerry, still holding the gun but seeming to forget that. "You really did a fine job on that adaptation, Jerry."

Jerry puffed up. "Why, thank you." Theatrical ego knows no bounds at any level.

Frances looked annoyed again as she turned back to me. "It was really the fact that the stupid informant had drawn attention to my prescription business. I would have been indicted if they'd found evidence, and that would have meant real jail time."

Okay, Frances had some serious crazy going on here.

"That's right," I recalled. "You had a son who's a pharmacist. A connection when you needed one. But Jerry"— I felt that Jerry needed to be spoken of kindly at this moment—"was also kept overnight on suspicion over the prescription thing, too."

Jerry looked sheepish. He coughed a couple of times and said, "I thought it would deflect suspicion from me if I implicated myself. I didn't have anything to do with the drug business."

That took a moment to sink in. Maxie flew out of the room but in the wrong direction, toward the kitchen. Yeah, she'd find rolling pins and frying pans in there, but Frances had a gun. We needed something a little more . . . immediate.

"I don't understand," Mom said. "Jerry, you were the informant?"

"Well . . . um . . . yes. I thought it would generate some publicity for the New Old Thespians if we were involved in a controversy. So I called in about the nude scene. But the police weren't interested in the nudity. So I told them about the prescriptions."

I looked at Frances, who was trying to process that information. "You killed Larry, and he hadn't even informed on you."

She heaved a breath and frowned. "It doesn't matter now." She gestured toward the bedroom with the gun. "Move. The bunch of you."

"Why?" Jerry asked.

"Because I'm going to shoot you all in there and then leave the gun in your hand, Jerry. Go."

Just as I was wondering why it mattered which room Frances shot us in, Maxie came back holding a kitchen knife in her trench coat, which she showed me as she passed. It was better than nothing, but knives are not the most accurate weapon, especially when the opponent is more efficiently armed. It occurred to me in that moment, however, that there was no reason to conceal Maxie's presence anymore.

"Maxie!" I yelled. Mom swiveled and looked at me in astonishment. "Go to the garage and find some of my father's old tools—something to hit her with!"

"On it!" Maxie shouted, and vanished into the wall.

"Who's Maxie?" Frances stared at me. "Are you out of your mind?" she demanded.

"Are you really the person to be asking that question?"

I'm sure that to Frances and Jerry, it looked like this: Before Frances could answer, heavy rope encircled her around the waist, pinning her arms to her sides. In surprise, she fired the gun; luckily the bullet went harmlessly into the floor (although I'm sure Mom's first thought was about getting her carpeting repaired). In the next moment, one of Mom's dining room chairs shoved itself hard into Frances's knees from behind, and a tire iron pushed itself into her midsection, forcing her to sit. The rope started tying her to the chair.

Jerry fainted dead away.

Maxie flew through the garage wall into the living room while pulling a huge wrench from her trench coat. Then she stopped and stared as the rope continued to wrap itself around Frances, who screamed and looked around for her unseen assailant.

That's not how it looked to Mom, Maxie and me. To us, it was even more extraordinary: We saw three more ghosts swoop into the room from the ceiling and subdue Frances while Jerry passed out. One of them was Lawrence Laurentz, carrying the rope. The one brandishing the chair was a ghost I recognized as Dr. Wells.

The third spirit, wearing an expression of absolute fury, dropped the tire iron only when Frances followed Jerry and blacked out. Then he reached out his arms to me and said, "Baby girl."

"Dad," I murmured, close to tears but only barely feeling the embrace he tried to offer. "Where have you been?"

"It's a long story," he answered. He glanced at Dr. Wells, who had his arms folded in front of him, and nodded. "One it's time for me to tell."

I stepped back from Dad so Mom could get closer to him. "Jack," she said. "I was so worried."

"I know," he answered. "I'm sorry. I've never been so sorry."

I swear, at that moment, the lights came back on.

Lawrence hovered over the scene, smiling as a cape appeared around his shoulders. "I *told* you someone murdered me," he said.

Thirty-three

"I couldn't look you or Melissa in the eye," Dad said.

We were in the kitchen at the guesthouse again. I'd secured a promise from my father that he wouldn't fly off into the clouds and leave me wondering, and Dad always kept—keeps—his promises.

There hadn't been time to have this talk, which no doubt would be a doozy, while we were at Mom's. Morgan had found Melissa and called in a connection at the New Jersey State Police. Those guys don't worry about snow. They'd made it to Mom's, gotten the power restored and contacted the plowing service at her complex, so they could speed in and arrest Frances. This had the added benefit that the roads were cleared by the time we'd sorted things out.

It pays to have friends in high places. Speaking of which, Lieutenant McElone called ten minutes after the state police must have posted a report on Frances's arrest and apologized for not calling back in real McElone fashion, saying, "You should have mentioned it was an emergency." Clearly, it was my fault.

Frances was very, very arrested, particularly after my voice recording of her stating in no uncertain terms that she'd killed Lawrence and was going to shoot the three of us was played. When she came to, Frances denied it, said we'd been rehearsing Jerry's latest play and was put in a trooper's cruiser in rapid succession.

Jerry, who owned up to snitching on just about everybody in the New Old Thespians, was not arrested but had to change his clothing after the scare he'd gotten. Before leaving, he said he thought his next production would be *The Mystery of Edwin Drood*. The man's an artist.

The troopers had been kind enough to give me a ride back to Harbor Haven, and I'd insisted Mom pack a bag and come, too, which took very little convincing, since she wanted to hear Dad's story. Many of the large roads had been plowed by now, but there were still hardly any cars on the road, and we were home in no time, much faster than traveling by ghost. Maxie and Dad tagged along in the trunk. Well, their legs were in the trunk, anyway. If I'd been driving, it would have been disconcerting to look in the rearview mirror and see my late father and my deceased tenant staring through the back window, but luckily the trooper didn't have that problem.

We'd had to leave Lawrence at Mom's, since he wasn't able to travel beyond the community's boundaries. He'd explained that he'd been lurking out of sight in the powder room when Frances had begun threatening us and went off to find help. He couldn't leave, but he apparently could tap into the Ghosternet like Paul, and Dad had come running (flying?). They'd met in the garage, grabbed the rope and gone to work.

Dr. Wells had been at Madison Paint, having been alerted by the grumpy ghost, an old patient of his (a painter crony of Dad's named, incongruently enough, "Sonny"), where Dad had been hiding the whole time, and heard the call from Lawrence. (Lawrence had not tried to contact Dad, having gotten no response in any of his previous attempts. But he'd heard Mom discuss Dr. Wells and, in a Hail Mary play, focused on the doctor.) There hadn't been time to sort it out, and they'd both answered his plea.

The doctor turned out to be a very nice man haunted by Dad's case, for reasons he wouldn't discuss. But Dad put his arm around Dr. Wells and thanked him (asking him to pass the sentiment along to Sonny). The doctor gave Dad a few more stern looks, said something about "coming clean" and went off.

Melissa had been clearly relieved when we'd returned but strangely shy around her grandfather. She was spooked (pardon the expression) by his odd absence for all this time and seemed wary of what he was going to tell us, though despite my concerns that the conversation might be upsetting for her, she would not be moved. Frankly, I couldn't blame her.

"What do you mean, you couldn't look us in the eye?" she asked Dad.

Dad looked absolutely forlorn when he turned toward Melissa. "I was ashamed, honey. That's the truth. I was so ashamed, I couldn't even talk to you or your mom. I thought you'd hate me."

"Dad!" I shouted. Maxie, hovering near the ceiling, started at my volume. Luckily, after a lengthy briefing on the Laurentz case, Nan had insisted they go out to explore the blizzard and forage for food. If they weren't back in two hours, I would call the National Guard.

"It's true, baby girl," he said. "Your mom knew I was upset, but she still doesn't know why, and I'm sorry for that, too, Loretta. I shouldn't have handled it the way I did, blocking out our daughter and granddaughter, and not telling you the reason."

Mom looked over at him and sniffed. "I still don't even

know what we're talking about," she said. "It's time to unburden yourself, Jack."

Dad nodded.

"Dr. Wells sent your friend Sonny here after he died, and he wrote two things, Dad. He said he knew where you were, and then he said you didn't die the way we thought. Is that what this is about?"

Dad looked like he was mortally wounded, which under the circumstances was impossible, but he nodded. "The doctor knew exactly what was going on, and once he passed away and found me again, he tried to get me to tell you, but I refused, so he tried to push you into finding out. I'd been bragging about my daughter the detective."

"So you went into hiding," I noted.

Dad waved his hand. "Hiding? I didn't go into *hiding*; I just managed to be away from you and Mom for a while so I could think. Wells guessed where I was from conversations we'd had in the hospital room . . . back then . . . and he sent out a message. Sonny heard it. The two of them have been badgering me at the store for days."

"You were there the whole time?" Mom asked.

Dad nodded again. "Mostly. I knew you wouldn't look there, Loretta," he said quietly, then looked at me. "But it didn't occur to me that *you* would come looking there. I had to duck out pretty quick when you showed up there. And what's this about you and Josh Kaplan?"

"This is *your* confession," I reminded him.

"It's true," Dad agreed. "And I have a lot to confess."

"Like what, Grampa?" Melissa wanted to know. "You can tell us anything. We won't be mad." Twenty years from now, when you meet my daughter, don't judge her for being a successful prosecutor. Judge her based on her heart.

Dad smiled, but it was a sad smile, if such a thing is possible. "Okay, Lissie."

"Nobody calls me that anymore," Melissa told him. But after a beat, she added, "But you can."

"Thank you," Dad said. He seemed to gather his thoughts and said, "Dr. Wells was right. You really didn't know what happened when I died." He turned and looked at me. "You remember, Alison, what kind of shape I was in at the end."

Paul, all stiff-upper-lip restraint, was having a hard time watching the scene from the area around the stove. He seemed to be fascinated by something on the ceiling. Except there wasn't anything on the ceiling.

"I remember you were in a lot of pain," I said. "It was so hard to watch. I felt awful for you."

Dad nodded slowly, remembering.

"We know that, Jack," Mom told him. "And it's natural for a family to be upset when someone goes the way you did. But you have nothing to be ashamed of." She reached out to Dad, but he was a few feet up out of her reach.

"Yes, I do," he answered. "I didn't want to leave you, not the three of you, at all, but it got so bad—the pain—that I couldn't stand any more. And that night, Dr. Wells told me it could be six or seven more days before I . . . before the pain ended. That sounded like forever. So I asked . . . No. I *begged* him to make the pain stop."

"Didn't they give you medicine, Grampa?" Of course I questioned my decision to let Melissa in on the conversation. But I believe that children are stronger than we think and that they can handle things as long as they're told the truth. That was the excuse I was using today.

"You asked the doctor for something that would put you out of your misery," I said, in an effort to word it delicately that ended up not being so delicate.

Mom bit her lip, but she didn't cry. "It must have been awful for you," she said.

Dad closed his eyes and nodded. "He didn't want to; he held out for what seemed like a very long time." He opened his eyes and looked at me to make his point. "But he really is a compassionate man, and he couldn't bear to see how I was suffering. He waited until the nurse's shift was changing and put something in my IV drip. And the next thing I knew, I was . . . like this."

"And that's why you haven't come here or talked to us in five years?" I asked, incredulous. "But you came to see Mom once a week, on Tuesdays. If you could do that . . ."

"I couldn't see you," Dad said, his voice quivering. "A husband is different from a father, baby girl. Believe me I wanted to all the time. But I thought . . . well, I broke my promise to you. I looked you right in the eye and promised you I'd fight until the end. Besides, just because you didn't see me doesn't mean I wasn't here. I was with you sometimes when Melissa was at school, before you met your two friends there." He gestured toward Paul and Maxie, who were uncharacteristically silent. "And sometimes I'd sneak in and see you, Lissie, when you were sleeping or from a distance. I couldn't *really* stay away from you.

"It wasn't until Dr. Wells was here, like us"—he gestured to Paul and Maxie—"and he was saying you needed to know, and if I didn't come clean, he'd tell you himself, although he insisted it wasn't his place to do that. But I couldn't get the courage together to do it until that Laurentz guy told us your lives were in danger. Then I had no choice," Dad said. "But if you can't forgive me for being so weak at the end, I'll understand." He looked at me. "You don't ever have to see me again, Alison."

It was very hard to fight back tears, and Dad was right—I was angry at him. But not for the reason he thought I was. "The only thing I won't forgive," I told him, "is that you didn't give us the chance. I understand how much pain you had, and I don't blame you a bit for asking Dr. Wells for help. I didn't ever want you to suffer like that." I made serious eye contact with my father, something I'd wished for desperately over the past five years. "But you assumed we'd never want to see you, when that was the one thing we wanted most of all. Don't you *dare* ever go away again, Daddy."

I don't think there was a dry eye in the kitchen, among those of us who still have tear ducts, anyway. The others weren't faring much better.

"I won't, baby girl. I promise."

Josh Kaplan called a little while later to see how I was dealing with the snow. I shoveled out the front porch and the walk (with a little help from some "invisible" shovelers) and left the rest for Murray to do the next day.

"It's clear enough for you to come over if you want to," I said.

Josh sounded his usual amiable self, but there was a hesitation I hadn't expected. "I don't think so, Alison," he said.

I knew I shouldn't have involved him in all this, ushering a guy I'd just gotten involved with into this crazy life with my family, my guests and my criminal investigations (he didn't even know about the ghosts!) so soon. Another huge miscalculation. "I understand," I said. And I did. I didn't *like* it, but I understood.

Josh chuckled. "No, I didn't mean it like that. I'm just exhausted from shoveling two and a half feet of snow from in front of my house and the store. I'll be happy to come by tomorrow, and maybe we can do a patch on that plaster wall that self-destructed in your house."

"You know how to show a girl a good time," I told him.

"Mr. Smooth," he said. "That's me."

Phyllis Coates loved the story of the naked senior arrests, the contraband Viagra and, by extension, the murder of Lawrence Laurentz for ratting out people when he hadn't done so at all. She did some digging, however, and said the police investigation into Frances Walters had turned up a stash of illegal prescription drugs and enough "medicinal marijuana" to have kept her in jail for some years even if she hadn't killed Lawrence.

"Her son the pharmacist was the supplier, but Frances was the dealer," Phyllis reported. "And when she thought Laurentz ratted her out, she went crazy."

"She was crazy long before that," I said. "You weren't standing there with the gun pointed at you."

"Well, a gun wasn't her weapon of choice. She went to Lawrence's house that night straight from a *Peter Pan* rehearsal, and Jerry asked her to take the fishing rod home with her because he had no room in his car. She went to see Lawrence, found out Penny was there, and decided she had a patsy to hang it on. She'd practiced with the rod and reel, so it wasn't hard. Problem was the cops questioned Penny and let her go, so there was no obvious suspect. Frances just kept her head down."

"And almost got away with it," I said.

Phyllis's call came just after Nan and Morgan Henderson heard the Garden State Parkway was once again open to traffic and had decided to head home. But Morgan had one last question: "We never found out who left those messages for you all over the house."

"Frances confessed to leaving them," I lied. "She knew Mom well enough to make insinuations about my father's death. Thought she could scare me off or distract me."

"But you didn't know who to be scared away from," Morgan noted, shaking his head. "And that business card of your father's?" he asked.

"We'll never know how she got hold of that," I told him. We *would* never know, because it hadn't happened. It's a way of looking at things.

"It's a crazy world," Morgan said. He had no idea.

He and Nan packed their bags into the car and we all hugged at the door. They promised to come back again sometime. I told them the next stay would be on the house, but Nan wouldn't hear of it.

I had called Jeannie with the news of Frances's arrest and the story (minus supernatural elements) of how it happened. She said she was happy the case was closed but that she wouldn't be able to join my firm on a full-time basis, which I found comforting, since I'd never asked her to. Jeannie said she was thinking about returning to work as soon as she could find suitable day care for Oliver (as if). "It's important he learn to separate from his mother before preschool," she explained.

Phyllis was clearly taking notes. "Yeah, how did you get out of that whole situation, anyway?" she asked, bringing me back to this conversation. I could hear the pencil scraping on some old receipt on her desk. A good reporter is never off-duty. "The cops weren't clear on how Frances was subdued, just that she was already tied up and groggy when they arrived."

"What did Frances say happened?"

Phyllis barked a laugh. "She claims the rope tied itself around her." We shared a chuckle over that. "So what really went down?"

"Jerry Rasmussen risked his own life to save me and Mom," I told her. "The man's a hero."

"Uh-huh." Phyllis, somehow, did not sound convinced, but that version would appear in the *Chronicle* the following week, complete with information on the arrest of Frances's son Philip the pharmacist (read: supplier of illicit prescriptions) and the announcement that Jerry was considering writing an opera based on the saga called *Laurentz in Water.*

"What about Penny Fields?" I asked Phyllis.

"She's in the clear. Always was. Talking about moving to an active adult community herself, though," she answered. "Says she's lonely."

"Frances's house should be available soon," I pointed out. *Then Lawrence could come visit.*

"And what about Tyra?" Phyllis asked me.

"Back at the Basie," I said. "I think she got fired from the tire job, something about mouthing off to a customer who wanted to know why they don't make white walls anymore."

Phyllis said she was glad everything had worked out and apologized for not having gotten that clip file about Dad together for me yet.

I told her there was no rush.

Lawrence himself couldn't stop thanking me via text on Mom's phone once she got a ride (in Murray's truck, as he'd come to plow late and deliver an exorbitant bill, which I paid immediately) home for the evening. We'd tried to get her to stay, but she looked at Dad, Melissa and me and said we needed some time together.

I told Lawrence repeatedly that I'd just been doing my job and that he had, in fact, helped save my life, but he didn't take that for an answer and promised to haunt Mom's house whenever she would have him. Dad, of course, felt that Lawrence should send a note and ask permission before showing up.

"What if she's in the bathtub or something?" he asked me late that night after Melissa had gone to bed and the other ghosts were elsewhere, giving us time. Dad was floating high above the floor of the hallway, widening the hole he'd made in the plaster above the library door.

"I think Larry is going to stay away from all bathtubs for a very long time," I told him. I pointed at the rectangle he was creating in my wall. "You know, you could have come up with something less cryptic than 'stop go up.'"

Dad shrugged. "It made sense. You wanted to widen the door. You couldn't. But you can get more brightness in the room with a window here. You needed to stop what you were doing and go up. Take out a piece of the wall above the door, bring in more light."

"You're a master," I told him.

"You're my daughter. You're supposed to think so."

I watched him smoothing the edge of the plaster he'd sanded down. "In this case, I happen to be right," I said.

Dad looked at the hole he'd made, which would eventually house a stained-glass panel made from light colors, which I'd found in the basement of the guesthouse when I'd first moved in. Tony had said he'd install the panel for me and offered to make the sturdy brace to hold it, but Dad was already at work.

"Do me a favor, baby girl," he said. "Go get me a two-foot level, would you? I need to make sure this is right."

"Sure." I knew just where that was in my tool room in the basement. I went down the stairs quickly, headed straight for the level, found it hanging on a pegboard and rushed back up the stairs. I stopped at the basement door and took a moment to ponder. A drop of anxiety hit me just as I opened the door.

But when I swung it open, Dad was still there, hanging up in the air, smoothing the joists he'd cut to get ready for the four-by-four brace he'd put in sometime later in the week. I smiled.

"Don't just stand there," he said. "Let's see that level." So I handed it up to him.

We stayed up talking until very late in the night.